Learning to Fly

V M Taylor

This edition published 2017
V M Taylor 2017

Copyright © V M Taylor 2017

The rights of V M Taylor to be identified as the author of this work have been asserted by her in accordance with the Copyright, Designs and Patents Act 1988.

Cover Design by flamin ape © 2017
Other Credits by Local Photographers

All rights reserved. No part of this publication may be reproduced, stored in or introduced into a retrieval system, or transmitted, in any form, or by any means (electronic, mechanical, photocopying, recording or otherwise) without the prior written permission of the publisher. Any person who does any unauthorised act in relation to this publication may be liable to criminal prosecution and civil claims for damages.

This is a work of fiction, based on real events. Names, characters, places, and incidents either are the product of the author's imagination or are used fictitiously. The author nevertheless welcomes contact from anyone connected with those represented in the book.

A CIP catalogue record for this ebook is available from the British Library.

ISBN 978-1-9997361-1-8

Acknowledgements

As this is partly a family history, the first people I have to thank for encouraging me to take on the task of bringing Captain Fred Dunn's story to life are my family. My aunt, Angela Bourn first suggested the idea after she, my parents, Michael and Margaret Taylor, and their cousins, also relatives of Fred, Sheila and June Priestley, visited the First World War commemoration events in Wylam, Northumberland in Summer 2014.

An article in the Northumbrian Magazine in July that year had related the story of the 54 men of this village on the banks of the River Tyne who had gone to fight in France and other territories, and whose names are to be found on the village's three war memorials. The article also related how the local Wylam history group had tried to find out more about each of the men listed on the stonework and plaques. The enthusiasm and detailed research of this local history group was a fantastic help to me in trying to piece together Fred's war record and early life. Roy Koerner and Aubrey Smith were unfailingly helpful, and provided invaluable information, as well as lovely tea and scones along the way.

I am also indebted to the archivists at the National Archives in Kew and their records. To find Fred's file and see his signature on the various documents was a humbling moment in this journey. I also had enormous support from the RAF Museum at Hendon, and in particular Andrew Dennis. He guided me through the various publications which unearthed some wonderful revelations about a young pilot's life.

The volunteers at the small RAF museum at Farnborough were helpful in showing me all their information about the Tarrant Tabor crash. Thanks, too, to the British Library staff in their Newsroom. Their resources are a national treasure. I was lucky that my own cousin, Julian Bourn, also a distant relative of Fred's, is a Captain with British Airways, and trained with the RAF. He helped me with the aviation details and was a companion on my many visits to the National Archives.

Any mistakes in flying technicalities and, indeed, in any historical detail are mine alone.

I also thank my editor Martin Godleman at Zitebooks, who guided me through the process of being a debut novelist.

Lastly, Keith, Matt and Hannah, thank you.

V M Taylor
London

In memory of

Frederick George Dunn (1894-1919)

and

Eva Taylor (née Dunn) (1907-1986)

for

Michael and Margaret Taylor

'The rank stench of those bodies haunts me still.
And I remember things I'd best forget.'

Siegfried Sassoon, 1916

Contents

Acknowledgements	*iii*
Dedication	*v*
Quotation	*vi*
Chapter One	*1*
Chapter Two	*8*
Chapter Three	*13*
Chapter Four	*18*
Chapter Five	*24*
Chapter Six	*29*
Chapter Seven	*37*
Chapter Eight	*46*
Chapter Nine	*50*
Chapter Ten	*57*
Chapter Eleven	*61*
Chapter Twelve	*67*
Chapter Thirteen	*74*
Chapter Fourteen	*80*
Chapter Fifteen	*84*
Chapter Sixteen	*92*
Chapter Seventeen	*97*
Chapter Eighteen	*106*
Chapter Nineteen	*110*
Chapter Twenty	*117*
Chapter Twenty-One	*124*
Chapter Twenty-Two	*129*
Chapter Twenty-Three	*136*
Chapter Twenty-Four	*141*
Chapter Twenty-Five	*147*
Chapter Twenty-Six	*153*
Chapter Twenty-Seven	*159*
Chapter Twenty-Eight	*165*

Chapter Twenty-Nine	*173*
Chapter Thirty	*178*
Chapter Thirty-One	*183*
Chapter Thirty-Two	*187*
Chapter Thirty-Three	*192*
Chapter Thirty-Four	*197*
Afterword	*202*
Author's Note	*205*
Bibliography	*207*
Gallery	*209*

Chapter 1
Hendon, August 3, 1914

The weather on that August bank holiday seemed to be hurrying away from the summer into the cold, damp months ahead. The grey clouds lay heavy above the aerodrome and the aviators knew flying would not be easy, with the strong gusts making their lightweight machines twist and turn in the squalls. In spite of this, the airfield was determined to make it a day out for the visitors.

The wooden stand with its red and white striped bunting set out around the perimeter fence looked pretty, and inside each pavilion, laden on white clothed trestle tables were the tea urns, cucumber sandwiches and little cakes that the crowds would come for once the flying displays were over.

Girls with their long white aprons bobbed back and forth adding more and more to the tables. They were in a hurry to complete the task and give them time to look out and see these amazing flying machines.

For the great and the good, the weekly display at the London Aerodrome at Hendon was a place to be seen, to be part of the new technological adventure, marking them down as thoroughly modern. Colindale Avenue, the road into the airfield was filled with chauffeur driven cars and the sound of the carefree chatter of the very rich. The underground and motor buses from Victoria brought the less well-off professionals, who were no less noisy and no less curious.

Fred Dunn was anxious. He had only passed his pilot's licence in January and at nineteen had not the experience of the older airmen, already famous for their skills in the air. Some had been born into this world of privilege and showmanship, of public schools and chauffeur-driven cars. Some even had their own machines. For Fred, though, it was a far cry from the pit village in Northumberland where he had grown up. On that unseasonably cold August day, Fred felt a million miles away from the neat brick terraced homes and wide open countryside along the banks of the River Tyne. He felt his palms, which he noticed were a little sweaty, and adjusted his scarf for the tenth time and tried to make a perfect line against his neck. The cotton of his shirt collar was worn slightly and he wanted to hide its imperfection. Looking around, he could observe the stylish people who were there to see him, not just him of course, but his name was on the programme. He had felt a shiver of childish pride when he had seen that, his name among all those heroes of his, now on equal billing.

Fred's bright, youthful face could have been called handsome, so defined were his features, as if they had been measured by a meticulous architect. He was not tall, but that was an asset in a pilot who had to fit into the small cockpits of these machines. He carried himself well and almost gave the appearance of height. Looking at him in his tweed jacket, crisply ironed beige trousers and tweed cap worn rakishly back to front, no one in the crowd that day would have realised he was anything other than a relaxed, and supremely confident airman.

That Monday Fred was not bothered by the thought of any antics he might perform in the air. His concern was that Mrs Edith Perkins would be there.

Fred wouldn't have been at Hendon, preparing to perform for the crowds, if it hadn't been for Mrs Perkins. She had given him the £75, more than most people earned in a year, to cover the cost of learning to fly at the Grahame-White flying school.

Edith Perkins had seen in Fred a way with engines and mechanics that few boys of sixteen could match and she had recognised talent in a young man that she had the chance to develop. She relished the fact her money had allowed Fred the opportunity to study engineering before going on to Hendon to learn to fly.

Today Edith Perkins was coming to see the fruits of her financial commitment. She had told Fred that she would be bringing her younger daughter Kitty too. They had never met, but Fred had learned from the society columns of the newspapers that she was beautiful and intelligent and he was intrigued, if not a little bashful, at the thought of meeting her in person. He knew she had married a wealthy military man, who owned a large estate in Hampshire. Their wedding had been in all the papers.

"It feels just like Ascot, but without all those dreadful horses, don't you think?" A high pitched voice could be heard above all the others, even above the roar of the engines of the machines in front of them, preparing for take off.

"I must say I do prefer it here. So exhilarating." By now Edith Perkins had reached Fred, a good minute after the clipped notes of her voice.

"Fred. There you are. You do look dashing. Quite the pilot. Do come here and tell us what is happening?" Fred took her hand and kissed it.

"Mrs Perkins. How wonderful of you to come. Thank you so much. I've been looking forward to showing you what happens here at Hendon. May I present my friend and fellow aviator Mr Robert Lillywhite? He's about to go up in the biplane, so we should go to the front to watch him, if it pleases you."

She looked up and down at Lillywhite assessing him like a piece of furniture in an auction. Satisfied, she held out her gloved hand.

"Delighted to make the acquaintance of another flier."

"Later Mr Noel will be taking people up for a spin. Some of you may wish to join him perhaps?" Fred said the last words with a broad smile, knowing that although the party before him was seeking thrills and a taste of adventure in Hendon, they were not likely to want to try it out for themselves. He was therefore determined to make it sound as exhilarating as he could.

"Afterwards Mr Lillywhite and I will be taking part in a target competition. I hope we can make it a memorable day for you all."

The confidence of his words hid the nervousness he felt. He was ready to lead the party to the front when he caught sight of one of the most striking young women he had ever seen. Self-consciously he adjusted his scarf.

"Oh Kitty, there you are, do hurry up, you'll miss all the action," Edith Perkins said. "We are going to see Mr Lillywhite set off in a few minutes and do a few spins. Come and join us. Here, Fred, make way for Kitty."

Edith seized Fred by the arm and turned him with slightly more pressure than was necessary to face her younger daughter.

The newspapers had not lied. Kitty Burrell was indeed extraordinary. Unlike her mother, who was tall and rather too large-boned to be called beautiful, Kitty's slim figure gave her an added elegance and poise. She wore a pale blue dress in soft chiffon, the colour of a blackbird's egg, with a woollen shawl held together by a silver brooch at her chest. Her wide hat, under which her long brown hair was swept up, flaunted a single peacock feather, which seemed to bring out a deep green in her eyes. Only her tight black laced boots and pale leather gloves gave any hint that she had been expecting unseasonal weather.

Kitty had about her a splendour and sophistication which even at Hendon among her own glittering set, stood out.

Fred's was not the only head to turn as she walked up to her mother.

"Well, Frederick Dunn. I've heard such a lot about you from mother. And to think you are now a real aviator. You must be brave to go up there into the sky. Or maybe you are just a little bit reckless?" Kitty, spoke with a cut-glass accent, its edge softened, with just the hint of mischief. She was someone who had learned from her mother how to command an audience. Fred had never encountered someone like Kitty Burrell before.
"Mrs Burrell, I'm delighted to meet you," he said. "I wouldn't call it bravery. Just luck and lots of hard work." He sounded complacent, almost arrogant. He was conscious of his voice and its drawn out North-East vowels.

"Well I wish you and your friend here lots of luck flying today," she said. She turned to join her mother and the rest of the party who had moved away to see the first machines getting ready to take off. Fred was surprised at how glib her reply sounded.

"Blimey, Fred, she's stunning!" Lillywhite said. Fred nodded, unsure of what to say.

"Can you organise it so I'm sitting with them at tea?

Shame she's married though. She doesn't have a younger unmatched sister does she?"

Lillywhite was a year older than Fred. He had left school at fourteen and become an apprentice mechanic at the aerodrome under Mr Grahame-White, who had agreed to allow him to learn to fly for free in return for his mechanical skills at the airfield depot. Lillywhite and Fred had got their Aero certificates at the same time and had become firm friends ever since.

Fred barely heard what his friend said. He felt a disabling mixture of embarrassment and attraction. He was now more nervous than ever. Maybe she had only feigned interest at his flying skills. If he had been forced to continue the conversation, such as it had been, he would have had little to say. He turned his attention back to the task in hand and tried to push the thoughts of Kitty Burrell from his mind.

Despite the gloomy weather, the day went well. Brock and Birchenough performed some good turns and even the light rain could not prevent them doing a few wide loops to delight those below.

At 3pm the announcer told everyone to get ready for the bomb-dropping competition. It was to be the finale of the afternoon's entertainment. The pilots would perform a single turn each and drop a bag of flour onto a target on the airfield below.

Lillywhite was first up in the aviation school biplane and got his drop within twelve yards of the target.

Barr, another teenage pilot, was next and got within fourteen yards. Louis Noel, the best-known of the aviators out that day in his Henri Farman aeroplane, got blown off course by a sudden gust of wind, and only managed 49 yards, so he was well out of the reckoning.

Fred was next. He walked up to the school biplane and climbed into the open cockpit. He pushed the tweed cap back on his head and after a few checks held his thumb up. The mechanic heaved at the wooden propeller, making it wheeze and splutter. The muscles in his arms danced as he pulled at the blades. The engine sparked into life, giving a great howl as the blocks were pulled away and the machine as if freed lurched forward. Fred took it slowly at first, conscious of the impression he would be making. It was not the best take-off he had ever managed, but once he had a few hundred feet between him and the ground, he relaxed and reveled in the sensation being above everyone else can give a man. He looked over at the diminished figures below, their heads bent back in unison looking upwards and felt a peculiar sense of security, there up in open skies looking down to earth. He waved, a salute almost. Perhaps down there he could make out a single peacock feather. After an elegant wide turn in the air, he swept down towards the target. He thought he could hear the gasps from the crowds below as he dropped from the sky. That sweet moment when you know it is only by your skill when to pull up that separates life from death. He was just above the spot now and carefully tipped the flour bag out of the side. It left a trail of white dust on the side of the cockpit and his gloves. Twelve yards away from the marker. The same as Lillywhite. The prize was tied.

He would have loved to have been the outright winner, but sharing with his friend Lillywhite was not bad. I'll beat him next weekend, he thought.

The clouds darkened and everyone crowded into the stands for tea. After a small presentation and much clapping and congratulating, Fred and Lillywhite were presented with the silver shield they would share. As Fred returned to his table, he caught Kitty's eye and found himself involuntarily smiling broadly at her. She smiled back, nodding in congratulation, a look which seemed to say so much more than simply well done. That shot through Fred and made the colour flow to his cheeks. Was that flirtatious or just being polite? Suddenly, unexpectedly, he allowed himself to look on Kitty in the way he hoped her smile had encouraged. This new feeling unnerved him.

What are you thinking about? he said to himself. Kitty Burrell is a married woman and her mother is your benefactor. Apart from that, a woman like her would never look at someone like you.

Forget you ever met her. Just… forget.

But Fred would not forget that day, not just for seeing Kitty, but as the day after which everything changed.

Nor would anyone else in the crowd forget where they were on that bank holiday in August 1914. The day after, the country declared war on Germany.

Five days later Fred and Lillywhite would join the Royal Flying Corps and, instead of the second round of the bomb-dropping competition, would be heading to Farnborough for military training.

The bombs they would be dealing with now would not be flour bags.

Chapter 2
Wylam, 1907

Fred Dunn was proud of the fact that he came from Wylam, a mining village on the banks of the River Tyne. It was George Stephenson, a local boy who had transformed the way the country travelled, and steam engines now took passengers up and down the country thanks to him. Fred loved engines too, how speed could be cultivated by the mere shift of a throttle. This love of engines and mechanics ran in his blood they used to tell him. His grandfather, who he had never met, had been an engineer in the mines in Lancashire and it had been his job that had taken the Dunn family to the North East where there were opportunities opening up for young ambitious men in mining.

The Dunns lived close to the mine at Hagg Bank, they could almost see the tall chimneys from their upstairs room. The front one where his parents Thomas and Adele slept. Fred was in the tiny back room where they was just enough space for a single cot bed and a chest of drawers. His window looked out onto the yard and the washing lines slung like a cat's cradle game between the neighbouring houses. On washdays, Mondays, the smell of soap and linen would float up to his room and he loved looking out onto the flapping sheets and noticing how they moved in the breeze.

Fred, looked up to his father like every boy he knew, but his father was especially important to Fred's young eyes. Being a deputy at the mine was a responsible job, and Fred liked to think that it was his dad who kept all the men in the village safe.

He knew that the stern looking man with his black bushy moustache, which sat regally on his upper lip, was a kind hearted and generous man. His father's serious face was kept for work, but it was a serious job, life or death, so that was only right.

Each morning at 4 am long before anyone else in the row was up, Thomas Dunn and the second deputy who lived two doors down would walk the half a mile from their terraced houses over the new railway bridge crossing the River Tyne to the pit. There, each morning at dawn they would be the first men to go down the mine and check that the pit props were stable, and the working areas of the mine were secure. Everything had to be in place to welcome the miners two hours later. The Wylam pit was the biggest in the area, employing over 1,000 men and since Thomas had started as a deputy, there had not been a single accident. John Appleby, his predecessor, had been killed in the mine in 1889 when falling timber from a roof fall had crushed him. John Appleby's death was a constant reminder to Thomas of what might happen underground and he tried to keep to himself how the nagging sense of foreboding and fear of an accident which often kept him awake at night.

The Applebys had lived in Hagg Bank too, number 4, and his two boys went to the village school with Fred. No one dared mention their own dads in the playground when they were around. It didn't seem right, what with them not having one.

Thomas's fear of an accident wasn't something he could discuss with Adele. He knew she thought the mine was a dirty, dangerous place anyway and she wished he worked anywhere but there. She had been a young, determined Parisian girl who had come to England to seek work as a lady's maid. Her job had taken into the interiors of the big estates in Northumberland lived in by the men who owned the mines and factories all over the North East, so marrying a miner had been the last thing she had imagined for herself. Her European ways and her French accent, suggested sophistication not generally seen around a pit village. But the couple, miner and maid, mismatched in many ways had married and Fred had arrived a year later.

Fred was happy in those early years, especially when the school day was over and he could go down to Henderson's workshop and watch as the men, smeared with oil and engine grease toiled over the farm machinery trying to coax them back to life.

In winter it was warm and a refuge against the biting cold, and Fred felt at home there among the dirt and oil. The owner, old Mr Henderson gave him milk in an old tin mug tea stained and smeared with the dirty marks of the hands which had held it last. It made him feel grown up drinking out of their mugs and listening to their talk. Although his mother didn't like him coming home every night bringing the smells of the garage with him, he knew she preferred that he was keeping out of trouble in the fug of the garage than wandering the banks of the river in search of entertainment.

There was no reason to think anything would move them away from this part of the world. So when Adele got a letter out of the blue from her old employer, Mrs Edith Perkins, it overturned their settled existence.

34 Elm Tree Road
St John's Wood
Middlesex

September 25th 1908

Dear Adele

I do hope this letter finds you well and that you are settled into work with Lady Parsons. I'm sure they are thrilled to have you there and that you are doing a marvellous job for them.

I am writing to ask you though, if you would consider a new position in London. My good friend Mrs Freemantle is looking for a lady's maid who speaks French and the position would be offered with a chauffeur's job for Thomas, if you were to consider it. They are the most delightful family and I thought of you immediately when she said she had a vacancy. She has been let down so badly by her staff recently, and she needs an honest, trustworthy woman like you to convince her that not all the French girls she has employed are out to steal her jewels.

They have a large house in Queensbury Place, South Kensington and plenty of rooms for you and Thomas. It would be good for young Fred to move to the capital. I do hope you will give this some consideration.

With warmest wishes,

Edith Perkins

Adele was astounded, and the more she read and reread the letter, the more the idea grew in her that this was an opportunity not to be missed.

"We'll be nearer to France of course, and just think Thomas, what it could offer Fred. He will have so many more opportunities down there. He was going to leave school in two years anyway, and there he can study engineering. Something good will come of it I'm sure."

"But Adele, our family are here. We have this house..." Thomas's voice trailed away. The chance to never have to go down into that damp, blackness again, to be free of the responsibility for the lives of a thousand men. He could take that boulder out of his pocket where it had been dragging him down each day he worked at the pit.

"A Chauffeur, she says. No mention of the cars this Mrs Freemantle has, is there? No doubt a Rolls Royce, something grand like that perhaps?" His mind was out of the mine now and on the roads, himself driving a gleaming Silver Ghost. A peaked cap, a smart uniform. Safe, above ground.

Adele's mind was in a different place. She was inside the drawing room of one of those grand houses in London she had read about.

Three days later, Adele wrote back.

2, Hagg Bank
Wylam
Northumberland

September 28th 1908

Dear Mrs Perkins

Thank you so much for your letter and recommendation. You are always so kind to have me in your thoughts and I cannot thank you enough for this offer of employment with your friends, the Freemantles. We are delighted with the idea and would very much like you to make the introduction for us.

Fred will also do well in London with all the opportunities there. Thank you for remembering him.

Thomas and I send you our very best wishes,

Adele Dunn

It was all arranged.

It was a cold frosty December morning, as 1908 came to its end, that Thomas, Adele and Fred arrived at Newcastle Central Station, their meagre possessions in three battered leather cases. Adele had their three tickets in her hand and anxiously scanned the station for a porter to help them. One of George Stephenson's puffing steam trains waited there. With a sharp whistle and a screech of clanking metal, belching smoke filled the glass dome roof, and the Dunns set off on the 300 mile journey down to London, and to a new life.

Chapter 3
Learning to Fly, Hendon, 1913-1914

Instead of the red brick four-roomed house, with its view of the Wylam mine, the new home for the Dunns was in a mews flat at the back of the elegant Queensbury Place, South Kensington. The white stucco five storey townhouses were ostentatiously grand, built to impress, with their porticos and first floor balconies in perfect proportion, facing their mirror images across the wide asphalt street. Rather than miners and railway signalmen, their new neighbours were now the politicians, diplomats and aristocrats of society London.

It had been a wrench for Fred to leave his school friends and the men at the garage, but he soon found a new outlet in the small engineering works just a short walk from their new home.

It was in these works among the oil and grease and the noise of the tools clanking against the machines that he first read *Flight* magazine.

"You see this Fred, this fellow Bleriot, he's just crossed the Channel in this machine. Designed it himself. It's going to change our world, you mark my words."
One of the mechanics, Jimmy, who was just a couple of years older than him had brought in the magazines.

"How do you think they manage to keep up in the air all that way Jimmy? I'd love to be able to meet such a man as this Mr Bleriot to ask him. They say he has set up a flying school in north London, at Hendon. Do you think, we'll ever get to go there?"

Fred's dreams were of flying in one of these new contraptions, those aeroplanes. He could think of nothing else.

Adele witnessed this growing obsession with aviation with some trepidation. "What mother, would encourage her only son to want to go up in something so slight, so dangerous? It is not natural, Thomas, if God had wanted people to fly then he would have given them wings, not projected them into the sky aboard a metal tub with few pieces of fabric held together with glue."

Adele looked at her husband, who had his face in the newspaper. His lack of response irritated her.

"You should say something Thomas, make him take an interest in cars, show him the engines in those, not these aeroplanes."

Adele was moved by the fact that this hero of Fred's happened to be a Frenchman and it was in France where these new machines were being made.

"The fact he is a Frenchman doing this crossing is of course not surprising, but really, I do insist, aviation is not for our boy. Thomas, you see to it."

"I'll have a word with him Adele, that's all I can do."

Fred was lucky in that he had another unlikely ally in his new obsession. Edith Perkins.

The woman who had brought the family to London, was a regular visitor to South Kensington, especially to spend time in the new museums, and in whose cavernous room she loved to spend an hour or two, looking in amazement at the dinosaur bones and other exhibits. In another lifetime she thought she would have longed to study such things.

One afternoon, after a particularly stimulating visit, Edith decided to call on her old friend Mrs Fremantle. After a tea and a gossip, Edith asked after Adele and how the Wylam family were settling in. Mrs Freemantle took the same warm attitude to her staff as Edith, so Adele was soon brought up to meet up with her former employer.

"How is young Fred settling into life here?" Mrs Perkins asked.

"He is well and thriving, thank you Mrs Perkins. He spends most of his time talking about these new flying machines. He reads all the magazines and is obsessed with this idea of flying across the Channel."

"Yes, I know all about this marvelous Frenchman Monsieur Bleriot, Adele. I read he has come over to London to start a flying school here."

Edith was intrigued. She had always loved adventure and the new and daring appealed to her sense of a world beyond that of an upper class matriarch. Yes, thought Edith, aviation and aviators may be just the thing to interest her. She was fascinated that Fred had become interested in flight, hardly a hobby which a boy with no great financial prospects might ever hope to enjoy.

Just as well that her husband Charles had died a rich man she thought, as living on his eight thousand pounds a year made up somewhat for his early demise. Charles had always preferred his horses to humans. She had to be thankful at least she was still legally his wife when he had died in the crash. It had been hard at first; a wealthy widow can attract the wrong types. But she felt she had made the best of it. If only she didn't feel so bored. But now, for a woman who feared boredom, like many women feared germs, here was a solution. The new world of aviation could just be the answer.

"Well I have an idea, Adele. I too, like young Fred, have become interested in these machines. I would be happy to pay for him to learn to fly at this new school. Maybe in time, he will even take me up in one of these contraptions."

Fred could not believe his good fortune. He knew from Flight magazine that of those who were taking up the offer at the Louis Bleriot school, he might be the only one who came from a local village school, where his father had been a miner. But what did that matter, he was being given a chance to learn to fly.

The winter which brought 1913 to a close was bitter and not the best time to start a training in anything, let alone something which involved getting off the ground. But Mr Grahame-White who ran the school was not the sort of man to let a bit of snow and wind get in the way of his desire for flight.

It was well below freezing and a thin, perilous layer of ice covered the streets outside Queensbury Place. Fred took the underground to Golders Green and then a motor bus to the new airfield on Colindale Avenue. He had fretted over what to wear and what impression he would make, but had decided in the end to go for a tweed jacket, a cap, and heavy wool overcoat with thick leather lace up boots. He got off the bus just before 7am, and as it was still dark, he was not sure where to go. He noticed another young man, about his age heading north.

"Excuse me, sir, do you know the way to the Mr Grahame-White Aviation School?"

"I'm going that way myself, so follow me," said the young man. His easy manner and startling grey eyes made Fred soon warm to his new acquaintance.

"Robert Lilywhite. I'm an apprentice mechanic there by the way. What are you here for?"

"I'm signed up to learn to fly. I've got to meet Mr Grahame-White at 7am and was worried I'd be a bit late. It's not the best weather to learn to fly in." They both looked up at the colourless sky. It looked like it might snow later.

"You're right there. We'll not be going up in this. I'm learning too as it happens. He's a bit of a stickler, Mr Grahame-White, but he has been good to me and let me try for my license, so I can't complain."

Fred soon discovered that Lilywhite came from Chichester in Sussex where his father was a grocer. Fred felt a tinge of guilt and decided it was best to keep the story of his rich benefactor to himself until he got to know his new friend a little better. He hoped that Robert would not ask, though it would soon be obvious that he wasn't one of those public-school boys spending their father's fortunes, bored with shooting and fishing, and pursuing flying as the latest amusement. These characters usually came along in their own cars, or were even chauffeur driven by men like his father. They certainly didn't get the 83 motor bus to Colindale Avenue.

For the first few weeks the training consisted mainly of lessons in the hangar and a few cross country races to get them all fit. Mr Grahame-White insisted his would- be pilots spend hours drawing precise models and only after they had memorised the workings of each of the new machines at the aerodrome were they to be allowed their first taste of flight.

January 2nd 1914. His first flight.

He was to go up with an instructor in a Maurice Farman Longhorn, a two-seater with a 70 horse power French engine. They planned their flight on the ground, as up above the sound of the engine and the wind would be too great for conversation. They would fly in a straight line, with no turns or twists or 'showing off', and then instructor would hand over the controls to Fred for a few minutes.

Learning To Fly

It had stopped raining and most of the Christmas snow had melted. The runway was still bordered by small grit-stained patches of it. The instructor took off into the wind, gracefully, and with a signal forward with his arm, he took them up to about six hundred feet. Fred looked behind at the sheds they had left less than a minute before. It was a feeling like no other he had ever experienced. Not driving, swimming, not even kissing Lily Swinbourne, the girl who worked in the kitchens at Queensbury Place, could match this feeling of being like the birds, looking back down on the world below, the wind pushing against your face, its chill making your eyes sting so that tears formed in the corners. He felt the freedom of the empty space around him and a calmness, which was surprising, given the intense sound of the engine.

He felt no fear, not even when he looked over the side of the metal frame and could see the motor bus wending its way up Colindale Avenue. Everything was diminished, and the few people walking along, had become ant-sized. The hills to the north of London looked like mole hills in the distance. Cautiously when he got the signal, Fred took the controls. He held it steady, enjoying the feel of the engine through the metal wheel, its vibrations reaching through his arms and down into his body like a transfusion. The machine responded to his gentle touch and purred along, no showing off, the instructor had said. It was a long way from the five figures of eight he would have to do solo if he were to get his Aero certificate, but it was a start. A good start. By the end of the month he promised himself *I will be able to fly*.

Chapter 4
To France, October 1914

Fred had not expected things to move so quickly after the August Bank Holiday weekend. It was as if one moment he was a showman aviator in north London, where time was measured out leisurely between weekend displays. Now every minute was accounted for, every one making him ready for war. With just 40 hours in the air, Fred was to leave for France on October 2nd.

The day was not auspicious when he reported to the airfield at Farnborough to pick up the Bleriot 68. Most of the other non-commissioned officers and pilots were making their way across the Channel by steamer ferry and train but Fred and three others were flying there. The spare seat would be for his luggage.

He felt that same feeling of unease he had felt that first day at Hendon, that his clothes would mark him out as somehow different to all of the others The most important thing was to fit in, he told himself, let his flying speak for his character and hope that what he had ordered at Burberry would not let him down. He was glad of the long waterproof coat he had and buttoned it up to his neck. His brand new leather boots, polished like mirrors.

Mist and light rain had left the aerodrome with a miserable, pensive feel and no one came to wave off the latest men to head east to make the channel crossing. They knew they had to go via Redhill and reach Dover by lunchtime to give them enough daylight to make the French coastline.

"Right, see you in Dover. Let's get at them."

They took off just after dawn, heading east. The wind was with them for a while and the flying was straightforward. But then small woolly clouds appeared and it became more difficult to place where he was. Fred knew Lillywhite would be behind him, along with two others in Bleriots, but above the noise of his own engine he could not hear the other aeroplanes, and the cloud was obstructing most of what was behind and now in front of him. The low open cockpit felt to Fred like he was almost sitting on these clouds themselves. Alone in the great mass of air between heaven and earth, at this height with not even the birds for company. He assumed he was still heading east, but getting your bearing right in cloud was not easy. Fred knew he was now dependent on his compass and the few techniques the training commander had drummed into them in the seven weeks since the war was declared. He tried to steady the metal dial and cursed the ice cold pain in his fingers which made him clumsy. But still he felt no fear, flying did that to him. With every sensation activated, there was no tiny gap for that sliver of self-doubt to creep in.

After what seemed like hours bumping in and out of clouds, without the guide of railway lines or landmarks below, he came out into clear skies and could just make out the airfield at Dover below. He turned the engine off, and brought the machine down into a glide, flattening the descent out as he neared the ground before landing with only a slightly awkward bump. The others had already landed, their Bleriots lined up and empty outside the sheds. He must have gone off course by several miles

"You took your time, Dunn!" Lillywhite called when he saw his friend climb down from the cockpit.

"Just checking out a few things on the way, trying out my compass skills. We may need it over there." Fred knew his friend would see through the bravado.

"Well you're here now. Looks like we're here for the night." The relief was evident in Lillywhite's voice.

Lillywhite was right, since the Farnborough team had landed, winter wet and numb with cold, the weather had darkened, and a blanket of rain lay malevolently between them and their enemies. The war would have to wait another night.

As it turned out the men had to spend a second night there too due to the weather.

When they did leave the sky was still mottled grey like too-often washed underwear, but at least it wasn't raining. Visibility was even worse as they got over the pigeon grey sea, but one by one they flew on, a chain of birds heading south. For them it was not to an African summer, but a winter in occupied northern France. Fred had been there before and could speak his mother's tongue fluently. He felt a familiarity as the postage-stamp neat agricultural land came into view.

Fred could make out the packages of fields and hedges marking out small farmsteads, no different to how they would have been two hundred years ago, except now they appeared to be desolate, no lone farmer or worker brave enough to welcome them to their country.

They all swooped in like grateful sea birds, landing at a village just west of Calais to get their bearings. All four made it down, passing their first test as war time pilots. From Calais they had been told to hug the coast and keep low, around 200 feet, following the rocks and cliffs westwards to Boulogne.
They had been in the sky for four and a half hours, an eternity in an exposed cockpit, and their bodies were stiff with fatigue and hunger. The bar of chocolate they had last eaten in England was not enough to fill their stomachs and they landed at Etaples, bone cold and hungry, and decided to spend the night there rather than make the journey any further south.

Although Etaples boasted a small airfield bashed out of an open corn field and dangerously close to small groups of trees, there were no sheds or hangars for protection, so they curled up, and tried to sleep under the wings of their machines.

"First night in France at war," Fred said. "Doesn't feel like we'll be in any danger here, eh, Lillywhite?" But his friend was already fast asleep.

Fred pulled his long waterproof coat about him and tried to make himself comfortable on the rough ground. Sleep that night was difficult, but he managed to catch a few hours before the light woke them. It seemed strange to be there alone, in France, without any superior to monitor their journey. They had been told to make it to Abbeville and no 3 Squadron, but no one had specified how or when they were to be there. He and Lillywhite checked with the maps they had.

"I reckon we should keep to the coastline. That way we can be sure where we are. There looks like a flat beach at Le Crotoy, and we can go inland from there."

They landed in a field just south of Abbeville where

Learning To Fly

they had been told to report to A Flight, no 3 Squadron, under the command of Major John Maitland Salmond. He was not there to receive his new men of course. He was running operations from a hotel at Amiens while teams of his men tried to make an airfield out of the rough ground of a farmstead. The roads around had turned to a soft yellowish mustard-like mush and old abandoned farm carts littered the yard which was to become their base. The buildings were not equipped for anyone to sleep in, having just given up the cattle which were their previous occupants. The smell of their dung hung everywhere and coupled with the odour of the weeks-unwashed bodies of the labourers who were clearing the debris, the stench was almost overpowering. It was not the most auspicious start to the war for the young pilots and for the first week Fred and the others had to sleep again under the wings of their machines in the open air.

As the nights got really cold, they would all crawl into the nacelle and huddle down against the controls. Being able to sleep in the smallest of spaces was a skill all pilots had to acquire quickly in wartime.

"How far do you think we are from the fighting?" Lillywhite asked. He tried to sound casual, but now they were actually there, and the business of war was all around them, he was clearly anxious.

"Oh miles. No sign of the Bosch in this part. We probably won't even get to see them. It could all be sorted out further east and we'll be heading home in no time." Of course if that happened Fred would be disappointed. Waiting for the action had made it a strangely longed-for experience.

"I don't think there's any chance of that, Fred. It looks like we're setting up here for a few months at least." Lillywhite's attitude was different. He knew that if the war was to be over before it had even begun, he would not be disappointed.

It was in fact several weeks before the men got their first sight of the enemy. The Rumpler-Taube flew above them brazenly, checking them out, cheekily, testing them. One of the other pilots, Charlton, who was about to take off, headed off after it, cursing its German flier, keen to be the first to bring down an enemy fighter. But the machine was too quick, powered eastwards by the wind, he was gone long before Charlton could find him and claim his trophy.

So it began. The airborne game of cat and mouse. Up and down, from Abbeville to Bernay and on to St Pol, even as far north as St Omer, following the railway lines or the rivers. Their objective to observe any enemy movements. On the good days, the 50 miles of flight went without incident. It was easy to make out and avoid the sharp burst of artillery fire or the white puffs of smoke from the German guns below, a perfect indicator of where the enemy was digging in.

Up early with a mug of strong tea, on a two-hour patrol, and back for breakfast. Then two hours more duty, then back for lunch and the afternoon two further hours in the air, then back in the rooms before an evening in the mess. Very occasionally there were dusk patrols.

It was often too cloudy to see anything in detail, but on good days up above the fighting, observing, god-like, they screwed their eyes to make out any movements below them and reported back. Men marching, heavy traffic on the road, railway carriages being loaded. All information which could help win a war. Their greatest danger a stuttering engine or lack of petrol, not an enemy aeroplane.

October 12 1914 machine Bleriot 681. Passenger Sgt. Allen. Hours in air, 2 hours 40 minutes. Bethune, Lens, Lille and St Omer, 5,000 feet, 170 miles, good wind, going near to firing line for observation of artillery fire. Very cloudy. Machine did ok.

When he wrote up his day in his log book each night, Fred knew that it read just like an office job, with not even as many hours worked as his father had put in down the mine in Wylam.

He'd written, *Observing artillery fire*, surely the simplest of tasks, but what he didn't write was how his Bleriot was shaken as if in the jaws of a determined terrier and almost tipped over by sharp bursts of fire which whipped through the clouds when they had come lower.

What *Machine did ok* really meant was that it had saved Sgt. Allen's life. One inch was all that had separated him from coming back a dead man. That routine observational trip had been made longer by Allen not getting the course quite right. The clouds had made it impossible to see which small indistinguishable village they had just passed. Then just outside of Bethune when Fred had brought them down to find out where they were, a barrage of artillery fire had found them. It may well have been French soldiers firing. Whatever it was, that one stray bullet had pierced the side of the cockpit just inches from Allen's head. Another had missed the petrol tank by an even smaller margin.

But that evening, alive and intact, Allen was back in the mess with its warm fire and plenty of rough wine. He showed them all a graze on his forehead. They all laughed at that. It was not done to suggest what might have been if it had been an inch more to the right. They all knew what that meant.

It was exhilarating, this game of dodging death. Battling plummeting temperatures, weaving in and out of cloud and even snow, and fingers always numb with the cold, but every day in the air, flying. Then, in those early weeks the men in the Royal Flying Corps were giddy with the excitement of their new lives at war.

Before the real fighting started.

24

Chapter 5
Christmas 1914

The mid-winter trundled on, not crisp and even, just muddied and coarse.

Christmas was fast approaching. There was no hope of a break. Fred had been hoping for leave to get home to see his parents, but he knew that would be impossible. Two weeks before Christmas he received a letter.

Sutton Place
Hawley
Kent

December 15, 1914

Dear Fred

I do hope you like the small package from Fortnum's. I am sending it to you along with some silk gloves, which I hear are just the thing to brave the cold for young aviators.

I have moved to my house in Kent for the time being, and Kitty is staying with me. You may have heard that Captain Burrell was due to join his regiment in November. He was at Southampton when he was taken ill with pneumonia and he died in hospital there. It took us all by surprise, even those of our family who are used to tragedy.

Your mother writes to me when she hears from you, and I check the newspapers regularly, but they don't mention the flying very much. There is so much else going on and all those poor young men who won't be coming home. It really is an awful business and what with William dying before he even got to France, it doesn't seem very festive here at all. We all hope to see you back here soon, safe and sound.

Yours with admiration, and wishing you a Happy Christmas,

Edith Perkins

Fred had not expected a letter from Edith. Certainly not one which revealed the fact that Kitty was now a widow. Carefully, he examined his feelings. He had only met her for a few minutes. Of course she had intrigued him, but why did he feel lighter and happier as a result of hearing about someone's great loss? 'We all hope…' was the we Edith and his mother… or Kitty? Had something and someone unobtainable now become within his grasp?

The August bank holiday at Hendon had been on his mind increasingly. In the absence of any woman, or anything feminine, the image of her lithe, slim body, under that delicate cloth and her wide smile of congratulation was something he could not shake from his mind.

For the group of young men in France, most were unacquainted with any woman other than their mothers, sisters or maids, and sex was something seldom discussed, only occasionally joked about.

Fred had been with a woman at Hendon. She had been hoping to work in the theatre and had come to watch the shows and catch the eye of the dashing aviators with her coquettish smile and ruby red tumbling hair. It had not lasted and after a few weeks she had stopped coming to the airfield. Fred assumed she had met someone, an actor or theatre owner, someone who could be more useful to her career than an exciting but ultimately impoverished young pilot. It had been brief, un-noteworthy and not a subject he would ever bring up in the mess.
But Kitty Burrell, she was different.

British Expeditionary Force
France

December 20, 1914

Dear Mrs Perkins,

Thank you so much for the package. The pudding and pies are much appreciated here. We are going to eat the pudding on the 25th, and all the men in our Flight will thank you warmly at the thought of tasting a proper English pudding. I have already had some of the pies. They were delicious. We eat rather well here considering. There is enough meat for everyone and the French make the best bread and cheese, as my mother always says. We seem to be able to get everything we need, though I'm not sure it is true of our soldiers elsewhere. You are very clever to know about the silk gloves. I know some of the men have them and swear by them and they keep out the cold rather well. There is nothing like the feeling in your fingers go. There is a pilot here who lost a finger through frostbite. Can you believe it? I'm sure your kind gift will prevent any such thing happening to me.

Your news about poor Captain Burrell was such a shock to me. Please do send my deepest sympathy to Mrs Burrell. We lose good people on too many days here, and it is hard to act normally when you know a young man is not around one day after you shared a joke with him the day before. Perhaps it is a small comfort to Mrs Burrell to know how many other families are going through the same thing. The war in the end will be won, we all believe that. Although we only met briefly, I would very much like to write to Mrs Burrell with my sympathy if that would be appropriate.

Best wishes and thank you again for your kindness to me,

Fred Dunn

Fred realised as he finished writing that his heartbeat has quickened, and his hand was shaking. He couldn't understand what had made him feel that way. It could only be thinking about the beautiful Kitty Burrell.

He had meant what he said about it being hard to accept the deaths of the young men in his squadron. They all felt it when one of them didn't come back, and their meagre possessions had to be packed up, and the place in the hut or at dinner taken by someone else. But life went on. That was the only way.

What could he, a miner's son, her mother's ward effectively, ever mean to her? What chance was there she would even reply?

But now Kitty was single, she had returned his gaze and spoken with him, not as an inferior, but maybe as a brother figure or a friend of his family's. He remembered the moment

Learning To Fly

again and let his thoughts wander so that he could even imagine her presence there, among the damp smelling sweat-stained khaki and ingrained mud of his hut. He would write to her. He had not time to wait for Mrs Perkins' permission.

British Expeditionary Force
France

December 20, 1914

Dear Mrs Burrell

I heard from your mother about the terrible loss of your husband and immediately wanted to write to you, to send you my deepest sympathy. As I wrote to Mrs Perkins, we are facing up to so many deaths. It is very hard to make sense of it all. It must be so difficult for you. I do hope you are being comforted in your loss and will find solace in your stay with your mother in Kent.

Fred grabbed the letter ready to tear it up. His eyes raced over the words. It read just like an officer might write to the mother of one of the pilots who had been killed. Platitudes. Did they really offer any grieving parent or wife any comfort, to know their loved one had died fighting for their King and Country? What solace was there in that? He knew very few such letters ever gave away the actual details of a death. The country could not stomach that kind of honesty.

Pilots he had known had died hours after surviving a forced landing. Broken and near death, they had struggled on, wheezing, spitting blood and desperate for their end. They had not died quickly and painlessly as the CO's letter would put it. The flamers. Of course you would never mention how they went. The charred books and burnt cigarette case, with their assailing residue of smoke, would never be returned to those homes.

How could he find the words to show that this was not one of those routine letters? How would he convey that as he wrote, she had become something more to him than the daughter of his benefactor he had met only briefly?

He added a few more lines before he began to think too deeply. Their letters were censored, but he would have to be the censor now. He must keep his true feelings in check.

I enjoyed meeting you in Hendon and do hope you found the flying interesting to watch. Maybe as you are in Kent there is an aerodrome near, and if you see the aeroplanes you will think of us chaps out here.

With my deepest sympathy,

Fred Dunn

There, he thought, licking the envelope and addressing it to Sutton Place. There. A bit of a risk.

But what was there without risk? Risk was something he knew all about. Life was a series of calculated and sometimes unexpected risks.

Some nights he assumed he would be dead by the New Year, and as death had become a constant companion, it had lost some of its horror.

He sealed the letter and put it in the tray ready for the censors and Kitty.

Chapter 6
Paris, January 1915

It was a routine patrol, this time without his observer. The take off into the wind had been stomach-churningly bumpy, as if thrown by a catapult. Small gusts of wind nipped at the wings unsteadying the machine, and the rain was battering his helmet and causing his goggles to steam up. Fred had to hold tight to keep both him and the Morane upright. He cursed the weather under his breath. Out of nowhere, a group of clouds appeared, chasing him, drawing him in, and blocking all visibility. It was an enveloping grey mass, like an oversized overcoat still damp from being worn in a heavy downpour.

Fred decided to drop quickly from 2,000 feet and get out of the dark heart of the clouds. Now just a few hundred feet from the ground, he feared he would hit the tops of the trees in a small copse with the wheels, and tugged hard to pull up and over the obstacle. At this rate he would be able to read the road signs on the side of the lanes, and could end up impaled on one.

He could see houses and a church spire poking up in the distance. Then, as if a switch had been pushed, the engine stopped. He could feel the power drain away. Before he had time to assess why it had happened and whether it was as simple as not having any petrol, a raised area of muddy brown earth loomed up at him. He lifted the wing, presenting the underside of the machine to the fast approaching obstruction, but suddenly the wing tip was rammed hard against some boulder and folded back on itself, its slight frame unable to withstand the force of solid rock. The Morane tipped right over, its glue hardened linen wings crumpling like crushed tissue paper.

Fred remembered very little of what happened next. The impact must have thrown him out of the cockpit. His last conscious thought had been of the wing touching the rough stony earth. It was his first real crash since learning to fly, and although he'd had a few scrapes and forced landings, he had always had time to think to himself in those few seconds... so, this is it.

"Monsieur, Monsieur."

The pock-marked, quizzical face of a young French farmer was looking right at him. He could smell the sour combination of garlic, cigarettes and bad breath. He was alive then. Though in a bit of pain, he could move his limbs. He surprised the young farmer by speaking his language.

"Thank your sir. If you can tell me where I am, and how far from Bethune? I will need to get word to my Squadron to come and collect me and what bits of the machine we can save."

"Monsieur, you are 40 miles from there. I could not believe it when I saw you come down like that. We thought you would be dead. Thanks to God you live."

The younger of the two men, who had spoken to Fred ran off. Fred offered the older farmer, maybe he was the father or even grandfather, a cigarette. Without uttering a word, the old man pocketed it deep inside his dungarees' pocket, and stood silently, staring back at the wreckage. He reminded Fred of the poem by Thomas Grey.

And aged peasants too amazed for words Stare at the flying fleets of wondrous birds

"It won't fly anytime soon, this machine. It is too badly damaged, but we will salvage some of it if I can get help."

The conversation with the older man would not be as easy, he clearly had never seen an aeroplane that close up and looked confused as to why it had landed in his field. Fred knew he would have a long uncomfortable wait in the field for the tender to arrive.

When Fred got back to the base, it appeared in darkness, only a few lantern lights glowed through the mess hut windows. He was told that two of the four machines which had left that morning had not made it back. Hanlon, and Davidson had been seen coming down, and the other machine, with no observer, was last spotted heading north to St Omer.

The weather had got worse since then and the rain which had buffeted Fred had turned into a downpour nearer to the coast. They were waiting to hear whether Powell had managed to make it. The news, coupled with his own crash, was crushing. He felt guilty to be alive in the face of the news of the two dead airmen and another missing. Hanlon had given him the thumbs up when he took off. Was that a sign, he was saved and Hanlon wasn't?

Fred was too tired and sore to sit with the few still left in the mess that night listening to awkward jolly ragtime tunes, drinking pastis. There were no words left for that day; he merely longed for sleep and oblivion.

Fred was given 24 hours to recover before he learned of his next task. Rowden the adjutant put it to him, with a knowing glint in his eye. Paris and the Rhone engine factory. He was to spend 10 days there learning all he could about the new rotary engines. The mechanics Webb, Bowyer and McCudden would go too, but by road. Fred would be flying a Morane back to the factory to have its engine checked.

Fred couldn't believe his luck. All those hours in the garage and engineering works back in South Kensington would prove worthwhile. Fred was considered one of the most technical of airmen and even the mechanics themselves had to admit that for a pilot, often the butt of most of their jokes and derision, he knew his engines as well as they did.

The three engineers left the next morning and arranged to meet Fred at the factory on Boulevard Kellerman, on the south side of the city. None of them had been to Paris before, so it was an opportunity to learn not just about engines, but about the other things the city had to offer.

"Just think, a haircut and a hot bath. Gentlemen, lady luck is with us now." Bowyer pushed his hand through his unkempt hair as if to prove his point.

"Clean sheets, for the first time in months." Each man had many reasons to be thankful to be in Paris.

"What about a show and maybe one of those bars I've heard about." Webb winked at the others, who smiled knowingly.

Fred knew Adele would most certainly have advised her son to avoid those places, but they drew soldiers and airmen like magnets.

Paris, in early 1915, was untouched by the war which was raging just north in Flanders. It was hard to believe it was the capital of a country at war. Its wide avenues were thronged with people, young and old, well-dressed, smiling and apparently carefree. The cafés and bars were well-stocked, and the monuments, that January still stood majestically, showing themselves off to the young airmen.

The Germans had got quite close a few months ago, but now with the new year the city appeared impregnable again. The motor taxis bowled along the elegant streets, they were back from their service transporting soldiers to the front when the enemy had appeared almost at their gates. Now their fares were the gilded ladies and the aged top hat wearing gentlemen who accompanied them. The tall thin trees were leaf less and the air crisp with the January chill, but there was a positive sense of a city still able to practice its favourite pastime of showing off.

Just beside the factory in the neat rows of tall pale-stoned properties, seamstresses behind the closed doors of the fashion houses cut, stitched and embellished silks and satins to create the outfits for their wealthy clientele. War had not sated the desire for the rose pink and eau de nil fabrics carefully created into long luxurious gowns. Fred passed their windows and observed their provocative styles with amazement.

Even in London, there were no windows offering such a view to a mere passer by. Before he had met Kitty Burrell he had not noticed the effect an expensive figure hugging gown could have on the feminine shape. Now he could admire the cut of the cloth draped over the mannequins in the window and imagine it on her. When he reached the factory sign at the end of the boulevard he was relieved to be in the more comfortable domain of metal and motors. Their work was no less sensitive to the feel of shape and motion and the best engines responded to human touch as haute couture costume does to a model's movement. He knew here, he could feel at home.

Later, the men ate at the Café de La Paix, there were no rations here and they ordered lavishly. Oysters sea salt fresh, fat pink prawns, and then thin strips of tender beef in a deep red burgundy sauce, with mushrooms and shallots, so perfect and succulent, the feast brought the table to silence. Who knew if they would be in Paris again? They were unlikely to eat like this for months, maybe ever. With enough of the heavy wine and liqueurs to make their steps unsteady, the men stumbled back along the banks of the Seine. They made their way by the wall, holding onto the cool sides for support. Bowyer and Webb held each other up, their faces under the lamplights showing an eerie green tinge uncannily the colour of the crème de menthe each of them had sampled for the first time a few hours before. Compared to how each had felt just two days before, stumbling through the city filled with her best food and drink, gave them a sense of lightness, as if a shoulder bag crammed with tools had been taken off their backs.

They had forgotten how it felt not to expect to die and be surrounded by death. That was a birthmark or more rightly a deathmark they each now wore, but tonight perhaps they could almost feel they had become invincible.

Tonight in Paris, Les Aviateurs Anglais were a long way from England and their lives before the war. A long way from the coarseness and daily grime of the Squadron and the spectre of death which hangs around it, abiding its time till it takes its next young victim. At the next corner, lured by the light through the port hole windows of its dividing doors, Bowyer led them into a bar.

It was a wood-paneled smokey snug, like the inside of a small ship, and Fred could tell from the other people huddled within its over heated interior that this was the place where they would get what they were looking for. Inside were a small group of army officers, carrying that glazed look that documented both shame and exhaustion. Shame at what they had done and seen and exhaustion beyond anything they had ever experienced before. Only those who had seen four months of real fighting would understand. They raised their heads only slightly when four uniformed men came in.

Four or five gaudy women, some waiting at tables and the others leaning against the small bar area, watched the group of men with interest, occasionally laughing or pointing at them. Fred spoke to the older woman in French, the owner maybe, her massive bosom held aloft like the prow of a ship by the tightness of her frilled black top which strained to meet over her deep set cleavage.

She signalled for some of the younger women to bring the newcomers brandy. Unlike most of the men in the squadron, Fred had not yet visited the brothel in Amiens, where a mother and daughter who by day sold bread from a small shop front had a second job upstairs in the two dark dingy bedrooms, and took the virginity of many of the British Expeditionary Force for a few francs.

The painted women in the small Parisian bar greeted the new arrivals unashamedly, briskly even, aware that to these men, they were goddesses offering nectar. Business was business, and it was especially good when there were foreign military men around. The older woman issued some more orders and made sure the newcomers had room at their table for some of her girls who had been propping up the bar. Takings tonight would be good.

When the brandy bottle level had dropped sufficiently to build up courage, the three others left Fred to go into the dimly lit side rooms. Another young woman, her long dark hair hanging loose, with just a simple pin holding it away from her forehead, sat down at Fred's table, clutching a new bottle of brandy and two glasses. He noticed the chipped red paint on her nails and cheap bangles on her wrists which clattered as she set the bottle down.

"So your friends will be happy for tonight, at least," she said, in a thick accent, one from much further south than Paris. Although she was young, his age probably, around 20, her voice and demeanour was that of a much older, world-weary woman. Funny, thought Fred, this war is ageing all of us, even prostitutes.

Her name was Marie-Louise. Fred's flawless French surprised her. She had not been expecting it. It unnerved her and made her feel exposed. Far better in the circumstances to have no common language but the business in hand.

"Military men don't usually ask names. You are a bit different. You have very good French," she said. She poured them both another brandy, glancing over at the older woman for consent. The liquid was rough and stung the back of Fred's throat as he gulped it down. He took another cigarette out of his case and slowly lit it, thinking it rude not to make conversation, though both knew where it was all leading.

"My mother is French, so I spoke the language from very young. I didn't think it would come in useful in this way." They both smiled at the understatement.

Minutes passed, the brandy was drunk.

Finally, she took his hand purposefully. She could see he had long thin fingers. Aviator's hands. She led the way, through a heavy tapestry drape to a corridor from which he could make out a few rooms on either side. Fred could hear her breathing, her deep, raspy breaths.

How many times had she done this, today, this week... during this war? Fred felt overwhelmed by a total absence of desire, a kind of dull inertia. His head felt light as if still at altitude. For just a minute he wondered where he was and had to steady himself against the damp wall. Marie-Louise led him to the last room in the corridor, which by day he guessed was used as a storeroom. He could make out the empty wine bottles in crates stacked around the edges and smell the dregs of red wine still left in the bottom.

There was a single mattress on a wooden bed in the corner with a brightly coloured knitted blanket thrown over it, as if to add a touch of colour to disguise the room's original daytime purpose. A candle was already lit, burning itself down slowly, spilling its wax over an upturned crate. She pushed him back onto the blanket and he fumbled with his Sam Browne belt and trouser buttons. He felt that maybe they both just wanted to get it over and done with. When it was, he finally pulled away to rearrange his clothes, it was with relief, not pleasure. He left ten francs on the side next to the candle.

"Goodbye, Marie-Louise."

At least he had remembered her name.

He didn't want any more conversation so he staggered out into the sobering cold of the night air. It must be well after midnight. The others would have to make their own way back.

Chapter 7
Neuve Chappelle, France, March 1915

After the respite in Paris, the next few months were a return to the daily drudgery of patrols, interspersed by misery at each loss and the forced jollity in the company of their replacements. Any lightness felt after a good sing song or a win at cards was offset within hours by the news of a crash or a headache inducing, frost-biting flight. Those were the flights which left you numb with pain.

The monotony of reconnaissance flying coupled with the terror of having to spot enemy planes before they picked you out was gruelling. When the war had been in its infant months, roles to observe from above and report back were easily defined, to be the eyes and ears of the artillery. Now with the enemy in the skies too, each circling the other like Medieval Knights, their roles had become offensive. For young men, some still in their teens, this was a new and terrifying change.

The Germans had learned to arm their aeroplanes, to make them fighting machines. The battles now would not just be fought on the rough ground separating the trenches, but in the skies too. Men who just months before had been showmen aviators performing for adoring crowds were now expected to be killers.

"It's lasted seven months already, and looks like it will be another seven months at least. Sometimes I cannot even remember the names of some of the first ones to go. I can see their faces.

"Charlton, Dawes, and that other Officer who talked about his horses… who was that?"

"Munroe, went down in flames, poor bugger. But his observer, who was that, from Lancashire, I think?"

"I don't mind admitting Fred, I dread the end of patrol when you count the machines back in. Even if they have been shot to pieces, I'm still mighty glad to see the six line up. It's not what I expected to be honest, back then when we joined up."

With Fred, Lillywhite felt he could say more than he would in front of the others.

"It's a roller coaster you're right there Lillywhite. Sometimes I think we will be dead by the Summer, then I think surely it cannot last a whole year. Someone has a plan to win this bloody thing. We just have to believe that Robert. Let's get a drink, old boy, we are making ourselves miserable with all this talk. Good job no one can hear us. Not sure Salmond would approve."

A letter on thick paper the colour of clotted cream was handed to him as he and Lillywhite made their way to the mess. It smelt fresh and clean, unsullied by war.

Sutton Place,
Hawley,
Kent

January 25 1915

Dear Fred,

It was so kind of you to send your good wishes and sympathy to me after the death of my dear husband William. This terrible war has turned too many people into young widows. I know William would be sorry not to have even reached France and fought the enemy like all you brave young men out there. We do read the papers, and each day mother scans the columns to see if she knows any of the names. I'm sad to say that very often we do. I do wish we could do more.

I have been staying in Kent with mother, and although I know I should go home at some point, for now, I am happy to stay here. We are not so far from France of course, and sometimes we think we can even hear the fighting. Do you think that is possible? We also see the aeroplanes fly overhead on their way out to join the Royal Flying Corps. I do think of you all out there when they go past. It seems so long since that August bank holiday at Hendon. A lifetime ago.

You asked if you could write to me, and the answer is yes. We do long for news and I know mother would want to hear how you are getting on. Perhaps you can tell me what I can send you from Fortnum's.

With best wishes,

Kitty Burrell

Fred felt like he had suddenly come out into open sky, He could be in touch with her. She had said so. Could he dare to hope they may even meet again if this cursed war ever ended?

Despite what he'd said to Lillywhite, from the air, they could see the German army was not going to give up easily. Like ants colonising dark earth mounds, they could see the mass movements of heavy military machines, trainloads of them, coming and going up the lines, and Germans digging vast stretches of trenches across north eastern France. A scar with its tributaries stretching out like small bleeds was forming right down the middle of the country, as from above the airmen watched these two enemies, sometimes only yards apart, gathering more and more the means of killing each other.

There was to be a big push around Neuve Chappelle and the Royal Flying Corps were to play their role by indicating the German positions and trying to bomb the enemy from above to improve the chances of an Allied advance over ground. They had a new addition to their tasks, they were to try out the new cameras to get photographic maps of any movement below.

Photography in the air wasn't an easy operation.

"It's like a bloody tea chest strapped to the side. Did nobody think it would make keeping these buses in the air a bit more difficult with that weight on one side."

Hill, his new observer, gunner and now photographer was not impressed by the new technical challenge they'd been given. The transfer was the worst bit, getting the plates out and new ones in, all the time keeping low.

"And the Hun knows where we are, course he bloody

does, wobbling around, taking the plates out, putting them in. I hope someone bothers to look at them, what with us being sitting ducks and all that." Hill kept this monologue up as he struggled with the new contraption, confident in Fred's flying skills to counter any imbalance his actions might cause.

Captain Conran led the bombing party out after the aerial photographers had done their bit. Grey volcanic plumes of smoke came up towards them as their firepower hit their target and blinded the fliers coming behind. Day after day it went on. At night, faces bore the strain of the operation, ears were becoming deaf with the constant noise of shelling, nerves were straining just a little bit tighter. Each of those single days in early March stretched out like a decade. No one got any sleep, there was never any let up in the noise, of shells or machines. The knock on the door to rouse them came it seemed minutes after they had put their heads down, and eyes crusted and drowsy and wearing the uniform they had slept in, they would crawl into their cockpits and fly into the eye of another storm.

It was enough to curdle the smiles of the most gung-ho, and even Conran, the bravest of the brave, was etched with tiredness and exhaustion. They were told not to mourn the men who died, but to face forward. Salmond had been insistent.

Somehow they had to press deep down inside themselves the horror at what they saw below. They had to forget when good men like Wadham didn't come back. Conran had seen it. A deep spiral after being hit, from 1000 feet to a sickeningly loud crash. Did he die in the descent or on impact? At least he didn't die in flames, the worst of all deaths. That was the darkest of all the pilots' nightmares, and for which many of them kept a revolver in the cockpit. Better to shoot yourself, than die that way.

Fred didn't carry a revolver, so he would have no choice in the matter. Deep down he knew he would have found it hard to pull the trigger. He had seen two aeroplanes downed now, both bursting into fireballs of crackling yellow red and white flames. No time even to scream for them. It did not do to think about it. That way madness lay, Fred knew that, but often at night he thought madness was where he and a few of the others were heading anyway. A form of insanity was the only way to explain the turmoil in his mind.

Although the battle had lasted only three days, only yards had been gained in a see-saw barrage which had not pushed them forward any great distance. Over 11,000 were dead. A whole village or small town lost in three days. It could always get worse, that was the only true lesson of war.

March 12th was cold and damp, like most days that March. All colour had been drained from the sky leaving it a grey gruel.

At 5pm Fred returned from a particularly wet and uncomfortable patrol and a few of the others, including Conran, had gone off out again. Cholmondeley and his mechanic were loading up their Morane outside one of the sheds preparing to follow them.

"See you later chaps," Fred raised a cheery wave to them as he walked back to his hut.

A fierce blast caught him in the back, forcing him to brace hard to avoid falling flat.

Turning round he saw smoke filling the space he had just passed, rising into the air. Acrid, oil laden smoke. He felt sick. Two more loud sharp explosions followed. It was the most heart-stopping of sounds, right there on their own base, miles from the enemy. Where Captain Cholmondeley had been standing by his aeroplane minutes before was now just a massive fire ball. The whole of the machine was on fire, though it was hard to make out its shape under the erupting flames. The mechanic must have taken a direct hit, as there was no sign of him. There had been at least three people near the plane. He hurried back to 'A' flight's shed, but already the other mechanics, rushing over, were waving people away.

With potential fire hazards in the other machines, laden with petrol, it was easy to see how much worse this disaster could become. The whole shed could still go up. On the ground there were maybe a dozen men; mutilated, unrecognisable. Only a few items of clothing were identifiable, a pair of goggles or the metal of a spanner held tight in a hand unattached to a body. The unique and ghastly smell of burning flesh filled the air.

Fred had seen death before, in many of its guises, but

never on this scale; so close, so hellish, and so horrible. A few of the men got near enough to pull away what and whom they could from the cauldron. Some of the most badly injured were carried to the first aid area. Major Salmond, brought out by the blast, stood there, ashen-faced. He instructed the fitters to make a cordon around the area. Once the badly burned men had been dragged away, he ordered everyone else to leave.

Hours later when the flames were extinguished and the smell of burned flesh and scorched fabric still hung in the void, the full extent of the explosion became clear. Eleven men had died, some of the very best of the band. Costigan and Bowyer, NCOs like Fred, both fine men. Bowyer, who had tasted crème de menthe for the first time in Paris and had kept them entertained with his tall stories. He had managed to get himself back to the Rhone factory the next morning after their night out, fuelled by girls and alcohol. A bystander to the machine which exploded, he had been caught up in the tragedy by being that yard too near.

Fred grimaced at the thought of his fiery death, and tried to push the image from his mind. Bowyer, now scorched and in bits on the tarmac. Chomondeley, too, and his observer. More good, decent young men. The men left knew all eleven. Each had a friend, a favourite among those who had gone. No squadron had ever lost so many, a carnage not even in the sight of enemy or in the skies. An accident in your own backyard. It was beyond comprehension.

That night all the men were in the mess, wide-eyed with shock, their clothes still reeking of smoke and oil. This was not a time to distinguish between ranks. A massive punch was mixed in an old farmyard bin. There was no thought of the flavour, or the combinations. Anything and everything was poured in: gin, brandy, wine, and blackcurrant juice to dilute the intensity of the flavours.

Tonight they would drink purposefully to forgetfulness. One by one they filled their glasses and downed them quickly, praying for the feeling of light-headedness to take over. Those who could told stories about those they knew the best, trying to make light of the moment or to use the blackest of humour to

Learning To Fly 43

take the edge off the evening. Soon it began to feel more like a wake.

Fred toasted Bowyer's conquest in Paris, nearly choking on his words. He'd had his hair cut as he wanted, at least he'd done that. The Major couldn't deny them their grief that night. It was hard to see how you could go forward. Hard to sleep, to eat and even to fly, when so many would not be there at breakfast.

As the men drank to near unconsciousness, Major Salmond outside in the scorched wreckage cleared the offending area with a few hand-picked helpers. He knew the men who did that job would not be able to erase the sight of their grisly task from their minds, and it would be better if the fliers going back up the next day were not the ones to bear witness to such a gruesome business.

After midnight and enough of the punch to cloud his thoughts and unsteady his walk, Fred went back to his hut. Lillywhite was there and he could hear in the dark the tight sobs of a man who didn't want anyone to know he had been crying. He too had been close to Bowyer.

Fred knew he had to write what had just happened down to try and make sense of it, to make sure he recorded it. The censors would surely take some of this out, he thought, but he had to tell the truth, to someone.

British Expeditionary Force

March 12, 1915

Dear Mrs Burrell

I wish to thank you very much for your letter, which has been a great comfort to me. I always long for news from England and your letter was the highlight of what has been a very difficult time.

Perhaps you will not wish to read all that I write here, but I will write it anyway. We have been engaged in heavy fighting. I cannot say where, but you may read in the papers how the RFC was in the thick of it. I hope we did some good by giving useful information to our side and stopping the Hun in their tracks. You do hope what you do is worth it. I don't want to sound despondent, as it is thoughts of you and the fun we had at Hendon which cheer up the dark days here. We have had a terrible loss at the squadron tonight. It turns out it was a tragic mistake. One of the bombs being loaded onto a machine accidentally exploded and the whole thing went up. The noise was so loud that it would have been heard miles away. It is a sound I will never forget as long as I live. Many young, brave men died including some good friends of mine. It touches you when so many go at once in such a dreadful way. At times like tonight, one does wonder how long we might have left. It does seem to be a matter of chance who lives and who dies.

Do please write to me. Your letter will bring some cheer out here in France. Do send my good wishes to your mother. I hope the next generation don't get to experience a war like this one. That is what we all hope and pray for.

You are so kind to offer me a parcel. Whatever you send to me will be marvellous.

Yours,

Fred Dunn

He sealed the envelope. Perhaps it didn't explain honestly what had just happened or give any deeper indication of his feelings for her, but Fred knew that he had to share what had just happened with Kitty. How else could she understand what he had experienced if they were ever to meet. He would never be able to talk about what had happened. It would never do to go back to this, and like many of the things he was witnessing he would have to bury it deep within him.

The last and only time Kitty had seen him he was a fresh faced, carefree young man, buoyed by the competition and the occasion. Now only seven months later, he looked a decade older. His skin was sallow, his eyes bloodshot. He had lost weight and his face, once open and smiling, was now etched with immovable dirt, and had gained the creases of an old peasant.

That night he had the worst of nightmares.

He was going down in flames, but never managed to hit the ground, even as the flames became hotter and fiercer, as he spun in a ceaseless descent. He could feel the air pressure pushing against his flesh. At one point he felt himself scream out, but no actual sounds were made, and the effort woke him up. He was drenched in sweat and the bedclothes were twisted into a long sausage roll. The thin over-washed sheet was torn in two places where he had tugged at it. Feeling wrung out, Fred lit a cigarette, drawing in large lungfuls.

Usually this would be calming. Not now, in the middle of the night. It made his eyes sting, his head throb, his heart race. Quickly he stubbed out the cigarette and tried to lie back on the soaked sheets.

Sleep would not come. In two hours he would be woken for the patrol.

How long can you go on like this, he thought to himself. Was he alone in feeling this despair? He knew, as he could hear the screams and the calls, that the other men had nightmares too. He could tell from their faces in the mornings that many of them had been in their own personal abyss in the night. He could tell by how many drinks they all went through, and how they pulled fiercely on their cigarettes, that nerves were frayed all around. One poor soul had had to tie his pyjama strap to his bed to stop him jumping out in his sleep. Maybe it is the same in the German huts just before dawn, Fred thought. Before setting out on their missions to kill us.

Chapter 8
Neurasthenia, June 1915

Troubles come not as single spies, but in battalions, they say.

The deaths kept on mounting up. Pilots, observers, friends of his. Now he heard about men he knew in the infantry. Fred had seen what they had to go through in the mud and gore. He was the lucky one; in a proper bed at night, with decent food and the chance to go into the town; with days off whenever the weather made flying impossible. The lads in the trenches had no such luck. Up at his vantage point you could tell they were living like rats in sewers, without being able to run away and find better accommodation.

An officer in the Northumberland Fusiliers he met in a bar by chance, had told him that John Adams and many others in the group had died near Moyenville, just six days after arriving in France. John, in his class at school, with his shy smile and easy manner, the boy who had wanted to be a grocer. He would have made a good shop keeper, and he would have had his own shop in the end.

John was reported missing at first, but it was not long before they realised he had been killed. Fred felt this loss keenly and wondered how the Turnbull brothers were doing. Had they been with John? Had anyone been with him?

The thought of dying alone, fully conscious and afraid was like a fever inside him, burning him up. He was afraid of dying in flames, everyone was, but Fred had a worse terror that once shot down, there were those terrifying few minutes before death when you would know your fate. Up there alone in the skies, you would know that your life was about to end. He wanted to believe that he would face death with dignity, not reduced to an animal state, terror opening bowels and emitting howls. He'd seen men do that and it was unendurable.

His terrors about his death in the air were becoming increasingly difficult to hide from the others. Fred, who had been so confident in his flying, could not explain why now he felt insecure every time he slipped into the cockpit. He had

Learning To Fly 47

started to shake and each flight he came back drenched in sweat with his fingers bent rigid. Many times he had to wait two or three hours before he could peel off his gloves. Worse still he had developed a stutter.

He had always been conscious of how he spoke, particularly as his now softened Geordie accent still made him stand out from the other men in the mess. Now he couldn't even get the words out. Fortunately, nobody paid much notice and on some nights it seemed like everyone was stuttering so much that it had become a new and acceptable way of speaking. No one tried to fill in the gaps. There was no point. It was as if men in the Royal Flying Corps were creating a new strange language. A Morse code for the sick at heart.

Fred was becoming fluent in it.

Middleton Hall
Hampshire

April 28, 1915

My dear Fred

We read yesterday in the papers about your Commission and wanted to congratulate you on your great achievement. It is magnificent that you have become an officer, and I have been told to pass on congratulations from all the family. My nephew John asked what we were talking about when we read the newspaper and we told him about the brave aviators who are fighting the war for us. He was very impressed and said he wanted to be a pilot one day, just like you.

I have returned to Middleton Hall. The house feels enormous without William and as several of the staff have signed up too, it is quite empty. We are very quiet here now, and I am at a loss what to do much of the time. I have already spoken to the Red Cross, and have offered some of the rooms for the poor injured young men to come to. They said they would write back to me. The hospitals are finding it hard to cope and if I can do anything to help, I am glad to. I do want to do something.

I am sending you a fruit cake and trust it will remind you a little of life back in England. I am sure it is very hard for you out there. I did feel for you when I read your last letter. It must have been the most terrible of accidents. How very disturbing to have to carry on as if nothing has happened, when there are so many empty chairs after one's friends are killed. I think it is impossible for us back in England to understand what you might be going through out there in France.

If it makes you feel better to write down what you are experiencing, please do write to me. I will try to understand.

With warmest wishes to you,

Kitty Burrell

Fred felt his face flush. It was a very different tone from her previous letter. He was not so new to correspondence with a woman to know instinctively when things had changed between them, albeit subtly.

Was it because he was now an officer? Would she now treat him as an equal, not the recipient of her mother's generosity? The son of her domestic servant? He could not dare to hope so. But how would Kitty react when she saw this shell of a man? How would anyone who was not out here seeing what he had seen understand? He could not bear to tell even a tenth of what he had seen.

What Fred didn't know was that his CO had noticed Fred's nervous strain, and that he was not alone. Six others in the squadron were showing the same signs. They had to be given leave or they would certainly kill themselves and put other men's lives at risk. Every time one of them went out with an observer or mechanic they would now be putting them in harm's way.

They used the term Neurasthenia on his leave form, though no one knew what that meant. All they knew was that it had spread, and like the measles they'd had in the squadron recently, it had infected enough men to require action. Like measles, evacuation was the only option, and the men had to be sent away to recuperate.

Fred sailed on the Salta on the 19th June 1915, arriving back in Southampton two days later. He was not even 21, but already his hair was greying at the temples, and his jacket once a perfect fit, now hung off his shoulders as if he'd borrowed it.

Now, under someone else's steam, no hero, but a troubled and war-damaged man, his return to England was doubly crushing. He had become reckless about whether he lived or died and felt ashamed of his need to seek help. In a pit village, having trouble with your nerves was seen as an affectation, or as the act of a malingerer. Far better to have died than be thought of as a malingerer. Such thoughts flew in and out of his mind as the boat docked. The country he had left in innocence would be very different now. It felt as though he was going to another world, a pure world. Pre-war. Pre death. He was not sure how he would find it, or how he would be received.

His colleagues had been sympathetic, the six of them leaving without difficult questions about their treatment. He knew he had some awkward and inevitable questions to answer when he got back to London. He would face a medical board in six days and have to explain all over again. He would have to frame words and phrases to describe exactly why, when he had been a man who loved, even lived for flying, who could fly any type of machine, day or night, why he was now unable to fly for more than half an hour without suffering headaches and shakes in his hands.

But first he had something important to do. Something he was sure would be good for his sanity. He scribbled a telegram and went to the nearest Post Office to send it.

Mrs Kitty Burrell
Invalided home. Not wounded. Going to Kensington Palace Green hospital. Fred Dunn

Chapter 9
Medical Boards, Summer 1915

The motor bus rattled along Knightsbridge towards South Kensington. Everything seemed just as he remembered it, so normal. It was as if here the war was distant, unconnected. The grandeur of the buildings was unmolested, their very neatness and lack of scars mocking the last few months of his life. The contrast with the scorched rubble and pitted roads struck him like a slap, and he wondered how everyone and everything could seem so unmarked.

People appeared to be going about their everyday business. The only sign, if you looked more closely, was that nearly all of the people out that day appeared to be old. All the young men had disappeared behind a military Pied Piper, leaving only the women and the aged. Those that were left still walked purposefully, in their ignorance, intent on their daily tasks of reaching their small businesses, to the museums or the shops. He envied them and wondered what it would be like to not really understand this war.

For a moment, he missed the men in his Flight and the shared memories that bound them. They were safe together in the knowledge of what they could reveal and what they had to hide away. A symbiotic relationship that came only with someone who had served. With anyone else there would be always be a gulf, as wide as the Channel which separated them.

Fred got off the bus, and turned into Queensbury Place, left into the mews, a row almost hidden behind the grand white houses. He drew up slowly towards the narrow bottle green door and leaded windows of number two where his parents were still living. Throughout the war they had remained in employment with the Freemantles in their London house around the corner, anxiously waiting in case one day the telegram boy would stop, rest his bike against their wall and ring their bell. They knew Fred was lucky in many respects to be in the RFC and out of the trenches, but they also saw in the names listed that even pilots and observers were dying at an alarming rate. Names they recognised appeared, some of the young men who were with Fred at Hendon. They wept for them and for the relief they shamefacedly felt when they saw again that this time Fred's name was not on the list.

Fred had decided not to be too frank about the reasons for his return. The condition, which was written, was so new and so little understood that he decided to say he was on home leave for a rest due to his headaches. It had an element of truth about it as his headaches had initially come about because of flying at altitude and the daily nausea from the smell of the fumes. As a result, they could not now be relieved by simple pain killers and a few hours' sleep.

They were now a constant companion.

As he stood in the cobbled mews, Fred saw his father Thomas, polishing the Rolls Royce Silver Ghost at the end of the narrow lane. For a few moments he stood quietly, unobserved, watching his father as he carefully rubbed at the headlights, standing back to check he had not left any smears. The scene was so typical of his father, meticulous and earnest, serious even in the most trifling of tasks. Fred felt his chest tighten and his eyes sting.

His father had aged. The dark hair was still neat and close-cropped, but his full moustache was now speckled with grey. He was a tall man. Fred had often wondered why he was himself so short. It was of course a bonus as a pilot to be short, but as his father stood up, he wondered again at his long, lean shape.

Fred coughed.

Thomas turned his head and looked over towards him. A smile spread from ear to ear. He dropped the waxed cloth and ran over to his son, taking him in his arms and holding him out before him, momentarily, as if to check it was his own returning flesh and blood stood before him.

"Fred, lad. You're here. Why on earth didn't you say you were coming today? We were expecting you tomorrow." Fred mumbled something about the speed of the train, but the words were jumbled and his father stared at him, for a second, trying to piece together what he'd said.

"Well, no worry, you're here now. Let's get you to the house then. Your ma will be there. She's been so worked up wondering when you were coming."

"It's good to be back, dad." He squeezed his father's hand. They stood like that in silence for a few seconds, embracing with just their two hands.

It was as if the years were going into reverse and he was a child again. He felt bathed in their happiness at his return and soaked it up silently, letting it wash over him. For that hour, drinking strong black tea and eating slices of thick fresh bread and butter, Fred could almost forget the reason he had been sent back. He told them he had to report to the hospital at Palace Green, just along the road from the Albert Memorial the next day. He didn't go into any more details. They did not have to ask too closely how he was feeling. A parent's intuition filled in those gaps. The reports they had read in the newspapers would not convey the full reality of what was happening in France. These were horrors that no man should see, they knew that. Especially a man of just twenty years. They could glean from Fred's sunken eyes and the stutter, which he was trying so hard to suppress, what months of war in the air had done to his young mind.

Fred asked about the family.

"Your young cousin George died of diphtheria this past winter. He was only seven. And a few more in the village, the poor mites. Your aunt and uncle have taken it very bad." His mother wiped her eyes as she gave him the news. It seemed as though a whole generation was being wiped out by war or disease.

"I'll write to them," was all Fred could think of to say. Death again met with inadequate words.

Adele spoke of Mrs Perkins. Fred was grateful that she had her back turned at the kitchen sink so the crimson flush which spread from his neck to his face could not be seen. Although he had chosen not to reveal that he had been writing to Kitty, Adele knew he had written to Mrs Perkins and seemed to be pleased about it.

"Mrs Perkins did say you're welcome to spend time with

Learning To Fly

her in Kent to help you recover from your headaches. Maybe a bit of rest and some sunshine in the country would be good for you?"

"That is very kind of her. I owe her a great deal."

Yet again, a woman who by all rights should be separated from him by her wealth and privilege was offering him a sanctuary.

The next morning, determined that no one observing him should know he was about to be treated for nervous shock, and dressed in his now brushed-clean khaki uniform, Fred strode up Exhibition Road towards Hyde Park, turning left along its metal railings towards Kensington Green and the hospital. The war was sending so many wounded and sick soldiers home that temporary hospitals were being created all over the country, out of any building the War Office could procure. 10 Palace Green belonged to the King, and was in a small row of houses at the side of Kensington Palace.

The only sign this was not currently a Royal household was the sight of a large metal desk in the tiled hall and a matronly woman wearing a blue cape and white cap crossing off names on a long list.

Lieutenant William Pretyman was the officer in charge of the medical board, a brusque man, not really suited to sickness of the mind, having spent his early medical career in Devon working in a small hospital where farm injuries and diseases brought about by poverty were his main concerns. He was nevertheless not unsympathetic, and in four months had seen enough young pilots like Fred to know that this was not a ruse to get away from the Front.

Many of the men who were sent to him, wanted to return and covered up their shame at being in front of him by insisting they needed to be declared fit for active service. Twisting their hands together, beads of sweat gathering on their foreheads, they would sit before him staring blankly. It was more eloquent a presentation than any report from their commanders. Pretyman knew that what the pilots and observers who came to see him were experiencing was equally as much a threat to their survival as a severed leg or infected lung. The difficulty was how to treat it. The doctor had to admit that he was new to this psychological field.

"Frederick Dunn, isn't it? In your own words try to explain to me how you feel when you are flying?"

"I love flying, it's all I've ever wanted to do. It's just, I just get these terrible headaches after just a short time. The vision goes and my hands start to shake. I'm sorry if that sounds stupid, sir."

"No, not stupid. And sleeping, how is that?" Pretyman knew the answer from Fred's notes.

"Not too good, sir. I have these nightmares. Lots of us do. You hear people in the night calling out."

"These nightmares then, Fred. Tell me about them?" Fred looked at Pretyman, shame coursing through him. He had to tell the truth now, there was no hiding it.

"Sir, it's hard to describe to you, but the worst ones, are about being shot down, sometimes in flames, sometimes not. But the machine doesn't hit the ground. I wake up before that. Just goes down and down… Red hot, it is."

"And you've seen that happen to people in your Flight, being downed in flames?"

"Yes, sir."

"What do you think when you see men you know shot down like that?"

"I mourn them, of course. I pray for them. I hope they went quickly. It makes me feel guilty still being alive."

Pretyman knew he could do little more with talking. He decided to declare Fred unfit for general war service, but fit for home service. That way he could stay out of whatever was going on in France and maybe get the rest he so obviously needed. There was not much else Pretyman could offer a young pilot in this frame of mind. He had heard that some of his medical colleagues were offering electric shock therapy, but he had an aversion to what seemed like a barbaric practice and preferred to give his patients time off, not electrocute them.

"Well, I suggest you spend a few days here just resting and we'll try to get rid of those headaches for you, then you are free to stay wherever you want. Get some fresh air and plenty of sleep. Where are you going to be staying?"

"Sutton Place, in Hawley, Kent."

He said the words automatically, and then checked himself to confirm that he had really just given the address which would bring him nearer to Kitty. Pretyman scribbled it on the form and signed his name.

"Right. You've got until 31st August. Then present yourself back to the War Office for another medical board and see how you feel then. Good luck, Dunn."

The next few days in the hospital were a blur.

Fred assumed the painkillers he was being given were a strong sedative, but he was glad for the deep untroubled sleep they brought, usually in the afternoons after the lunchtime dose. The others in the ward, appeared dazed and uncommunicative. Fred welcomed the sense of anonymity.

Nights were still difficult and the recurring nightmare seemed untouched by any painkiller, but the scene he was reliving now was viewed through a smeared window. It wasn't as bright and real as back in France.

Thomas and Adele visited each afternoon and brought small pastries and fruit which Mrs. Freemantle had given to them, but he mostly left them on the side or gave them to one of the nurses.

One afternoon, with the sun strong and direct, he was sitting in a wicker chair in what had once been the Royal stable yard. It still had the sweet smell of horses and remnants of its previous life. Fred was wearing his uniform, having refused to wear anything which might suggest he was a patient, but had taken his tunic off in concession to the heat.

Another officer, also in uniform, was in the far corner in his chair dozing, his head fallen into his chest. From the other side of the cobbled yard, Fred saw a nurse pointing him out to a shimmering elegant figure in a wide brimmed cream hat.

The figure inclined her head in thanks and was now walking over towards him. The sun behind her partially obscured her, but also cast a golden glow. She came out of the sun like an apparition, fuzzy around the edges, wafting towards him in a long cream dress with a high collar and a thick blue band at the waist.

He felt his heart in his mouth.

Kitty.

Chapter 10
Convalescing in Kent, July 1915

Life had moved on quickly at the hospital after Kitty had swept in to take command, effortlessly and naturally, with often just a word or a smile to the right person. It did not take them long to bend to her will as besides her determination they knew full well that a spare bed would be filled almost as soon as Fred walked out into Hyde Park.

"You will take the train from Victoria to Farningham and Wilkins will meet you off the train. It's all..." Kitty stopped, aware that Fred was staring at her as if she was speaking a foreign language. Clearly his thoughts were elsewhere. She assumed, wrongly, that they were back in France.

"Mrs Burrell, you have been too kind. I cannot ever thank you enough."

"Kitty, please call me Kitty. We needn't be so formal now. There is no need to thank me. Mother was insistent you came."

"Kitty, yes of course. And, well, will anyone else be there? Will you... possibly..." Fred seemed to have lost the power of speech.

"There are no house guests just now, just mother. It will be very quiet. But I will come as soon as..."

"That would make me most happy of all. I will look forward to that."

Their conversation had veered precariously between polite formality and unsaid possibilities. Two months in Kent with the chance to spend even just a few hours with Kitty, even if on half pay, was a trophy Fred had not imagined would have been his.

Fred dressed carefully in his uniform, pinning his 1914 Star to his tunic, which meant people on the train looked kindly on him. Some even offered him sweets and cakes from their baskets. He read the looks of those who had men like him at the Front controlling desperate thoughts about their own sons and lovers when facing a man in military uniform.

On the rattling journey through the Kent countryside, Fred thought of all the men who had gone before him towards Dover and onto France. The great adventure, eight months into this war, was now a very different reality. What they had seen would never be the stuff of stories in the pub, or comic tales to school friends. He would have to try not to recall the severed limbs, blasted flesh and mangled wreckages of the last few months, even trying to explain it to the uninitiated was impossible.

Fred felt his spirits lift with the thought of heat on his skin and long bright days ahead. He had swapped the thick sodden French soil for a verdant honeyed England. It was this countryside which he and the other men had dreamed of, cooped up like hens inside their huts. The lanes, the hedgerows and that most English of smells, cut hay and blackberries. Now it was to be his nurse and medication.

Hawley was a tranquil English village with the river Darent running silently through it. It nestled confidently in its corner of Kent, picture-postcard perfect. It was an untroubled spot, despite being only twenty miles from London, and still in the range of any bombing mission Germany might decide to send. It gave the impression on that summer's day that the war was a distant event, and that its inhabitants would still carry on regardless as they had for centuries: growing, ploughing and surviving.

Sutton Place itself was a large cream stone building covered in wisteria, its purple beads and graceful foliage hung around it like an elegant feather boa. The wide drive up to the house was fringed by meticulously trimmed beech hedges, and Fred saw at the side an orchard and tennis court. For him it was like one of those films they had once watched on the borrowed projector in the mess. A fairy-tale country estate, where the gilded few played croquet and filled their days with pleasure. It signalled opulence and wealth, but at the same time giving the impression of a much-loved and cared for home. It was so far removed from his real life, and he had to pinch himself to believe that this would be his home for the next few weeks.

Edith Perkins was in the garden and Fred, after being

shown his room and carefully checking his hair was neat and his boots dust-free, was taken out to meet her on the front lawn. Although not far off her 60th birthday, she was still an impressive grand woman. She was wearing a fine grey cotton blouse over a long dark grey skirt, with a full brimmed straw hat. Against the sunshine everything about her appeared to be polished silver. Her long hair had escaped in places and tiny strands fell down onto her shirt. She dabbed at her face with a handkerchief.

"Fred, welcome. You do look tired. Do come and sit. Hickman will get us all some lemonade, or tea if you would prefer."

Fred felt over-dressed and his tunic itched his neck in the heat. His knee-high leather boots were totally out of place in this summer garden in July. He was not used to afternoon tea on the lawn of a great English country house and felt clammy in his thick wool uniform. He knew he was looking flushed and awkward.

"Mrs Perkins, thank you for letting me stay with you. It is really most kind. You have always been too generous to me." He blushed a little knowing the false pretense, longing as he did to see his hostess's daughter.

"I understand you've been having a rotten time out there. Kitty has told me a little of what has happened to you. Anything I can do to help restore you to your best health I most certainly will. You must take time here just to rest and forget about this beastly war for a week or two."

Fred smiled.

"I will try. This is the perfect place to recover." Here in the lush garden of Sutton Place, where everything was cut and teased to perfection by a team of gardeners, the war was indeed if not literally then metaphorically a million miles away. He was not certain how this grand old lady would take the knowledge that he had fallen for her younger, widowed daughter, in status and eligibility as far away from him as this house was from the terraced house he had grown up in. It was fair to imagine that she would be shocked and displeased. He would have to be careful about that, but he knew he was not mistaken when he had seen in Kitty's kindness to him at Palace Green hospital more than an efficient, wealthy woman trying to do her bit for the wounded and sick soldiers back home. He had at first assumed she was offering him this sanctuary just as she was offering her own home to the Red Cross as a hospital, but she had now shown extra warmth and tenderness to him. Could he hope that she was doing it with the knowledge that they could get to know each other a bit better, here in Kent?

He had until the end of August before he had to report back to the War Office to find out.

Chapter 11
Summer with Kitty, August 1915

The next few weeks went by dreamlike, in a kind of timeless suspension.

For the first few days Fred had been left on his own, meeting Edith in the evenings for dinner. Days were spent sleeping in the summer chairs on the lawn or in his room writing letters. Occasionally he would include a small sketch in his letter. At first he drew the aeroplanes he had flown, but that made him think back to the men who had flown in them and who would never be coming back to England.

In the late afternoons he walked around the country lanes for miles, crossing the little ford over the Darent River, careless of where the paths took him. It was as if time had stopped, and he soon felt the heavy burden of the past few months' lift as he walked among the horse chestnut trees and overgrown hawthorn hedges.

Here everything seemed to be full of life; the plants, the fields, even the shops seemed to have enough produce to sell in their windows, and displayed it shamelessly. He could not help but contrast it to what he had seen. The hedges there had been trampled or cut down to make way for the heavy military vehicles, trees were scorched, or felled either by weapons or men. It seemed that everything green and verdant had been sacrificed for the war, and everything colourful drained to black.

Fred walked aimlessly, enjoying the lack of purpose or orders to be carried out. He crossed the single plank bridge, past the watercress beds there since Roman times. He might stop off at the Chequers Inn for a pint and a smoke. Out of uniform on these walks, he hoped not to meet anyone who would question or report him for his rolled up shirt sleeves and loose cotton trousers.

He got quizzical looks from some of the locals in the bar. Old, bent-double and red-faced farmers who wished their sons were still there to work the land and let them retire as they had expected. He didn't want to get into conversation with them. They could think what they wanted. A young and apparently able man out of uniform was not something they saw these days. The war had emptied the villages of any male under 35. He knew the admiring glances from the young women cycling around the village were at the novelty of seeing anyone male and youthful who on the surface didn't appear to be maimed.

One early evening after his afternoon amble and pint at the inn, Fred returned to Sutton Place to see a new car in the driveway. He could hear the sound of people laughing, and knew at once Kitty had arrived. He examined his crumpled clothes in horror. He looked like the gardener finishing up after a hot summer's day, not an Officer of the Royal Flying Corps just back from service with the British Expeditionary Force. There would be no chance of avoiding the new arrival. He would have to go through the front door and present himself.

Self-consciously he pressed his hair and wiped his hands on his trousers. As he feared, it was Kitty, still in her summer driving coat, cloche hat and gloves. She looked up as he came to the door, and he noticed the smile which he hoped said: you are right to wear these clothes in this heat; don't fret about how you appear to me.

Edith spoke first. "Here's Fred. I do hope you had a good walk. Kitty has just arrived, so we will have quite a gathering at dinner. Usually we are rather quiet here. But that is what we all need just now, a little celebration, although it doesn't seem the time to be having parties." She sighed, the unspoken presence of the war hanging there between them.

It was Kitty's turn now to welcome him.

"Well, Fred, you do look much better since the last time I saw you in that hospital."

"Yes," he said, self-consciously. "I feel much improved thank you. Everyone here has been so thoughtful. But if you don't mind I think I am in need of a wash and clean up."

Before anyone could contradict him Fred headed up to the first floor two steps at a time and threw himself on his bed. He felt grubby and could still taste the beer in his mouth. Kitty Burrell deserved better.

A few hours later, cleaner and in his mess uniform, he headed for the drawing room. Mother and daughter were already there, drinking dubonnet. The smell of the drink brought back images of the bar in Amiens where the men went to drink and meet the local mademoiselles. He pushed away the uninvited memory.

Hickman, who knew his evening drink by now, handed him a gin, it swirled against the ice as Fred made his way to the sitting area. The vicar of St John's and a local landowner and his wife were already seated there, cradling their drinks. Edith was holding court, but soon ushered Fred into the gathering.

"Everyone, here is Frederick Dunn, who has been serving with the Royal Flying Corps out in France. He's just back for a period of leave."

He knew, from previous evenings when Edith had had visitors, that she would expect him to tell a few tales of life at the front to her guests, who would hang off every word he spoke, bringing as they did the war and their loved ones a tiny bit closer. The landowner's son was in France and he and his wife lived in daily fear of the worst news. Fred knew his role and had perfected it in his few weeks at Sutton Place.

"It is a great contrast to France and a tonic for me to be here in Hawley."

"Where are you based?" the vicar was the first to ask.

"St Omer for the most part, but we started off near Abbeville, then near Amiens. We fliers move around. We are luckier than most, we know that."

He always tried to keep his stories neutral. He spoke about the French farmers and villagers and how they would help the pilots if they lost their way and had to do a forced landing in one of their fields.

"*Les Aviateurs Anglais* they call us and we can be quite a local attraction, if we come down, they always come out to see us. Most of them look like they've never seen anything like it. Dropping out of the sky like that," he said.

Fred made it sound like their six hours in the air each day was nothing exceptional, just as if they were at Hendon, Gosport or Farnborough. You could not tell such people the truth. Without a conception of what the war was really like, above or below ground, there was no point. He had become his own censor in public and increasingly now in private. He was getting better at it.

The assembled guests seemed satisfied with his performance, and dinner passed off pleasantly. He tried to avoid Kitty's eye, and spent rather too much time comparing French and English agriculture methods with the landowner.

Later when the visitors had left, Edith said she was going to bed and suggested Kitty too might need an early night after her drive from London. Kitty said she was just finishing her coffee and would go up shortly. She didn't move from the large sofa, though. Did he imagine that Edith hesitated, about to say something, but thinking better of it? She turned and spoke to him.

"Well goodnight, Fred. See you tomorrow. Sleep well. I do hope telling all those stories didn't tire you too much. You are here to forget the war, I'm sorry we are all so desperate to know what is going on. The trouble is we feel we never get the whole story in the papers."

She left the room, and they were alone.

Fred had made a half-hearted attempt to follow Edith out of the room, but Kitty, signalled to him to wait and beckoned him to sit down. Now it was his turn to hesitate. He felt very young and very inexperienced, but he returned to sit on the sofa opposite.

"You seem a bit nervous, Fred. Please don't be. I was hoping we might have a proper chat without everyone dragging information out of you about this beastly war."

"I don't mind really... Talking about the war, that is." Fred looked back momentarily towards the door, surprised to see Mrs. Perkins had pulled it almost shut behind her.

"Well, yes, I am a little nervous. It's hard to believe I am here with you like this. I've thought about it a lot recently, being alone with you, but now I'm here, I feel speechless. I'm sorry Kitty. I am not the showman you saw at Hendon." He gave her a nervous smile.

Kitty had moved across to join him, like a swan

moving through water with that calm and impressive way which suggested a more deliberate purpose. Fred felt his stutter returning. He could not think of anything to say which would not betray his feelings, so he took her slim hand in his, stroking the underside and looking shyly at the patterned design of the thick blue and gold carpet.

They sat like that for some minutes in silence, the clock ticking loudly in the background. Kitty eventually gave his hand a small squeeze before she stood to leave. She kissed him softly on his forehead and left the room. All this had been done without a word being uttered. Something had changed, though, irrevocably. Fred felt something tectonic and wondrous at that moment, not just for him, but for Kitty too. They had crossed a divide which before the war, she would never have dared or wanted to cross. They now had an understanding from this moment on. He was sure of it.

This slow and secretive liaison carried on for a further week as they managed to grab short moments alone, either on a stroll in the village or by the river, fishing. Edith, seemed to know nothing of their growing attraction. She would organise picnics for them all, games of croquet were played on the lawn and they sat together as tea and cakes were brought out to them.

One afternoon, Kitty, out of sight of the rest of the party on the lawn, leant over and kissed Fred's cheek. There had been no indication she was about to do it. Fred felt at that moment as if he was floating above the earth. A feeling not unlike the sensation of flight and being held up in a machine, in some way suspended and looking down at all those below him.

It took his breath away.

He had known his attraction for Kitty from that August bank holiday, but to think that she might have been interested in him was little short of a miracle. When life could be so swiftly taken from you, with a wrong turn, a loose burst of artillery or even a dud engine, he must grab this chance of happiness with all his might.

On Kitty's last night at Sutton Place he scribbled a note to her which he slipped into her hand. They would meet in

London away from her mother and this idyll, with its frustrating veneer of innocence.

She was a widow, he a young pilot who may be dead in a few months. They had nothing to lose and everything to gain.

Chapter 12
The Savoy, August 1915

Aircraft Inspectorate Department Military Aeronautics Directorate,
War Office
Whitehall
London SW

6 August 1915

Dear Dunn,

Would you kindly drop me a line to say how you are getting on? I see from your Medical Board papers that you have been granted leave to 31st instant, but if your health has improved, you may like to take on light duty at an earlier date. There is a position in the Aeronautical Inspection Department which it is thought you might fill.

Sincerely Yours

WW Warner

Fred was still at Sutton Place with Kitty when he received the letter. He already knew he would have to face a second medical board and could be sent back to France immediately, even though his sick leave wasn't due to end until August 31st. A brief spell in the AID may be just what he needed to keep him near London, and Kitty.

Fred presented himself at Caxton Hall for his medical board. It was a far less daunting prospect that it had been just two months before, and the panel appeared sympathetic. Perhaps they always were. He wondered how many men they had seen. Only a few weeks away from the deadliness of the daily patrol and the horror of knowing each day might be your last had made a huge difference to how he felt. His stutter was barely noticeable, and his sallow skin and deep set eyes had been transformed with the Kent sunshine, and his new love affair. It was only when the panel pried a little deeper into his nightmares that the damage done in France resurfaced. Something showed his recovery was not complete, no matter how hard he tried to disguise it. After ushering him out of the room, with a friendly pat on his shoulder, the head of the panel Hamish McIntyre went back to his seat.

"There is clearly evidence that his nerves are not fully recovered, wouldn't you agree gentlemen?"

"I don't disagree with you McIntyre, but the RFC have made it clear they want us to send as many able pilots back as we can, they were sounding desperate in their last communication."

"They will just have to wait. We have ten men to see today, and if all ten are not fit, then we cannot send any of them back. They are not malingering, I'm sure of that. If we can keep them out of France for a bit longer, they are still being useful to the war effort here in England."

After a few words of agreement from the others, he wrote on the form, 'He has considerably improved and is now fit for general duty at home.'

Before the war he had been glad he had stuck with his profession of psychiatry. This war had turned this upside down. He was not one who assumed those presented were trying anything to escape the fighting in France and grab a cosy desk job in the War office. Stable, sane young men, who would otherwise be carrying on with their professions, their love lives, their education, were turning up like sea-hollowed shells, drained of whatever life force they'd once had. There had been no text books for this in his Scottish medical school. He signalled for the next young man to come in.

The next day Fred got the news about being fit for home duty and though it was what he had hoped for, a small part of him felt ashamed. He knew squadrons were desperate for pilots and that his place would be taken by a young boy with barely enough experience to get off the ground at a training airfield, let alone in the heat of war. He also knew that the war,

Learning To Fly 69

if it was to mean anything at all, had to be won and soon and needed all the fighters it could get.

He had to do something to make what they were all doing count. Otherwise, Bowyer, Graves, Smith, Chomondeley, all those young, brave men would have died for nothing. It was unthinkable. Fred wrote to Warner to say he would welcome work at the AID and looked forward to helping the service win the war in the skies in that department. But first he still had some leave.

To: Mrs William Burrell, Middleton Hall, Hampshire
Savoy Hotel, August 21st, 7pm. I will be waiting. Fred

Kitty received the telegram when she was supervising the arrival of 100 metal framed beds into her drawing and dining rooms. With their drapes and rugs removed and stored away, the rooms appeared vast, echo chambers to new sounds. She tried not to wince whenever the metal caught on the wooden floor leaving long black trails like fingers across the polished and once pristine surfaces. They were expecting the first casualties in just a few weeks and already the smell of the house had changed, with paraffin and sharp antiseptic taking over from cut flowers and beeswax polish.

A matron from the local hospital had been sent to manage the transformation from elegant rooms of a grand house to hospital wards. She did not look like the sort of person who would take kindly to interference from the head of the household, particularly a beautiful young and rich widow. Kitty read the situation perfectly and decided to put that perception to bed.

"Matron, I think it best if I go away for a few weeks while you settle things here. I'm sure it would be more difficult for you if I was to stay."

The matron nodded curtly, not wanting to get into conversation. This Mrs Burrell was far too striking to be around desperately sick men. Too much of a distraction.

"Well if you need me I'll be in London, and the housekeeper can answer any immediate questions." Kitty was about to add something about helping the poor soldiers, but by then matron had already moved on.

Widowed at the age of 21, Kitty Burrell had not expected her life to take the turn it had. Looking back to that August day at Hendon, she had to admit to herself she had been intrigued by the young aviator and had found him dashing. There had been something about him, his braveness perhaps, which she could see covered a deeper vulnerability. She had been drawn to him, even then. But she was just married, and it had not crossed her mind that her gentle teasing of him could have masked a deeper attraction.

It was only when she had received his letters from France and the descriptions of what he was experiencing out there, that she had begun to see Fred Dunn as someone other than her mother's maid's rather attractive son, the pilot. She found in his words a natural instinct for honesty towards a woman which many men of her class and circles felt unable to show, and a thoughtfulness, which softened her to him.

On hearing that he was being invalided home, she surprised herself by making arrangements to be sure she was at his hospital in Kensington. She had walked into the courtyard that morning with the intention of doing her bit and offering some support to one of the men fighting the war, but had left knowing it was not a charitable act she was performing, but that she was doing it for Fred, and only for him.

The week in Kent had thrown everything she had ever thought about herself and her place in society into confusion. An emotion and sexual intensity she had thought buried along with her husband had been awakened. She had found it hard to disguise her feelings for Fred and, try as she might, she had to accept that she had fallen for this young man.

Why else she asked herself, did she feel so light-headed when he came into the room? Why else did she now dress so carefully each day? Why else had she allowed herself to behave so recklessly, it was she after all who had been so forward with him in Kent? Kitty blushed at the thought of kissing him on his forehead and the look of surprise and delight in his eyes. But she didn't regret her actions for a second.

Furthermore, she knew that meeting him in London would mean only one thing. They would become lovers. She who had not considered the prospect that she might marry again, had suddenly and irrevocably fallen for someone who might be seen as unsuitable. The thought of the word made her laugh. Let them think what they like, she thought as she packed. This horrible war has made those snobbish views ridiculous. This country will be a very different place after the victory.

Kitty was tired of conforming. She could fall for whomsoever she liked, from wherever she liked, and Fred had more than proved himself a brave and patriotic officer. She had always been strong-willed, someone to follow her own mind and not be swayed by convention or tradition. I will do just as I please, she thought, and what I please is to be at the Savoy at 7pm tomorrow.

Fred was already waiting in the American Bar when Kitty arrived. It was if they were on parade for each other. Kitty had chosen the same pale blackbird egg colour she had worn at Hendon, and it set off the aquamarine choker she wore at her neck. Her thick dark hair was swept up high in the latest fashion, pinned by two sparkling combs.

Fred was still in uniform, every part of it polished and pressed. Kitty had to smile approvingly at the transformation from his summer wear from their walks in Kent. They kissed openly, on the cheeks, unabashed and confident. The Savoy had become used to such meetings between would-be lovers; men just back from the war, grabbing what comfort and happiness they could within the silk brocades and black and white marble interiors of the hotel, and women who knew that very soon there would be few attractive men left who could take them to cocktail bars.

The fighting in Europe had given the place a party atmosphere as if it were New Year's Eve, with everyone clambering to be with someone special as the chimes sounded midnight. Fred had taken the precaution of booking a room. He used the name Bowyer as he felt poor Bowyer, his companion in Paris, blown up in that terrible explosion, would appreciate the joke. He'd closed his eyes to lose the image of the charred hangar as he'd signed the name.

"You look wonderful, Kitty. I wasn't sure if you would come." The mismatched sentences tumbled out awkwardly.

Kitty smiled, warming to his shyness. "Of course I wanted to come. We had to meet away from Sutton Place, with everyone looking and judging. Here no one will know us, and if they do, I don't care."

Fred had ordered champagne to wash away any nervousness they might be feeling.

"Six months ago I thought I might be dead by now. Drinking champagne here with you this evening, my life doesn't feel real. Sometime I wonder what is real anymore."

"This is real, here and now. Living. Don't think too deeply about it Fred, just enjoy this moment, this music, this champagne." She gestured around the pristine room, full of people like them, banishing demons and finding chinks of happiness, and her confidence pulled him gently into a make-believe world where war and death were unwelcome.

They agreed she would go up to the room first, she was wearing a wedding ring after all and no one paid any attention to the married woman leaving her husband in the bar to go on upstairs. The concierge nodded as she waited by the elevator. Even though he guessed this glamorous woman was not Mrs Bowyer, he was clearly not offended at the thought. Her face was vaguely familiar, but he could not place her. He looked away as the elevator doors closed on her neutral expression.

The room Fred had booked was a suite with a small sitting room and large bedroom, with a balcony looking out onto the Thames. The blackout meant that the river itself was the only thing offering a gleam of silver light. Fred had already ordered more champagne for the room and Kitty had opened the bottle and poured two glasses by the time Fred arrived. They clinked the crystal, the sound cementing what they knew was ahead of them.

The glasses they had had in the American Bar had made the edge of apprehension pleasurably fuzzy. Fred felt a slight dizziness and wished they had eaten, though it had seemed silly to prolong the evening with food. Kitty in contrast appeared relaxed and luxurious. He wondered if she had stayed here with Captain Burrell before forcing the thought away and taking her hand, leading her to the bedroom. The champagne coloured satin bedcovers had been turned back in invitation.

"You do want this, don't you?" he asked, almost too nervous to hear her answer.

She pulled him towards her and kissed him. He felt as if an electric shock had passed through his body, and as he reached forward to hold her face in his hands like a precious vase, one of the sparkling combs fell onto the bed and her hair tumbled down on one side. They could not stop it now.

They had stepped into something, so natural, so primeval, that to stop now would as if cutting off a limb. Fred knew he would never be the same again. Whatever happened to him now in this war, whether he survived it or not, Kitty was right. He would always have this night. He wondered how he would be able to keep this a secret, this intense happiness, the irrational feeling of completeness.

Chapter 13
Home Service, September 1915

The anniversary of the start of the war had been and gone and there appeared to be no let-up in the fighting. Still more men were needed. It was obvious that the war effort in the air was running perilously short of pilots. Kitchener's call to serve the country had driven thousands of young men into the infantry, and some who had seen the horror of trench warfare had already moved over into what was thought to be the lighter option of the flying corps. But still the numbers were not enough.

As the life expectancy of pilots dwindled to less than three weeks, young men, boys really were now going out there with less and less experience. Crucially the aeroplanes they were expected to fly had often been built in haste, and were very different from the two-seaters Fred had trained on. Many died without even seeing the enemy, just trying to take off or land in their own aerodrome.

Since Bleriot had flown his single seater over the Channel, aviation was restricted to wealthy private individuals. Men like Handley Page, De Havilland, and Sopwith who had cultivated their interest in flight before it became obvious that what was required was no pleasure machine for the derring-do adventurer, or one to win races, but a lethal fighting weapon.

Experimenting and innovating as they went along, the pioneers of flying adapted the flimsy machines with new features which meant they could now fly higher and for longer.

For Fred the next few months at the Royal Aircraft Factory at Farnborough were like being back at Hendon. He recorded each flight he made, testing rates of climb, loads, speeds and the ability to twist and turn, filling pages and pages with pencil-written notes. Having seen the war in the air first hand he knew how nimble a plane needed to be, but stability was important too. Young recruits could end up cartwheeling the machine with a tad too much pressure applied one way or the other. Speed alone would not get these inexperienced airmen out of trouble either, as even the swiftest of machines could stall, cruelly and inexplicably, ending up in an unstoppable spin to death.

They needed to rely on a machine not crumpling under them in the heat of battle; one which was stable enough to not punish an inexperienced pilot. So Fred, along with Captain Hucks and Lieuts Hooper and Lerwill, also back from France with nervous shock, had to face a new even greater terror of testing these raw machines with features which had barely left the design desks. They were not facing the artillery fire of the Germans, but the same risks as they deliberately put a machine into a spin to push it to its limits. It was as real a danger for the young testers that Autumn as they had witnessed months before over northern France.

Set against this, Farnborough was a short train ride from London and Fred was at least able to meet Kitty regularly. Hucks, Hooper and Lerwill were always up for a trip into town to meet girls and go dancing. The war had put everybody in a decadent mood and even the subdued and shy in peace time were finding a new vivacity.

In uniform men knew their chances with the young women they met in the London bars were higher than they would ever be in another life, so they grabbed at it. Although the uniform was meant to signify a certain type of behaviour and (officially) no dancing was permitted while wearing it, no one took any notice of those rules and the most drunken and riotous people in the darkened downstairs clubs and bars that September 1915 were in khaki and had very likely been in France just weeks before.

Fred would usually meet Kitty at a small grill bar off Kensington High Street and go to a club just south of the Cromwell Road where they could dance and drink anonymously until the early hours. Kitty wore her wedding ring, but no one in the places they chose to go to cared to check or pass judgement on an unchaperoned woman. They had made no promises, offered no declarations. It was just enough to be in each other's company for that night.

Their meetings were based primarily on desire; they

were unashamedly open about that. It wasn't just physical, but the wider desire to live and to survive which mattered more to them now. Fred had known fatalism in France and he had seen it in many other pilots. It was often this fatalism which heralded death, but now Fred shuddered to think that he could have been so reckless with his life now Kitty had made it meaningful and precious.

After two months of this near normal existence; a job and a lover he saw at weekends, Fred heard he was to be posted to Coventry aerodrome for more testing of new machines, with engines coming out of the Daimler factory there.

First, his next and hopefully last medical board. This time, as he was based at Farnborough, he faced a new, less sympathetic panel at the Connaught hospital. They had not seen as many cases of neurasthenia as those back in London, and one of them in particular was in no mood to keep men out of the war effort if he could help it.

W. M. Bunyman was a thin, anxious man who felt life had not dealt him the hand he deserved. He had hoped to be a psychiatrist in one of the best London hospitals, but had found himself in Aldershot, far away from any place where he might make his name. He would not let a few nightmares and stutters persuade him that a young man could not go and do his bit for the county.

Bunyman was the chairman and tried to bring the other, more junior doctor along with his point of view. They perused Fred's notes and could see that the last board had suggested he had improved considerably. A fulsome report from the AID chief inspector said he was a valuable test pilot and should be kept on there, even if declared fit.

The junior doctor, intimidated by Bunyman, kept to himself his opinion about whether Fred should be given an extra two months as they discussed the reports. His voice alone would not be enough to cast any doubt.

"There is no reason as far as I can see for you not to go back on active service. So that is my recommendation which I will pass onto the Air Ministry today." Bunyman gave the decision curtly, allowing no trace of emotion to cloud his sharp features. His junior panelist decided to keep quiet and nodded his agreement, unable to voice what he really believed; fit for general service, fit for war, to kill or be killed. He felt as if he was a judge sending a man to his execution and did not have the heart to look up as Fred left the room.

It was the day before his 21st Birthday. Fred had been told to leave Aldershot to head for Coventry that very afternoon. His 22nd now seemed a lifetime away.

The mess at any airbase was always ready for a party, and Coventry was no exception. Like Fred, many of the men were passing through having a few months' home duty, as a respite from the war. Fred's 21st birthday was an occasion for celebration. They drank neat gin, toasting each other endlessly and refilling their glasses, all against a background of gramophone songs, so that for a night in the mess in Coventry, they recreated a small piece of northern France. Although Fred yearned to be with Kitty celebrating, a party was a party, and he was happy to be the cause of it.

The next morning groggy, and with only a few hours' sleep, a group of officers had to drive a tender to the Daimler works to pick up parts. One of the new recruits, Private Joseph Hibbert, was to accompany them. Everyone was in high spirits left over from the night before. They did not expect much traffic that day and were likely to be back at the base for lunch. A horse drawn dray ahead was ambling along; the driver was bent over as if examining his hobnail boots, his whip loose in his hand, the end casually flicking the air. Fred pulled out to overtake. He looked at his speedometer. He was going at 28 miles per hour.

Suddenly, ahead of them, as if conjured up by a magician with evil intent, a glistening motor car appeared as if in a mirror reflecting multiple images of itself back at them. Fred, dazzled by the oncoming vehicle, had no choice but to swerve and aim for the grassed verge, trying desperately to avoid the tramlines. The tyres squealed in protest and the horse pulling the dray, startled by the sound, tried to pull away, clattering his huge hooves on the road.

A moment passed.

A calm before the storm.

The tender hit the front of the motor car, thumping into its front headlight with such a loud crash that the horse finally pulled the dray away, and its startled owner, his whip thrown into the road by the momentum was unable to stop the beast in flight. Fred was not sure what happened next, but he recalled later young Hibbert flying headfirst out of the back of the tender and striking the iron railings at the side of the road like a dart.

If you had recreated this scene a million times, what happened that instant would never have been repeated. It would be statistically miraculous. But here was Hibbert's limp long body thrown headfirst, impaled on the iron railing where it hung like a limp rag doll, his arms draped loose, unable to save him. Barely seconds earlier he had been sitting in the back of the vehicle. Now he was lengthways. Not standing, not lying, dehumanised like a carcass in a butcher's shop, a grisly metal spike through his white neck.

Afterwards, whenever he closed his eyes, Fred could see this scene replayed and replayed, Hibbert's neck gushing coursing rivulets of his red life blood over his khaki tunic. At first no one moved. A paralysis of shock made instant action impossible.

Fred screamed, "My god, Hibbert! Oh no, no. Help…"

He leapt out of the driver's seat and rushed to try to lift the private's dangling body off the rails, flesh tearing off the spike as he did so.

Hibbert was unconscious but still breathing, deeply, in throaty gulps. Fred tried to stem the bleed with his silk scarf and together the officers managed to haul Hibbert's body back into the vehicle, his blood splashing onto their boots and clothes, leaving a trail across the grass over the scar left by the tyre marks. It was a desperate journey to the nearest hospital, the horn blaring to clear the road and allow them through. Hibbert died, cradled in Fred's arms, in the back. A long last gulp and then nothing.

Fred felt something deep inside of him die, too. Hibbert who had just signed up to the RFC barely three months before. A young man who had looked up to Fred.

Now he had killed him.

In front of the other officers, failing to keep his upper lip stiff, Fred felt bitter tears run down his face. They dripped onto his collar, shamelessly. He had held dead bodies, many more badly damaged than Hibbert, but to have witnessed a man die in this most horrific way and to know you were the driver of the car he had been catapulted out of, pushed him into a deep shock which caused his body to judder as if it had taken on a life process of its own.

He was convulsed with the shakes, Hibbert's blood oozing through his trousers to his skin. He began rocking to and fro, cradling the now lifeless, but still warm body. Hibbert was too young to have found a wife, but even if he did not have a sweetheart, he would have parents who would have been proud of their son joining the flying corps.

How could he face them and admit that it was his driving which had led to this? Someone would have to ring on their doorbell and tell them how he had died. The police would come.

Fred's sobs were now audible, wracking and animal-like. Young men of nineteen were dying every day in France, so getting used to an absence, and getting used to the reality of death and the horrific ways people might come to their end, had become second nature. But if a single death could be felt more keenly, more savagely, Hibbert's end was one those who witnessed it would never forget. The fact he had died, thrown from a motor car, and had been impaled, not in the skies, or in the mud, it seemed so senseless and unfair.

More than anything it was such a waste; a ghastly tragic, incomprehensible waste.

Chapter 14
Court Case, November 1915

Coventry Evening Telegraph
WARWICK ROAD FATALITY
Sec. Lieut. Dunn Fined for Dangerous Driving.

Evidence had been taken from everyone involved. The driver of the dray, the owner of the motor car, the two other officers who had shared the tender that day, and a couple of passers-by. Mattocks, his solicitor, had been helped by a passer-by who said he thought the motor car driver would have moved to allow the three vehicles - dray, tender and car - to pass side by side.

The irony of the accident was that Hibbert had been supposed to have been the driver. As a private he was chauffeur to the three officers that day and it had been a last minute whim of Fred's to get behind the wheel. He had not driven much in France, and although he had been able to drive since he was 16, perhaps he wasn't used to the tender and the lightness of the vehicle. He was after all more used to a joystick and the sensation of flight. Why had he made that decision on that day?

He cursed his stupidity. Why, he kept wondering, did the other driver not pull over as he had believed he would? There had been room, a witness had confirmed that.

It was torture reliving the moments when he knew he was about to hit the other car, and when he had realised Joseph Hibbert had been flung out of the vehicle. The sight of the limp body impaled on the railings. His CO at Coventry had been understanding but from his position of authority he had been forced to harden himself against unnecessary young death and move on. He had made it clear that he did not want the accident or Hibbert referred to again.

It would be more difficult to know how to explain it to Kitty, or to his parents. His father, who had taught him to drive, was himself a chauffeur and the most careful of drivers. How would he look on a son who was to appear in court charged with dangerous driving? How could he explain to Kitty that the person she had fallen in love with had done such a terrible thing.

It was with some relief then that he was put in charge of delivering machines out to the front to keep him busy when the court case was being heard. Returning to France and putting his own life on the line seemed to be the most appropriate response to what had happened. He felt he deserved it and the more difficult the flights became the more he felt he was paying back his good fortune to be alive when Hibbert was dead.

Fred was glad to have escaped the ordeal of hearing the events recounted again. In the end, he was fined £10, but faced no further punishment as the judge told everyone he believed he was being useful in the present crisis.

Useful.

Fred had to grimace at that. How 'useful' could it be to take out machines, many of which were indeed dangerous crocks and which in all likelihood would lead to some young pilot crashing to their deaths. His faith that this war and his role in it was adding to something grander with a definable purpose was becoming harder and harder to maintain. The fine, which was meant to have brought an end to the crash, only underlined how fragile life was. At 21 he felt, not at the prime of his life, but at the end of it, looking back. He knew he must have been responsible for the deaths of many people when dropping bombs on unsuspecting Germans and even when making a direct hit on a German pilot and his observer in the air in a duel and seeing them spin to their death, there was no sense of remorse at being a killer. This was different.

The war was making monsters of them all in ways no General could ever have predicted.

Something dramatic would have to happen before an end to the war could be imagined. Over the battleground, a pilot could see what perhaps no commander could, that the fight for a few yards of earth was not being won by either side. It was a soulless stalemate, and one for which so many had already given their lives. In the air, the Allies were being taken out by a far superior German air force. Their new Fokker planes, nimble, fast, able to climb higher and armed with a front firing gun, were decimating the Allied ranks. They could not disseminate aeroplanes fast enough, and many were being written off before they got up to meet up with the new Fokkers. They didn't have the right machines, they didn't have enough men, they didn't even appear to have the right training in place for the men they did have.

Fred, who had never questioned the way a finely balanced machine was held up in their air, often felt at the mercy of the latest experiment to rush out something which was plainly far from an improvement on the Moranes and Bleriots they had set off to France with in August 1914.

He had other reasons to be fearful. With all the squadrons out in France, there were precious few involved in any defensive patrols over England. London had already been hit by a dreaded Zeppelin monster plane five months ago. Audaciously, following the light reflected in the Thames, it had headed west from Margate just before 10pm, and had randomly, with no means of knowing who or what they were above, thrown out its fire bombs over the east end of London. Seven lives taken; some asleep in their beds, others hoping for a kiss from their sweetheart in the stalls of the music hall or walking home unsteadily from the pub after a night out, all fragmented by the force of the blast. Ordinary people, not in khaki, were now legitimate targets and it made them scared and vengeful.

On his last few trips to London Fred had seen for himself the damage done in Soho and around Charing Cross station. Nowhere was safe any more. Fred thought often of Kitty, of Edith Perkins at home in Kent and his parents in South Kensington, all tiny prey to the killers overhead with their lethal loads.

Over in France just near the coast at St Omer, Fred thought he could hear the bombs landing on English soil. It would be his imagination, drawn tight by the events of the past few months. It would be shelling much nearer to him, on French or Belgium soil, but still he imagined them raining down on those he loved most, and it made him weak to think of it. The numbers killed there would never match the scale of whatever horror was going on out in France, but it made London which

Learning To Fly

was his place of escape and sanctuary, no better than where he was now.

British Expeditionary Force

November 20, 1915

My dearest darling Kitty

I have been out here for over a week and am thinking back longingly to our last fleeting meeting. Our time together is always cut too short. I'm sorry too that I was so distracted by this terrible court case and could not find the words to describe how I was feeling. It has quite wrung me out.

What keeps me going through it all, the cold, the terrible headaches, the thoughts of what we're doing, and what I've done, is that you want me? I can hardly bear to know it will be weeks, maybe months, until we meet again. Please do write. I will be back and forth for a few weeks more and then maybe I will be sent to another squadron here. No one seems to know where they are going. The base here is like a waiting room. We are all here before going someplace else. You get to know a chap over a few nights then he is off. You'll probably never see him again. Lillywhite is off to Egypt. Who knows whether I'll see him again. Sorry I'm being maudlin now. I need you to cheer me up.

Write to me, my dearest.

Yours with affection,

Fred.

He sealed and pocketed the envelope. He would send it tomorrow. The present was all he had now. It was no good thinking of life after the war. It could only be the next flight, the next patrol, the next leave. Life had ceased to have any distant attainable horizon, there was only the journey inching towards it.

Chapter 15
Croydon, Early 1916

The next posting, when it came, was back to England. To Croydon.

Fred supposed he should consider himself lucky that he would be swapping the constant presence of death, damp huts and relentless cold, for a comfortable bed and the chance to visit the people who had come to matter to him the most in this war.

Already they were in 1916, it seemed hard to comprehend. Fred and a small band of fellow pilots sent to home service duty were tasked with training the new recruits up into half decent airmen before the war swallowed them up. Croydon was a bonus, just outside London. The base was a grand if dilapidated country house on the edge of farmland. It still retained some of the remnants of its recent past; a bell pull to servants who had moved out when the war started and faded grey outlines on the yellow painted walls where framed landscape oil paintings had once been on display. The air strip had been formed from agricultural fields on the estate and take-off and landing was across short stubble, just another hazard for the thin rubber tyres. The recruits themselves were barely out of school.

Fred at 21, but feeling older and wiser as war could do to a young man, thought these school boys just past their 18th birthdays were too young and fragile to be thrown into the cauldron that was a fighting squadron. Flushed with idealism and the thought that the battle in the skies was a mirror of the sports fields at their public schools, these still spotty boys arrived with their new Burberry flying kit as if going on a school outing.

Fred had never felt so responsible for so many other lives before. Up to now it was just the observer behind him or the people he ferried back and forth, but now all these young delicate lives relied on him to keep them living. The death rate from training young pilots was terrible. He'd heard stories of the trainers who refused to go up with the young recruits at all, leaving them on their first solo flights totally unequipped to manage the aircraft if they managed to get airborne.

Second Lieutenant Robert Hadley was such a man. He'd spent the first year of the war in France and had seen it all. He'd been at Neuve Chapelle with No 3 Squadron and like Fred had come back to England to recover a sanity fractured somewhere over that particular battle field. It was something in Hadley's case not easy to find again once it had been shattered over the blood dark mud of France.

In the mess at night he still shook as he held his glass and he drank, steadily and noiselessly, to cover it up. But at night, through the walls of the old house, Fred could hear his heavy sobs as he relived whatever horror he had faced. It was not something they could ever discuss. Hadley saw this time in Croydon as a respite, a semi-retirement at 25, and having dodged a flaming death over Bethune, he was determined not to lose it over Sussex with a sixth former who still thought the war was a heroic adventure.

Hadley was older than Fred by just a few years, but had come into the RFC from the more conventional route of Sherborne, the army and a commission. His father was a military man as his grandfather had been before him. The expectation that he would carry on the noble tradition was drummed into him from nursery and through school, but as he left in the first batch of pilots to head for France in August 1914 he had quickly realised that the inherited view, like many of the assumptions he was expected to have made, was all hot air. In France he had seen the very worst of human nature and had quickly realised that this war was not one that he was ever going to want to remember. He had soon set about building a layer of cynicism that no amount of military success would ever break down.

With no siblings or offspring Hadley would not have to pass on the shattering burden of failure he now carried with him. As he surveyed the new recruits, some from his old school, polished and expectant, he felt no kinship with them, just a weary despair. He was very likely sending them to their deaths and the thought added another layer to his flinty exterior. Inside he was weeping, but they couldn't see that of course. To the young pilots he was gruff, unfriendly and liable to explode at the most minor misdemeanour. He was the unpopular master at school, the one they least wanted to learn with. Fred had been appointed Acting Flight Commander, so although younger than Hadley, and a newcomer to Croydon, he was his senior and had to organise the training. His first meeting told him all he needed to know about the problems ahead.

Fred asked about the training programme.

"What do you mean, programme? What bloody programme? We try to get them off the ground and back down without killing themselves or us."

"Well. how many hours are they allowed to fly with an instructor present?"

"Dunn, whatever you may think with your personal ideals and bloody love of flying, these boys are not fit to fly me anywhere. The first time they go solo, they go solo."

The logs had confirmed what Fred suspected. Hadley had taken only a few of the recruits up, but had never let them take control of the machine.

What Hadley had been delivering was no more than the instructors back in Hendon had done for the society ladies before the war, taking them up on a joyride over north London. But these bright young women, who had paid two pounds for the privilege of the flight, did not subsequently have to fight in the air within weeks of their first jaunt.

Before Fred's arrival at Croydon, two young boys, George Adler and Henry Thompson had died going solo for the first time without having been given the right training to even give them a dog's chance. Fred read the letters his predecessor had written to their parents. Adler, he'd said, had died trying to land the aeroplane, crashing it into a hedge. What his predecessor had not mentioned was that before crashing he had been decapitated by a telegraph wire as the ground had rushed up to meet him. He may have been trying to land or just fly, it was not clear, and Adler's parents would now never know just how grisly his end had been.

Thompson, too, had died ingloriously, despite what the

letter said. He had failed to even get off the ground and had driven the machine into the hangar, igniting the petrol tank and writing off not just his young self and machine, but a tender which he had hit full on. Hadley had been the one who had judged that both these young men were ready to go solo, each with less than six hours in the air.

Fred knew he would have to do something to try and ensure that if the new batch were to go to France, then they would go knowing how to take off, turn, take action if the engine stalled and, most crucially, how to land the thing. He ordered that although Hadley would take them up, all recruits would only first take the controls in a two seater and would have a more experienced trainer pilot with them.

The mood among the trainers in the mess when they heard this news was subdued. They knew that allowing a fresh faced school boy control was as likely a way to death as strafing over the trenches in France.

When Fred walked into the mess all conversation stopped. He knew his decision was unpopular and waited for the first officer to challenge it. It was of course Hadley, now on his fourth whisky.

"Look here, Dunn," he said. "You might be happy to go on a suicide mission with these pimple-faced youths, but we have seen enough to know they will never make airmen. If the bosses want them to go out to France, then they can do so without killing us in the process."

Fred would not be sidetracked. The young pilots' solo training would involve flying with an instructor. It was the only way to put an end to the deaths of boys like Adler and Thompson. Each trainee had to have had at least 20 hours in the air, and no papers would be signed unless they had done so.

"This war will not be won if we keep these sending young men to their deaths. There is nothing glorious about dying in a field in Sussex. They will leave here, alive, and with a modicum of training to get them through what they are all likely to face. What happens to them after that will be someone else's business."

One by one the small group of trainers nodded in

agreement and went back to their poker and whisky. A small victory had been won, and Fred found himself wondering at his confidence in taking on the likes of Hadley. Before the war, he'd not even have spoken to a man like him, now he was issuing orders.

Fighting the Germans had been simple compared to taking on your own side, particularly when you had to bridge so many social gulfs. He took his own whisky over to the fireplace, determined to maintain his composure, and enjoy the sweet moment of an argument so easily won.

Fred's new tactics with the training were proving a success. At least in February 1916 there had been no deaths at Croydon, and although it was a short month, no deaths were a significant improvement.

When the month ended, the first batch of recruits he had trained was ready for France. They could do enough to get them up and down and a bit of rudimentary flying, but not nearly enough to get them out of a spin or to cope with the unexpected. Fred still felt comfortable that they were less likely to kill themselves or anyone else than if they had left in January. If only they weren't so sure that it was all a massive game and glory hunt.

Let them spend a few days at ten thousand feet with frozen hands and feet ruptured with frost and the agony of crater sized blisters and that sickening feeling which being exposed to altitude does to a man, then they would realise. War in the air is a combination of sheer terror coupled with extreme, hideous discomfort. It was a long way from sport. But for those young innocents bound for France, it was still a great game they had yet to play.

Fred would have been a much better instructor if he could have persuaded them otherwise. But they would learn. There was talk of a big push coming and a new and bigger role for the air crews. Too soon they would know it was not a playing field they were joining, but a killing field.

Hadley had reluctantly gone along with the new training regime. The news coming through from France was dismal and the toll on the RFC in every squadron in those first months of

Learning To Fly

1916 proved to be even more costly than the year before. Fred felt lucky to be in Sussex with the teenage recruits.

A new batch had arrived at the start of March. Some just out of school, some transferred from the infantry, seeking better conditions. Those that had seen the war before knew enough not to tell the schoolboys what it was really like. How the trench warfare was churning up young soldiers, boys just like themselves, sending them into unimaginable and foul conditions to have them cut down, like a scythe through hay.

It was not good for them to know that the life expectancy of an aircrew was a matter of weeks maybe even days, and that the death of a colleague was so regular, so predictable even, that all you ever got to know about your fellow fighters were their names. Sometimes not even their full names. Before, in the first few months of the war when their role was observation not killing, there had been time to make friends and find out a little about the men who shared the mess with you.

Now the turnover was so quick, you might know that someone was brave or could shoot or fly straight, but that was it. To know more meant to grieve more if they died, and very quickly you stopped asking: Do you have a sweetheart? What did you do before the war?

So the group which was due to be trained and had to get out to France before the end of April 1916 were to be thought of as just names. Little background information, nothing personal. All under 25, most under 20.

Hadley was to train one of the youngest, Hugh Yates. His family owned a small swathe of Sussex and often at the end of a day's flying he would drive off back to his stately home on his motorbike and return in the early hours of the morning with cooked hams, cigarettes and wine from their ample stores. Because of this and not because of his attitude, which verged on the arrogant, Yates was generally popular and despite his conceit, had been a welcome addition in the mess. Bred into him was the ability to entertain and generate a party atmosphere. At Eton he had been the class joker and he saw no reason to change this position now he was in training for war.

When Yates and Hadley flew together, he had come to

accept that their flights would be wordless. It was all too noisy anyway. Despite his showmanship, which may have suggested a lack of intelligence, Yates was sharp and a quick learner. He watched every twist and turn and asked endless questions of the mechanics about how the machine flew and what did what. The thrill of war and the wonder of flight were still a marvellous thing for Yates which not even Hadley's cynicism could alter.

It was mid-March when Hadley finally said that he was going to let Yates fly the machine, with him as passenger. It was a dead calm, though still wintry day, as spring had not quite come knocking. Both men strapped in and taxied along the runway, taking off towards the west.

They flew for about ten minutes with Yates at the controls, gaining height then dropping down, keeping mostly to a ram rod straight line. At times they followed the railway line for guidance and Yates took them low enough to count how many people were inside the carriages. He could see that someone was reading the Times and laughed at the sheer exuberance of it. He thought if they were even lower they'd be able to read the headlines, which would be a great wheeze, and would scare the passengers witless.

Suddenly Hadley tapped the side as they'd agreed and Yates pulled them up and back into the clouds. When they were back up and flying straight, Hadley signalled to Yates to take them down. He motioned to him to take a gentle turn, turn the engine off and glide back to the base. By now Yates was feeling confident and wanted to carry on further. What he really wanted to do was fly over his parents' house and show them what an aviator their son was.

The moment Hadley understood what he intended, he started to slap at Yates' flying helmet and shriek obscenities. Just then out of what had been like a clear sky, they hit a pocket of cloud and the machine bounced like a ping pong ball. Yates was completely thrown by this, panicked, and pushed the controls forward, sending the machine into a steep dive. With experience, he could have pulled them out of the heart- stopping descent, but cruelly the engine stalled and within seconds the machine was spiralling towards the ground like a sycamore seed. Then, no experience could have changed the inevitable.

They both saw flat fields come rushing up to meet them, and just had the time to acknowledge this then was it, their end, as the aeroplane crashed head first into the earth, its metal and wooden frame crumpling up like an unwelcome letter thrown into the bin, before exploding and sending the debris of men and machine back up into the air.

When Fred looked over from the aerodrome at the time of the moment of impact, he could see the smoke rising ominously above the hedgerows. Their clean slate at Croydon was a thing of the past. It had been a forlorn doomed ambition, he thought to himself. He found out later that Yates had died on the land owned by his family. The war was doing a very good job of writing off the next generation of landowners, not to mention many of the young men who did any of the work on it.

The news of the death of Yates and Hadley was greeted with solemnity back at the aerodrome that night. A few tried to recall raucous stories about Yates that evening and make light jokes, but after a while it became too awkward and they went back to their lamb cutlets in silence. They would get used to this. Better not to refer to it or Yates or Hadley again. Soon they would not even remember their names or their features. Their empty chairs at the table would be filled, another instructor and another pupil would come. There were enough pilots who needed a refuge from the war in France wanting to fill the gap left by Hadley. They could not know that this training operation in Croydon was every bit as deadly as the one against the Germans.

Another public school would empty its dormitories and more fresh faced young men would arrive, keen to play the great game, their headmaster, safe in his cloisters, having fed them on tales of heroism and duty. How soon would it be before they would comprehend it was not Henley, not Lords. It was a deadly brutal game without rules, and in March 1916, one still without a winner.

Chapter 16
Brighton, Spring 1916

Despite the toll the training took on the squadron, the young recruits, the trainers, and the massive support crew who kept the aeroplanes and the men going, life in Croydon passed rhythmically, far removed from the staccato pace of war. Once you got used to the new faces at breakfast, life took on the familiar, clubbable routine of any organisation where men, in their prime, are gathered together, with adventure and alcohol in equal measures.

As the nights lightened, they got used to lounging around outside in the early evening sunshine, tunics unbuttoned, long legs astride their wicker chairs, drinks in hand. If they hadn't been wearing the khaki uniform and silk scarves, it would have looked like any other country house party, enjoying a warm evening with the prospect of a languid summer ahead in pursuit of pleasure.

Fred had earned the respect of his small band of men, and though Hadley, Yates and two other young men were losses he had felt keenly, under his watch, there had been many successes too. Raw recruits who, when they arrived, only understood aviation from a blackboard description, had left for France, able pilots with an instinct for flying. Hopefully it would keep them alive a little bit longer. Fred had let them enjoy their flying too, jaunts to Brighton to bob around, swooping along the pier, and racing back along the windy country lanes.

They would never get the chance to really fly in France. They might as well enjoy the sensation of looking down on their country, which from 2,000 feet, looked so different from the small part of northern France they would be headed for. It would help to have this bird's eye view of England when war in France in all its horror became their reality.

On evenings like this, Fred felt a contentment and sense of purpose which he had not thought possible just twelve months ago. He had others reasons to feel cheerful too. He could be in London in just over an hour and snatched meetings with Kitty were becoming his regular antidote to the pressure of running a training programme. He would meet her, often in the RFC club in Bruton Street, and together they would seek out the small clubs and bars where they could dance and rekindle their romance, which was being forged in war and made more vivid and more passionate by it.

In London, in those smoky, alcohol fuelled and pleasure seeking late nights, they tried to forget for just those few hours that there was a war going on, a war which had left her a widow, and could very well snatch the life of her young pilot lover.

Kitty was showing signs of strain too, and felt as if she was being worn down by the growing pressure of having the hospital in Middleton Hall. The wards had moved into yet more formal rooms to accommodate the numbers needing a bed, so that the tension seeping out of every room and the harsh smell of dried blood and disinfectant meant that it was no longer her home. The financial demands that fell to her as the head of the household were becoming a burden too. The figures danced around when she looked at them. She feared money, which she had taken for granted before the war when she had a husband, was slipping away from her like sand in a timer. Her spidery annotations on piles of bills covered every inch of her desk.

She had fewer and fewer people to help look after her large estate, or help out in the hospital. Only the old men and a couple of women, who had served her husband, were left. They did not have the energy or the ability for the task. It seemed so pointless to be worrying about financial ledgers when so many people were dying, so she spent less and less time in Hampshire, preferring to be in London and the chance of a meeting with Fred.

At the end of March, Fred was made a Captain. He had now truly become part of the establishment. Without a war, the rank would have been impossible for someone of his origins. A Captain with his sweetheart who owned large chunks of the English countryside, Fred had to pinch himself to believe this was the same Fred Dunn who had been born by the banks of the River Tyne. A miner's son, who had left school at 14.

The war, however appalling, and there were times when Fred questioned the sanity of the whole operation, had opened doors for young ambitious men like him and the whole rigid class system, which for generations had kept people like him and Kitty apart, was crumbling away. He had many reasons to celebrate. He was alive, he was a Captain and he had found Kitty.

His reward was a few days' leave, and he scribbled a telegram to Kitty immediately to suggest they met in Brighton. No one would know them there. He booked a room looking out to sea at the Royal Albion Hotel and arranged to meet her off the London train. They had not spent the whole night together since that first one in the Savoy, which felt like a lifetime ago. They kissed briefly and chastely like long lost relatives. "Best not attract attention here Fred, that crowd over there waiting for the London train are staring at us."

Kitty, felt like a teenager again and did not want anything to spoil these few days. To her Fred looked and sounded much older, not a 21- year-old at all. In what he had seen in his short life, he was her senior in experience in so many ways.

She took his arm. "Come on let's get this taxi and head to the sea. I haven't seen the sea for over a year. Before the war…." But she stopped herself, that was then, her old life.

It was a tranquil, cloudless day, a perfect one for flying. The pebbles on the beach shone in the thin rays of sunshine as they walked arm in arm along the front, breathing in the salty sea air.

"The train journey was interminable. I thought I would never get here." Kitty squeezed his arm.

"I'm so glad you did. When we fly over this coast I often look down and think it would be the place to walk with a sweetheart, staring out to sea, arm in arm, just like this."

Kitty laughed. "For a fighter pilot you are quite the romantic, Fred."

"Well, this is not something I would ever have seen myself doing, I'll admit. This is a bit of a fairy tale."

"With a happy ending I hope," Kitty added. She had stopped by a small booth offering photographs and stepped inside. Against a gaudy striped background, like a fairground stall, she sat on a chair, almost coquettishly, aware to the photographer that she looked unnervingly sophisticated and glamorous. Fred stood behind her, his cane in his hand, the leather boots and breeches giving a formality to the fabricated seaside scene. The bulb flashed. Their two images stuck in sepia.

"I'll take this to France when it's ready. I'll keep it by me always, here in this pocket. You will bring me luck."

"You can have the photograph. I don't think I could explain very easily to anyone who saw it what it meant. I told Mother I was going to visit a friend in London."

Fred felt his heart clench at her words.

"Come on, what's the long face for?" Kitty said. "We have two days together. Let's not quarrel, please."

Fred soon forget the incident with the photograph and they strolled along the pier, and talked. It seemed to dissolve their nervousness and slowly they came back to that easy familiarity of a couple who had already become lovers.

Small gestures and intimacies gave them their own private language, and that night on the seafront in Brighton, with the sound of the sea coming through the open window, they got to know each other again. When he thought back to it in the darker months ahead he could almost taste the salty moisture when he had brushed her check.

Their talk was light. They had learned an unwritten truth for those times; not to stray into serious conversation or talk of the future. After the war was not a phrase anyone dared use that spring of 1916. Perhaps it was impossible to even think of a future. They had a war to outlast first.

Kitty had accepted that for their relationship to survive for now at least, it had to be kept a secret. It would take too much explaining to bring her attraction to Fred into the open. There was Edith and her sister to consider. All she could do now was to enjoy the moment. The world had indeed changed, but she knew, deep down, maybe not as much as it needed to if they were to stay together. Like her heavy leather accounts books she dared not open, she put such unwelcome thoughts aside and concentrated on the present.

When Fred returned to Croydon, he found a letter from

the War Office instructing him to report back, not to France but to Farnborough. He was to re-join the unit of the Southern Aircraft Depot as a Test and Ferry Pilot.

Machines were needed to fulfil the Home Defence obligation against the Zeppelins, and in France the numbers destroyed in action was growing every day. New experimental planes were being rushed out of Farnborough; the SE5, the FE, and the new Sopwith Camels.

Now that they had to have an offensive purpose, there was no let-up in the race to get the best fighting machines out to the allies. There was a sense of a massive build up to some unknown event. This had been the case for many months, but now it all felt more intense. If the war was to be won, some side would have to make a meaningful advance. This may well be it, the turning point, thought Fred. He packed his belongings again.

Chapter 17
Build up to The Somme, June 1916

It was just after dawn, so still cold and fresh with a few wispy clouds ahead, when the ferry pilots set off from Farnborough to Arras. It was only a few days short of July.

This time Fred didn't get lost and one by one they went over the Channel into France. All five made it, and after a brief stop to refuel at St Omer, they arrived in time for a late lunch at the squadron base near Arras. The CO there was amazed that all five had come as one group.

"I don't mind telling you boys that I'm mighty glad to see you all. It's been a grim few weeks. We had two write-offs yesterday. Four men in them. Came under archie and didn't make it down on our side. Poor buggers. Maybe they'll look after them, Fritz, I mean, but we won't be getting those machines back."

He and the squadron had the atmosphere of a place in desperate need of cheer. The arrival of five new airmen and some new machines was excuse enough for a party. The four bottles of Scotch they had brought out, and some Cheddar cheese, were welcome too.

"We have places to spare at the table now. If another one gets it today we can fit you all in without anyone moving up," said the CO. He was a tough-sounding man, who had seen too much action and witnessed too many deaths to mourn openly about what had happened to his four men or the tens of others who had not made it back. He knew just the right amount of black humour to use to keep those who were left alive entertained.

Fred was pleased to see two old colleagues from No 3 Squadron, Barry and Dawes. They had been on early patrol together and with their machine riddled with artillery fire had been forced to land in a field just within the allied lines. They were arriving back to the aerodrome in a tender when Fred and the others were heading to the mess.

"Dunn! My God! What brings you to this bloody shambles?" said Dawes, slapping him on the back. Fred grimaced at the strength of the greeting, but his expression soon broke into a smile at the sight of his old friend. Someone from a time before the fighting began.

Eric Dawes had been at Hendon, getting his certificate about the same time as Fred, and although one of the sons of the rich and a product of an English public school down to the signet ring on his little finger, he wasn't one to let background make any difference to his friendships. At least not when there was a war on.

"This calls for some serious drinking. Barry nearly copped it today. Here, Buster, show him your boot, old chap."

Generally known as Buster (Fred had never learned his first name) lifted his leather flying boot. A bullet sized hole had entered the back of the heel and then the sole, and had apparently exited through the floor of the machine.

"One tiny movement north and it would have taken his bloody foot with it. Maybe his leg. Got away with it again, didn't you Buster?"

It was something to laugh about now. Life and death, or having a limb or not. All just a miniscule matter of luck.

The three men walked over to the mess, arms over each other's shoulders, another day alive was reason enough to celebrate. The mess was in the cavernous kitchen of a large farmhouse the RFC had taken over at the start of the war. Two years of market finds and bartered furniture had made it feel more than comfortable. It had a bar, with an impressive pair of antlers hung above it, as if in a Highland shooting lodge, and a large ripped leather sofa stood opposite it, its horse hair stuffing bulging out in places.

The fireplace had a stove in it, in place of an open fire. The gramophone was on at full volume. A mess relied on noise and even the changing of records was done at speed to take away any awkwardness that silence might bring. Fred and the four arrivals from Farnborough were served their whisky with soda, and toasts were made.

"To Farman, whoever he is, and his new experiment,"

Dawes called out, and within minutes they were playing a drinking game which involved naming all the new models of aeroplanes they knew, and drinking to their creators.

Anyone observing this small scene just twenty miles from the front line might not have believed this was a fighting force every bit as brave as the men in the trenches. No mention was made of the men who had been alive and there at dinner the night before. Before they went into lunch, one of the four bottles of whisky they had brought over was empty.

The food was delicious; the meat tender and Fred could make out rosemary and garlic, a rare combination unknown to the cooks in Farnborough. He had forgotten the culinary advantage of being in France.

"The food over here is so much better than what we get back home. You chaps don't know how lucky you are."

"Swap you our cassoulets for your watery fat and gristle pies any day, old sport. You get to lose your taste buds around here."

It was true; none of them had put on any weight in France. Having to breathe in the oily fumes in the cockpit generally took the edge off any appetite they might be expected to have built up.

Soon it was mid-afternoon, and free as there were no patrols slated. Some of the men peeled away to swim in the river. Fred, Dawes, Barry and one of the men from Farnborough went to sit on the patch of grass at the back of the farmhouse, which at one time may have been a paddock for horses. Now a rudimentary cricket pitch had been marked out and the grass levelled as much as it could be, without the aid of a roller.

A few of the men who had been at lunch came out and started a match. They called over to Fred and the others to field. A couple of the men had played cricket for their home counties before the war and took it seriously. They even wore white trousers. How, Fred wondered did they know to bring cricket whites out here to a war? Had someone ordered and sent out for them? Fred, who had not had the luxury of an education where cricket featured on the main curriculum, was hoping to stand at the perimeter and try and catch the odd ball if and when it came his way.

"Coming your way... Move yourself!" the former Surrey cricketer shouted, and Fred lunged at the ball heading straight towards him. A momentary memory of a grenade being hurled out of a German machine. He lunged forward as he tried to catch this approaching missile. The grenade had passed just below his machine and exploded in wide open air emitting white brilliant flashes. He held his hands up expectantly, the ball smashed into them. Its hard leather caught his finger, twisting it back.

"Jesus, what was that?" he said, flicking his throbbing hand.

"Cricket, old boy. You never played it before? How very odd. You come under the ball not over it." The former Surrey cricketer ambled off unimpressed. Another indicator of the gulf between the men who were cooped up fighting the same war, forced to learn each other's rules.

In pain and trying to hide his embarrassment, Fred thought of how Kitty would have laughed at him now. William Burrell must have been a man to play cricket, perhaps she would think less of him, him not being able to perform even the most simple of sporting tasks like catching a ball. The unwelcome thoughts whirled in his head as he headed to the first aid room. The medic at the aerodrome thought it was amusing, an injury he could fix at least. How silly to have come out to France and been injured, not by German artillery, but by an English cricket ball.

Fred turned to the medic. "If I'd been hit in the head, and died out there, I wonder what they would have written to my parents? Died in heroic pursuit, taking the enemy head on."

"Yes, of course, you never write what really happens. We had a chap fell in the river after a drink too many and drowned the other week. Told his wife he had died valiantly in aerial combat. Didn't seem fair to say anything else really".

That night Fred was given a room with another of the Farnborough pilots in the main house where a couple of the younger observers and gunners on early patrol were sleeping. The moon was full and through the window, he could make out the pulsing red glow of a bombardment somewhere to the south. The deep throated boom boom of shelling went on all night and he found it impossible to sleep.

It was difficult to believe they had enough shells to keep up that level of assault for so many hours. Relentlessly, pounding and battering away. Surely at some point they would run out of firepower and they could all sleep? What about the poor men under the barrage, sleep for them would be eternal surely? He had never heard a bombardment of such intensity and duration.

This was the big push then.

"Get used to it," said one of the young men in the dormitory, when he saw Fred sitting up in his bed. "I've been here a week now and I never sleep beyond two or three hours. I don't know what they are planning, but they never seem to stop the bloody noise."

In the morning, the barrage continued. The base felt busier, with tenders coming and going. Although Fred's hand still throbbed from his cricket injury, he knew they had to get the old damaged machines back to Farnborough. After a breakfast of porridge and fried eggs, the five ferry pilots headed out to the hangar.

The weather, which had been so calm the day before had suddenly taken a turn for the worse, and the dark grey thunder clouds rolled ominously across the sky from the west. He knew they only had a small window of opportunity to get home and called to the men to follow him closely. This was not the time for one of them to stray over the lines.

They all took off safely and at 8,000 feet spread out. Fred could see the menacing clouds ahead and signaled for them to follow him. They would head north as there was no way round them. Inside the dark heart of a storm and enveloped by coal black cotton wool, the temperature dropped, and Fred's machine bumped and bounced around like on a roller coaster. He couldn't hear anything but the constant drum of his own engine, and his head was throbbing with the altitude.

He had forgotten just how rough flying in a thunder storm could be. All sense of direction and being upright deserted him, as he tried to head in what he hoped was a straight line. He had travelled through the cloud and out the other side when he realised only three of the aeroplanes had come through with him. He circled back into the clouds to see if he could see the missing airman. Nothing. He retraced his passage and saw the other three were continuing their journey. Perhaps he should go down and land. But, Douglas was still on their side so should be picked up. Going down was not going to help him. He caught up with the other three, signaling for them to go on northwards to England.

Out of the clouds and dropping a bit lower, Fred was suddenly aware that there was a different trouble. They had strayed a little too close to the German sides, and traces of artillery fire were flashing like a photographer's bulbs. Bright blips of light popped around him. One nudged the tip of his wing and the machine stumbled, dropping suddenly. Cold air whooshed past. Skin stinging air. He pushed on and seeing the other three, overtook them and motioned forward again. To Dover. Four had made it to the French coast.

Fred had flown this Channel at least fifty times. He was nearly home now. His finger still throbbed and he was finding it difficult to hold the controls with as much precision as he would have liked. England was just over the horizon, the band of grey sea meeting the washed out grey sky, making water and air fuse into one, was disorientating. The effects of the whisky and wine and brandy last night had made him feel a bit sick. The lack of sleep was also making his eyes feel heavy.

His goggles felt grimy and it felt as if he was seeing the world through streaks of grease. He had to keep the machine going, trying to wipe the raindrops off the screen with his glove. It made no difference, visibility was virtually zero. Suddenly the English coast and its white chalk cliffs were coming into view and he looked around to see if they were all still behind him. Only two machines were visible at his height.

Fred looked down to his left and saw something hit the water. Berridge must have lost control or had engine trouble, and his aeroplane had crashed into the sea. The horrible echoing sound of metal hitting water and the white capped splashes it sent upwards. He knew he couldn't do anything. With luck, someone in a passing boat would pick him up. It was not to be dwelt upon. He had to get to Dover and keep himself alive.

His life, as he thought for the umpteenth time, was hanging by a thread and it wouldn't take much to snap it.

What Fred couldn't have known as he crossed the Channel that first morning of July was that behind him the most brutal of battles was being waged. The sheer scale of the bombardment he had heard had to signal something decisive was happening. The artillery had done their bit. He had heard their efforts all night after all, repeated over and over. Fred had flown away from it as if from the scene of a grisly crime. He felt as if he was running away from something.

The men who got back to Farnborough did not doubt they had left behind something terrible, perhaps even a turning point in the war. But always there was this nagging unspoken doubt that it would not be as easy as the Generals thought. For the first days of that hot July though, a mood of optimism lifted Fred's spirits and it permeated through even the most war weary of the riggers and engineers. The papers spoke of a huge advance and heavy German losses. It had been, they said, a good day for the Allies.

Fred made several more ferry trips over the Channel to deliver new machines to the squadrons, mostly those near the coast. Each time he went over, the mood was a little darker and seemed to contrast with the news they were reading back in England. The men in the air could testify that fields of churned up earth had become the graveyards of hundreds of men. But men in British uniform. They had seen that. Arms stretching out heavenward from the mud, and other limbs casually left as if they'd been taken off mannequins in a shop window. Except these were now set in stinking, fetid soil. British men.

It was not the Germans who lay there just before the German trenches, but their own young men in khaki. Fred heard the talk as patrols reported more and more horrific scenes they had witnessed below them. There was just as much enemy artillery fire, the aerial battles were just as intense and they saw just as many German kite balloons as before. Surely, they would have all been wiped out in the initial bombardment or forced to flee under the strength of the onslaught? If they were still there to fight, the plan to bomb them into submission and then march over and take their lines, had failed miserably. Back in Arras on another ferry visit, and after a straightforward crossing, Fred was pleased to see Eric Dawes step out of his cockpit, but he didn't recognise his observer. He went over to greet his old friend pleased to have some familiarity. Dawes looked up, glassy blood shot eyes trying to focus through his goggles.

"Back again, Dunn? If I were you I'd stay out of this bloody country. Stick to testing these buses and maybe when this horror show is over we'll have an air display in Hendon again." There was a darker edge to his voice which had not been there just two weeks before.

"Buster copped it, two days ago," he added, as if to explain why the young man, a boy really, was beside him, with his tousled brown hair and large freckles, his big eyes wide with fear, his ghostly white skin streaked with oil. He looked as if he was about to be sick.

Fred did not know how to reply. He knew Dawes had relied on Barry as his talisman and together they had come through enough scrapes to believe they made each other invincible. There was nothing to say to make the news more bearable for anyone. Barry had been hit in the chest and arm by artillery and Dawes had flown his dying friend, moaning in pain and delirium, back to base. He'd died as they pulled him from the machine.

"The thing is, I wish they'd shot him straight out. It took us an hour to get back and all that time he must have known he was a goner. There was blood everywhere, sloshing around the floor."

Dawes spat at the ground and pushed his goggles over his head. They had left deep crimson marks which looked sore and inflamed. He looked shattered. He could only be 25 or so, but already looked like a man of 40. Fred could see his boots still stained with what he assumed was his friend's blood. No amount of polishing would remove that.

Fred had to look away. That day was not one to hang around. It was as if grief had worked its way into every pore of the men he knew and taken away what dregs of their devil-may-care insouciance were left. They cared, of course, who could not care? It didn't mean they would not go on, but as each person who had shared a drink or a dorm with them disappeared, so a little piece of the ballast that kept them stable went too.

This was not even a day when a bottle of Bells could wipe away what Dawes was feeling at the loss of his observer and friend.

Fred was glad to get into one of the machines he was taking back for an engine overhaul and head back to England. France seemed to be under quarantine, waiting for an all-clear, hanging there in limbo between life and death.

As he left, he spotted the CO and said, "Dawes has taken Barry's going a bit hard." What he wanted to say was, let him come back for a rest, but even though he knew they had a familiarity with their seniors that would never be accepted in the Army, he kept his thoughts to himself. He didn't say what he might have done: "He's been doing this full-on for a year now, time to give him a chance to recover." The Commander's voice shattered his thoughts.

"We all took it a bit hard. He was a good chap to have around. But he's the fifth person we've lost this week. We've not got the replacements yet. Dawes is a good pilot, he'll have to wait until the end of August. He'll get home then." The CO had answered the question Fred hadn't dared ask. He had been thinking it himself and spoke almost in self-reproach. Dawes was not the only officer who looked on the verge of despair and exhaustion. There was no room for him to be lenient. To be human.

The CO cursed the war. He'd been in South Africa, not flying then of course, and it had been a damn sight easier. You simply had to fight then, and get on with it. He'd never had to consider the nervous state of his men before or the scale of the losses. This bloody war. He threw away his cigarette and added, as an afterthought, "Bring us some gin, next time by the way Dunn. These young so-called pilots seem to prefer that. Just out of school it's easier to drink, I suppose."

Chapter 18
Bad News, December 1916

The five months of fighting on the Somme had sapped the strength of both sides. The mortal enemies, now weary of war and burying their young dead, could not fight for a moment longer, and had called for a break. The dark nights arrived too quickly, it was as if there was not enough daylight left to have a proper battle, and the accompanying numbing winter chill seemed to match the mood of the military from top to bottom. No one had stomach for another fight. Not yet. For some not ever.

Although you couldn't compare the number of pilots killed with the tens of thousands of infantrymen mown down or drowned in the reeking sulphurous French mud, the 252 deaths of the airmen were a weeping sore of a statistic, felt by everyone who worked in the Royal Flying Crops. In such a small force, each of those 252 would have crossed paths with every one of those left behind. Training and replacing such a vast number of men would put enormous strain on every part of the service.

Fred was still at the Southern Aircraft Depot, working on new machines to get them to the Front and build up the supplies again. He felt his spirits dropping with the wintery temperatures.

If only this lousy shattering year would end.

It was in late November that he received more bad news. Even after two years of this terrible war, a letter or passing remark saying that a former colleague or just someone he had flown with once or had a drink with in the mess, had died, caused him pain.

This time it was news of Robert Lillywhite, the man he had shared the bomb-dropping prize with that August Bank Holiday, on the day he had first seen Kitty and just hours before the country had plunged itself into this European war. If you could have a best friend in a war, Robert had surely been his.

Robert, so gently amusing, so unassuming, had died the way he had lived, not in a great flash of aerial combat, but on a routine training flight near Catterick. It had been one of those one in a million accidents. His De Haviland Scout, coming in to land and making a left hand turn at about 50 feet, had side-slipped, turned and Robert had broken his neck on impact.

He must have made that landing a hundred times. How then, that day, had that gust of wind caught him and turned him and his machine?

Robert was just 23. No age really. There had been no time to find a wife, have children, and get a job that wasn't to do with the war. There had been flying, hopefully some time for lovers, but nothing really of a life lived fully. He'd gone from being a mechanic in Hendon, to a brief stint flying there as an instructor, and then the war had taken them away before they could even begin to think what their lives might have become. They'd both out manoeuvred their working class origins to force their way into the very heart of the military establishment, in the Royal Flying Corps. Robert too had become a Captain and had been accepted into the service for what he could offer, not for where he had come from. Fred found in Robert's death a mirror of his own, and it was an ominous premonitory feeling.

The funeral was just before Christmas, and Fred was granted a few hours off to go to Chichester to say farewell to his friend. It felt incongruous to be standing there in this place, miles from a war, miles from any fighting, miles from where Robert had died, with people who could not hope to know how he had lived his life. Fred stood at the back not wanting to intrude and feeling out of place in this harshly austere setting.

There were no other men in uniform at the cemetery, and he felt his tunic and breeches standing out amongst the drab heavy wool coats of the mostly elderly mourners. He pulled his great coat tighter to him, a barrier against the biting wind whipping round the churchyard.

They mourned him of course, these neighbours, friends from school, his old headmaster, but they did not question his going. They still believed it was a worthy, noble death. The vicar said so and the congregation as one nodded in agreement. Later, Robert's widowed mother, bent forward to add soil to his coffin. Fred had not met her before, but Robert had talked of her and he could see a resemblance there. This unnatural early death of her only son had crushed her.

The disjoint of burying someone who by rights should outlive you and provide the next generation had become commonplace. A new genealogical fault line linking every family in the country.

It was the first funeral Fred had been to in a church. The others in France had been less formal, less religious. Over there a padre, his faith tested by the number of times he had performed the same task in the last two years, would say a few words about the dead man, and perhaps a brief verse. Within ten minutes they would be back in the mess, having a drink and a brief toast to the recently departed, before their name disappeared from any future conversation, if not quite from the collective memories.

Here in a corner of England, it was prolonged agony as the rites were read out in full, and they talked of the great sacrifice of a brave airman. Was this the best way to say farewell, or was their way in the fields of France with a cursory goodbye and a moving on, a better way to honour his friends? A hastily assembled propeller cross or an ornate stone angel, its arms outstretched? Which was the best way to mark the end? Both seemed insufficient, inappropriate even, but how to account for the deaths of so many men, how to mark their passing properly? He just knew that he had lost a little bit of himself, of his youth, in saying farewell to Robert.

This was going to be his third Christmas at war. Fred had allowed himself the sweet luxury of assuming he would be in London with his parents, with a chance to see Kitty. He had dared to look forward. A mistake. To plan your future. Something no airman should permit himself. Within days of the funeral he received the news he was to go back to France with no 43 Squadron and be there by Christmas Eve. There was not even time to say goodbye. To mourn Lillywhite with her, the women who more than anyone else he knew, would understand his grief.

Southern Aircraft Deport Farnborough

December 22nd 1916

My dearest darling,
I can hardly bear to tell you, but I am being sent back to France and must leave tomorrow.
I thought we would get this Christmas together and I wanted to give you a gift in person and see the sparkle in your eyes as you opened it.

We will have to wait until I get some leave. I don't know how long this posting will be. It seems as if no one is quite sure about anything these days. The thought of you and our times together is what is keeping me going, whatever might lie ahead. This will be my third Christmas at war, it is hard to believe. We thought we would be home by the first one. I think of poor Lillywhite when I think of that first Christmas at Abbeville. I'm glad you got to meet him. He thought you were the most beautiful woman he had ever seen that day!

But my darling we will try to make the most of it out there I know, it can never match the one I had hoped to spend with you of course. You shall be in my thoughts often. I am taking a pudding out and a few other items to lift the spirits, but it will be a poor substitute. I shall be in Candas for the time being and you can write to me there.

I long to hear from you and will think of you always. I'm taking that photograph from Brighton. It will be my mascot to keep me safe.

Think of me my darling,

Fred

110

Chapter 19
Back in France, Christmas 1916 - New Year 1917

"Shut the door won't you? And put that bolster back under it. It's the only way to keep the blasted place warm."

He was sharing his hut with another Captain, Hugh Rutherford, who had just arrived from England three days before. Rutherford was lying on his mattress, bootless, with his long spindly legs bent at the knee and his blonde fringe falling over his pale blue eyes. He was flicking through a flying magazine not really taking in the latest aviation news.

Hugh Rutherford had the same clipped voice as many of the men he had come across in the RFC, straight from the same schools, but rounded off by a few years in the company of Australians and Canadians. Fred held out his hand.

"Fred Dunn. Good to meet you. Happy Christmas."

"Hugh Rutherford. You too. Dammed shame we couldn't have a few more days' back home. They were expecting me back in Cumbria, killing the fatted goose and all that."

Fred assumed when Rutherford had said Cumbria, he meant a very large piece of it, not just a house in a small village.

"Where are you from?"

"Northumberland, but I live in London now. South Kensington."

He let his new colleague assume, as they always did, that he lived in one of the large stucco houses, owned by his parents.

"Lucky you. Handy for the centre of things. I bet you know all the good places to go to. If I ever get some leave, you'll have to show a country boy like me around. I could do with going somewhere different. Meeting a few girls. I only ever seem to go to the Savoy, and that's getting a bit boring to be honest. Where did you go to school then?"

He asked the second question nonchalantly. After the 'where are you from?" it was a map people could place a person by. An address and a school went hand in hand, a symbiotic relationship perfectly balanced for people like Hugh Rutherford. The unspoken rightness of how things should be. He hadn't meant anything by it, for him, South Kensington as an address should have been complemented by an education at Harrow or Winchester.

"Wylam School. You've probably not heard of it. Very small."

"No, can't say I have. I was at Fettes in Scotland myself. Didn't like it much. Too bloody cold. A bit like this place really. No hot water, lousy food. No girls. Glad to get away and come out here really. At least I was, back then in '14."

"We're not far from Amiens, twenty miles maybe, we could go there and see what is going on one night. There are a few good restaurants I know there."

Fred had managed to steer the conversation away from schools, and was saved from any more questions by the arrival of their batman Fidler, who came to offer to help unpack Fred's things. He was grateful for a chance to leave the confines of the hut and get to know the Squadron a bit more. Rutherford seemed a decent enough chap, though you could never tell in this war.

People were rarely themselves at first, and having to come to terms with losing so many people you might have called a friend, it was often easier not to give too much of your real personality away and just stick with the safe subjects. He'd get to know his new room mate soon enough.

"Come on. Let's both go and see if we can find somewhere warm around here and get a tea. I'll bring a few puddings I brought over and we'll see if the cook knows how to steam them properly".

Christmas Day when it came was better than Fred or indeed anyone else at Candas might have expected. Despite putting the Channel between himself and Kitty, Fred was glad to be back in France in action. Although he still doubted the war would be over soon, he had missed the camaraderie of the squadron bases in the British Expeditionary Force and the sense that the war was a near neighbour not a distant relative. There had been a lull in the fighting for the past few weeks that

December, and the lack of constant shelling meant that sleep was easier, so the men felt at least more rested than they had for the past year. Between them, the newcomers had bought enough food and drink to make it a feast of sorts.

For many of the men there this was a better spread than any they would have had at home. There was a crisp white cloth across the trestle table and someone had fashioned a Christmas wreath for the centre out of the branches of a fallen pine tree and some candles. Their light flickered against the gold edges of their plates giving a sparkling cheerful feel.

On big meat platters, stood a massive cooked ham and a rib of beef (from the Rutherford estate in Cumbria), with piping hot roast potatoes and carrots, all doused in French butter. With Fred's puddings from Fortnum's and enough French wine to wash it all down, they began to feel a Christmas cheer. Afterwards, slumped around on the tattered old chairs, those who could remember them started to sing a few carols.

"Funny old world, really," said Rutherford. "You wouldn't think we were at war would you, with bloody Bosch only a few miles over the other side. They're probably having a right sing song too, having feasted on sausages and cabbage."

"Do you ever think about them, those Germans who have Christmases together just like us, when you're up there flying, looking down at them?" Fred tried to put into words what few of them every dared discuss.

Hugh blinked nervously unsure where this conversation was going.

"Sometimes, at first, when you see a chap go down and you had got a good look at them. Those piercing blue eyes looking right at you. Those Hun are very good at eyeballing you, yes I do. It doesn't stop you, of course, trying to kill them, but it, well, it makes you think, doesn't it? Me or him?" Fred nodded. He knew exactly what Rutherford was trying to say.

"Come on Dunn, pass that bottle. It's Christmas after all. We'll be back home the next one. I'm sure of that."

Fred passed the bottle over. The German pilots were men, just like them, thrown into a war, trying to survive, and get back home alive. He hoped that they all had had a good

Learning To Fly   113

Christmas and a proper feast. The war would start again soon enough. This had been a lull. They all needed a little bit of calm before whatever was coming next. If the Somme hadn't brought either side even an inch closer to victory, and had caused so many to die, what other horrors would have to take place before they could ever talk again of peace?

Fred was now flying every type of machine in and out of the base to the other aircraft depot just 60 miles to the north or to squadrons all over the French countryside. Often it was easy, even pleasurable, skirting well away from the German lines and earning a night away at an unfamiliar base with a new crowd. "Captain Dunn, you have to get this Albatros back to St Omer, they want to strip it down and do some work of it, to see what these Germans are up to. They need to have a good look at these Spandau guns. Get there by lunchtime and then back here tonight."

He was given his orders tersely, and didn't have time to ask any questions. There had been talk of how the Albatros had come down on the Allied side and a young German pilot taken prisoner. It meant he would probably survive, and go home to his parents afterwards, maybe even back to school.

The Albatros itself had been patched up on the wing which had been damaged, and the six shot holes in the floor where Allied artillery had peppered the feet of the young German, were covered with rough wood, not quite managing to cover all the holes, but enough to ensure Fred couldn't see the ground below him. Some paint had been daubed roughly over the Black Cross, but not enough to erase its grey shadow completely.

He took off, in awe of the power of the Mercedes engine and quickly reached 12,000 feet. It was quick this machine and flew well, but he felt a twinge of apprehension as he pushed it through its paces. He knew the way northwards like the back of his hand. Bouncing in and out of thick clouds made the cold air whoosh through the cockpit, and he felt the familiar sharp pain in his toes, which always came before the cold froze them to numbness.

He thought about the warm lunch which would await

him at St Omer. The hot soup and thick French bread and eggs. He was smiling to himself as he pushed on, turning the machine to left and right, testing it, feeling relieved that the patches on the wings were staying intact.

It must have been about 10 miles from the No. 1 Aircraft Depot, even though the clouds made it difficult to pick out any of the landmarks he knew so well in this part of France. He dropped a few thousand feet, enjoying the relief it gave to his eardrums. The air felt clearer here and the headache he had started to feel even before taking off in Candas was easing a little. He closed his eyes, snorted and shook his head in an effort to clear his blocked ears.

Suddenly he heard a thud as if someone at the shooting gallery at the fair had hit the tin can. A bullet had clipped the tail of the machine and sent it into a fierce wobble. The wings shook, the controls swayed as if in the middle of a fit. Fred, now wide eyed, saw another flash to his right. It whizzed off, a yellow sparking arrow of light into the distance. He was coming under Archie, and could even hear the artillery fire from below. But it could only be coming from Allied guns. He hadn't strayed over the lines here; he was certain of that. He was being fired on by his own side.

Instinctively he took the machine back up, catching another burst of fire in the tail as he did so. He could feel it listing to one side and had to heave on the controls to right it. Then another short burst from another direction came up through one of the wooden patches in the cockpit floor. It missed his foot and skirted past the thick sheepskin of his boot leaving by the side panel where it clipped just below his elbow.

The pain was instant, like a skewer in flesh. His mind registered the sharp throbbing sting. He felt hemmed in on all sides. The gunners must have seen him and assumed it was a lone and lost Hun, an easy target. Had no one thought to say one of their own was flying an Albatros back to base?

Fred just had time to feel angry at the lack of communication on the ground when the engine began making strange clanking noises. It was now vibrating dangerously. One of the shots had hit the petrol tank and the cockpit was

Learning To Fly   115

filling with the acrid smell of fumes. He felt a wave of nausea. Automatically, he turned off the engine.

Going down on fire in a German plane. It was not meant to end like this. A flaming death was the worst of all. His stomach lurched and his heart raced, acknowledging the situation he was in. He had to be very close to St Omer now so gingerly, in an effort not to cause anything to move or snap, and grinding his teeth to take away the sensation coming from his elbow, he took the machine into a gentle dive. The clouds peeled apart to reveal the canvas tents of the base below. A sense of relief beyond any he had experienced before flowed through him like an electric current.

He levelled the machine slowly out of its dive. He could see a couple of mechanics with binoculars on the ground anxiously watching an Albatros approach. He tried to wave with his good arm. Surely they realised it was not the enemy? He was now level with the trees at the far end of the base and tilted the nose down. The ground came up quickly far more quickly than he was expecting. He had never flown an Albatros before, what a time to find out its idiosyncrasies.

In the split second he had left, he thought of Kitty.

He could see her face clearly. It was the first time he had seen her so perfectly when flying. Then the wheels touched the ground and he had to pull back with all his might. The runway was wet and rutted and it held the wheels tight. Within an instant he used his good arm to swing his body out of the machine and, clutching his other elbow, ran away from it. A tender was making its way towards him. He looked behind to see the Albatross in one piece, looking threateningly at him as if to say "This time you got away with it."

Inside the tender was a mechanic he'd worked with last year.

"Dunn! Blimey, we thought it was a Hun come to spray us to kingdom come."

"I got hit by our own Archie. I guess nobody said I'd be coming over in a German machine. They got the tank, but not that much came out, so it may not go up, but you need to get the fire team out there pretty quick."

He'd had his hand on the bonnet of the tender, when

the world lost all colour and he felt himself tumbling forwards, hitting the grass with a thud similar to the one the Albatros had made when it landed. Blackness seemed to fill the space.

When Fred came to he was in a bed in one of the first aid huts. His elbow was bandaged and his arm was in a sling. He struggled to remember at first and shuffled images in his mind like a pack of cards trying to get them in order. Slowly the landing came back to him.

He was in St Omer. He remembered the bullet which had clipped him and he touched the bandage to check. Then he felt for his head. That was bandaged too. He must have hit it when he fell. His hand felt an oozing of blood from the cut over his forehead.

"We patched you up okay. You had a lucky escape there, Captain Dunn. Not a great idea to be flying an Albatros around these parts, old chap." The depot Doctor spoke. He was a new face and from his cheery demeanour and eagerness Fred assumed he had not been at the Front long. The medics had a hard time of it in a flying base, having to patch up many things which were beyond patching.

"Thanks, Doc. Did anyone else get hit when it went up?"

"No only the Albatros. I'm Pierce, by the way. You got away with it. It could have been much worse. But I imagine you know that. You've shattered the bone in your elbow, but it will heal right enough. An inch or two further over and it would have got the heart. You can still move your fingers, I assume?"

Fred shuffled his fingers. The movement shot a pain up his arm, but they moved. He tried to make a fist, but only got half way. Enough to hold a control stick, he thought to himself. Pierce then signed a few papers and handed them to him.

"You really shouldn't fly for a week or so. Here's a week's sick leave. You could get the boat tonight if you wanted."

Fred looked up at him. He was clearly a new boy round here. The medics who had been around for longer would not have let a simple thing like a broken elbow equal a whole week's sick leave.

"Thanks very much, sir," he said, grinning. "I think I'll do just that."

Chapter 20
Sick Leave, March 1917

The Channel was flat and grey like pewter, moonlight catching it and causing brilliant shafts of white light to ripple along its flat surface. The hospital boat was uncomfortably slow, inching its way through the molten-like water, taunting him at the contrast in speed between this lumbering sea transport and an aeroplane.

Another time when he had returned, crossing by boat, he was a shrunken despairing man weighed down by what he had seen and the onslaught on the nerves that constant flying and witnessing death could bring about. He was going back now, from Calais, not Boulogne, no less horrified by what he had witnessed out in France, but now able to file it away in the part of his mind, labelled private and sealed.

His coping strategies since those early horrifying months of war, were to never dwell and to never look back. To keep friendships light, and accept that if today were to be your last, the life before it would have been full and worthwhile. He was managing it, sometimes only just, but he was alive. The only obstacle to this manner of coping was his relationship with Kitty. It unbalanced him like a faulty altimeter and the slightest tilt in her letters or silence could tip him over the edge to those old dark days and nights.

He had already sent a telegram ahead to say he was to be home for a week and would be staying at his parents' house until he heard from her. If he heard from her. His own lack of confidence when it came to Kitty was an enigma to him.

Adele and Thomas had not known what to make of his telegram, they could tell by the boy's knock on their door it wasn't the very worst of telegrams, but still it did talk about being invalided home. Did that mean terrible injuries he had been afraid to mention? Their nerves were drawn tight with the anxiety of having a precious son over in France and it made them twitchy. No news was not good news, it was just the absence of bad news. They had seen enough young men in uniform around the capital with missing limbs to know that that was a possibility for Fred.

It was nearly midnight by the time his train got into Charing Cross. Thomas left the Freemantle's car round the corner from the station. They now had a son fighting at the Front and understood the anxiety that a telegram preceding the return of an injured soldier brought, so had allowed Thomas to use the car to bring Fred back home to his mother. Thomas stood on the chilly platform along with a few anxious others, glad to be meeting members of the living, but worried what might emerge as the train steamed into the desolate station. It had become too much associated with the place for farewells and the last embrace to ever have an air of anything cheerful.

"Thank God," Thomas whispered slowly at the sight of Fred emerging with his arm in a sling. He walked unaided and upright. There was no other outward sign of his injury as he had taken the head bandage off so as not to alarm his parents. Thomas almost ran towards him, and cradled his son in his arms trying not to reveal the tension he had been feeling just minutes before. He wiped his wet cheeks against the rough wool of Fred's overcoat.

"We were a bit worried when you said you were coming home on sick leave after an accident. We didn't know…" It was best not to go on. There were other people nearby, not so lucky. A few were on crutches, the legs of their military trousers turned up, unnecessary now. Thomas had to turn away from them and lead Fred to the side street when he had parked the Silver Ghost.

"Well, I say Dad, this is the way to travel."

"Mrs. Freemantle said I could use it to bring you home and put your mother's mind at rest," he said, almost apologetically.

"She is a good woman and very fond of your ma. Their son Arthur is out there too now which is a big worry for them. He's not a strong lad, like you Fred."

The Dunns had spent all of the war working for the Freemantles as a lady's maid and chauffeur and as the only remaining domestic servants, had become their most loyal and longest serving staff. Now after nearly a decade in London,

Thomas Dunn could look back, with his son, a Captain in the Royal Flying Corps leaning on his arm, and know that moving to London had been the making of their young family. The war would have taken him if they had stayed in Wylam too, there was no escape wherever you might hail from and from whichever class you came. He'd heard that all the young men of the pit village were in France or fighting somewhere.

Several of the sons of the large houses like Close House and Holeyn Hall had died, some in the Somme. The seeping away of everything he had once taken for granted; that sons would outlive fathers, that each generation would follow the last, that this war would be won. Thomas carried it all around inside him like an ulcer. But now Fred was home, alive, he could put aside those gloomy thoughts.

"Let's get you home, son."

The weather that first week in February was bitter; every morning frost covered the cobbles outside their mews house and remnants of January's snow was still left in a few dirty patches. Fred was glad to sit by the fire, and read the newspapers, occasionally breaking off to tell a few censored tales about the war and the aeroplanes he had been flying. On the second day he heard the knock at the door, well after everyone else had gone to bed. He opened the door quietly and saw the young boy, he could be no more than 14, holding a piece of paper out. The telegram he had been hoping for.

Cannot get to London. Come to Middleton Hall. Will meet you off London train. Kitty

There was nothing there to suggest a love affair. In her telegrams, she could be addressing a brother at the Front. Although thoroughly modern in so many ways, Kitty knew the telegram could be seen by too many eyes other than Fred's and had chosen her brief message with care. She saw no need to take unnecessary risks. Their relationship, as it was, was risk enough. It was less easy to explain to Adele and Thomas why he was to visit the daughter of Adele's former employer.

As his mother was washing up the next day, drying her

hands on her apron, he decided to bring up the subject of his trip to Hampshire.

"I'm going to be going away for a few days Ma. Down to Hampshire, to stay with Mrs Burrell."

"Oh, that sounds nice for you, dear. I didn't know you knew Mrs Burrell well enough to stay with her though."

"We spent a bit of time together when I was convalescing with Mrs Perkins down in Sutton Place. We got on very well, so she suggested I spend a few days with her when I next got some leave."

Adele, being French, was not so easily taken in.

"Well I hope you have a good time there. She has a grand home I believe, a chateau even, a bit different to this Fred?" She motioned round their tiny galley kitchen with its stone sink and rough wooden cupboards.

Adele smiled inwardly and was genuinely happy for her son. She had watched Kitty Burrell grow from a dark haired feisty infant into an elegant young woman, who was now the mistress of a large estate. If her dashing son had caught her eye, well good for him. The war had turned all things topsy-turvy. Perhaps there was really nothing strange in this wholly unequal coming together.

Adele's years in England had not diminished her Gallic outlook and the romance between two people from two such different backgrounds did not seem to her the least bit unnatural. This war was pulling people apart. They had to find their happiness whenever they could. But Adele wondered how much, if anything, Edith Perkins knew and what she would say. She of course, would not have such Gallic insouciance.

Fred took the train from Waterloo just twelve hours after receiving Kitty's instruction, having telegrammed ahead to say he would be arriving at four. His arm was still in a sling. Although he thought he could remove it, it was a welcome barrier to avoid conversation on the train and allow him to sleep. He wondered how he would be received, and what it would be like to see Kitty on her home turf, her chateau as his mother suggested. Coming out of the country station he was met by an elderly chauffeur who waved at him. He could not hide his disappointment that Kitty herself had not come to meet him.

"Mrs Burrell is tied up with the hospital just now and asked me to meet you, Captain Dunn. She sends her apologies," the old man said. He had picked him out of the crowd at the station despite there being a few other military men there. Perhaps no one had the wings on their uniform that set them out as an airman. Perhaps there was a photograph of him at the hall? His imagination was playing games again; his confidence always seeking tests and affirmations of her affection.

"Here let me take your bag, Sir. We shall be there in less than half an hour, it's not that far."

Fred tried to talk on the short journey to Middleton Hall, but his mind was twisting and turning, trying to work out how Kitty would be with him, and if they would be able to recapture what they had experienced that brief weekend in Brighton. The private drive up to the Hall was long, and lined with thick yew hedges. They were as wide as some of the trenches out in France. Hundreds of men could live in something as big as these hedges.

The house, when it came into view, was magnificent, too big to be called simply a house. Compared to her mother's home in Kent, this was a far grander property, built to intimidate and impress. It achieved both as Fred looked up at it. It did look a little like a medieval castle with its large red stone turreted porch and smaller ivy-clad wings off to each side, each with their own castellated roof. Fred had never visited anywhere this imposing before, and felt cowed that all of this belonged to Kitty, the woman he loved. Inside the echoing hall, far larger than his parent's home, he was met by a pretty young girl in a tight black dress with a white frilly apron and taken down a long stone flagged corridor with stags' heads and other hunting and fishing trophies lining the walls. He felt their eyes watching him. It was too masculine and severe for Kitty.

In the distance the sound of raised voices, and ahead he could see a nurse hurrying across the corridor. The aroma was incongruous in such a setting, a smell of disinfectant which brought back memories of the field hospitals in France. The girl who he learned was called Mabel, took him upstairs to his room on the first floor, in the west wing of the house looking out onto the garden. It must be on the other side well away from the hospital, which appeared to be taking up the one half of the castle.

On the way, Mabel pointed out a sitting room, which he assumed had been created from a bedroom. It must face the grounds at the back of the house, although it was too dark to make out anything in the distance. Here in this room was the feminine touch the rest of the grand house lacked. Kitty had fashioned it into her bolt hole now her more formal rooms were lined with iron beds full of wounded men. As Fred stepped into it, he admired how Kitty had carefully rearranged it to make a comfortable oasis from the frenzy which was going on downstairs. A fire had been lit and the logs cracked with the intense heat, sparks threatening the pale blue Chinese rug.

There was a photograph of Captain William Burrell in his uniform in a silver frame on the desk in the corner. He was tall and handsome, distinguished looking. Of course he was, thought Fred. They would have made a striking couple, and he had an image of Kitty and William Burrell together, here in this room maybe? Could it have been their bedroom? He felt Burrell's ghost occupy the space and it made him more nervous than ever. He sat uneasily on the yellow high backed chair, his back to the silver photograph, arranging and rearranging his sling as if he couldn't work out which was the best position for the bandage. Footsteps were coming along the corridor. Soft, but confident taps.

Kitty, when she arrived, was in a long grey wool dress buttoned to the neck and cut loosely over her slim figure. He had not seen her in anything so plain before, and felt his heart fill as he took in how it made her look even more alluring than the chiffon cocktail dresses and wide brimmed hats. She stepped over to him and held out her arms, no hint of any embarrassment or nervousness on her part. Sensing her ease, he allowed the strain he had been feeling to recede.

She was still the Kitty he remembered from Brighton, from Sutton Place, from those grabbed nights in London. She may own this enormous castle and everything in it, but she was still the same person he had fallen for, the person he loved.

For the next few days they tried hard to conceal their delight in each other's company while they were around any staff or the nurses. Even if the servants did guess or see evidence that he would slip from his room into hers each night, returning silently to his own single bed just after dawn, they were discreet. They walked hand in hand around the sunken garden, but only when hidden from the view of the house, sneaking kisses, breathing in lungsful of the smell of skin and perfume.

The three days were over too quickly. It was if he had been in a dream, wrapped up in all his emotions, unable to take in the enormity of his surroundings and of Kitty herself marshalling the organisation of her estate as if she were a brigadier general. Yet again he found himself in awe of this amazing woman, his secret love.

Chapter 21
Back in France, March 1917

The ferry back to France was packed full, rows of men lined up like skittles in their unmarked and uninfested khaki. Fred looked at their scrubbed faces, with their ready for war masks secured over the darting eyes and tight lips which would have revealed their true fears. How many of them would make the crossing back?

There was much talk about another big push in the north, and many of these men were heading to their units near Ypres. Fred heard their cheerful, innocent banter, how they were going to push the Bosch back to Berlin and good riddance to him. They would be back by Christmas, definitely, this year. Easy to say, difficult to predict, he knew that now.

At Calais, he saw them march away feeling an overpowering sense of gloom, and boarded his train to St Omer. He'd be staying there a few days, trying out the latest machine to come out to the Front, the SE5 fighter. Pierce would want to see him first, then there was a new CO, another one to get to know. The last one had lost control on a short routine flight, insisting he could fly himself rather than wait for transport.

It was not certain what had brought him down, but a combination of poor weather and a machine he was unused to had ensured he wouldn't ever return to his club in Pall Mall, the only place where he had truly felt at home. Hardie, his replacement, was a tall, intimidating figure, and one used to getting his own way. He'd moved up the ranks in the RFC because he was good at giving orders and carrying out any he was given, however misguided or inappropriate they might have been.

Brought up in the Highlands of Scotland he wouldn't let a bit of French cold and wet put him off. Hardie had studied engineering in Scotland and may well have gone into the shipbuilding business his family owned if the war had not intervened. Although he was only a few years older than many of the men he was in charge of, he wore those extra few years heavily and to many he acted like a man of their father's generation.

His carefully waxed moustache and neat cropped chestnut hair made him look ten years older than his 28 years. He did not hold with the laxer COs at some of the bases who let the men go wild and turned a blind eye to it, thinking it was good to let off steam. Indeed no. Not that he didn't like the odd drink himself (scotch, of course) but these tales of the pilots on the rampage in some towns were just preposterous. Smashing up windows, chucking food around, drinking themselves senseless, not to mention the womanising. No, it wouldn't be happening under his watch.

So Hardie was not in the mood to welcome back a pilot who'd just had a week's leave, and couldn't hide his displeasure that that softie Pierce had allowed him home in the first place with just a fractured elbow. Fred, had been warned in advance about the character of his new commander, and had taken the precaution of bringing a couple of bottles of whisky with him. Hardie was momentarily disarmed as he accepted them, a bit too keenly Fred noticed, and put them under his desk. Single malt. They were too good to put in the mess. They would do for special occasions, though there were precious few of those. Hardie had to accept that having such a competent pilot back on the squadron would be pretty useful.

The wastage, as he reported it to HQ, was too high and they were running out of anyone who had flown a machine for more than four weeks, let alone four years. Yes, all in all, he needed men like Fred to get these new machines up and ready and out to the squadrons before the next battle, when it came. Perhaps he could get Wing Commander off his back now Fred had come back at just the right time.

"Welcome back, Dunn. You're just what we need around here. Someone who knows what they're doing. You have a lot of flying to do. This lot have been sitting on their arses while you've been away. Not one of them goes up with the slightest whiff of rain around here. We need a few people who can fly whatever the weather," Hardie grunted, and waved to Fred to go.

The bombardment followed the now well-rehearsed plan, beginning with the fierce and constant shelling. Grey cloying smoke was a permanent feature in the sky. The air seemed to be alive, peppered with yellow flashing. The land had become a bubbling stew as more and more firepower was sent up. Roads and fields were being turned to brown sludge, all to make a path for the infantry to march across. Except there would be no marching in this, boots would sink and squelch through this new unnatural terrain.

They'd tried that one in the Somme, surely they had learnt that it was never going to be that easy? The plan was to launch the next battle around Arras. Its majestic cathedral, which had been attacked in a revolution was going to fall victim, yet again, to fighting men. Soon all of France would be one big godless swamp. They'd been told the Hindenburg Line was to be broken, that the Hun would be pushed back and finally, that there would be an end to this interminable war. How often had they heard that? They were nearly three years into it now, as hard as that was to believe.

April 13 1917. Fred and Rutherford, who had been sent to Candas too, were told they had to return to England as soon as possible to ferry out some new machines to a fighter squadron. All of its Sopwith Pups had been smashed up, which left an aerial fighting Flight without any means of fighting. Three days later, exhausted from the constant flying, the two ferry pilots were sitting in a bar in Doullens, hoping the rough wine and thick slices of creamy Camembert on chunks of bread would help them forget the frenzy of the last few days. A Flight Commander, Fred recognised walked in, and called for a bottle of brandy. Fred remembered him; a serious fellow, who'd learnt to fly before the war.

You could always tell the ones who had. He'd been one of the cricketers that day another lifetime ago, not a flight commander, then, he was just a second lieutenant. Fred remembered his name, Leadbitter. Leadbitter snapped the top off the brandy bottle he'd been handed and took a long swig, before waiting for the glass to be wiped and handed over. Behind his shrunken eyes he looked like a man trying to knock himself out with drink, they were the familiar signs of a man almost spent, an emotional empty tank which he was trying to fill with brandy. Fred and Hugh moved across and Fred pushed the cleaned glass towards him. They acknowledged each other briefly, but Fred saw this was not the time to talk cricket. Leadbitter was with the squadron which had lost the ten Pups.

After downing the glass of brandy in one gulp, he looked over at Fred, who had explained that they had just brought out the new machines to his unit. Leadbitter raised his glass, a half acknowledgement, perhaps a thanks for the new machines, perhaps for that shared memory. He kept his gaze away from them as he spoke.

"It had been a routine patrol, over the Hindenburg line, just to get the picture of what was going on. The weather was perfect." Leadbitter spoke slowly, deliberately weighing each word before presenting it to them as if in a courtroom. "If the mission had been to observe and take photographs, we would have come back with a very fine, perfectly clear set. It should have been straightforward. Bad luck, yes, very bad luck". Flight Commander Leadbitter was one of the two survivors, his observer now in hospital with multiple injuries. It had been the blackest day.

"Two were flamers you know. Horrible that was. Then, one of them got shot up, landed in a German trench, taking a few of those poor souls with them too I bet. But the worst bit, I saw this myself." Leadbitter filled his glass again, and downed it in one. "Snowy, that was the worst. Snowball his name, the gunner, he must have undone his straps, to get the gun round and get a better shot at them. I don't know what happened then, but I saw him fall out, like a spinning toy, you know, like one of those tin ones that just fall over in the end."

He stopped again and this time Fred filled the glasses and pushed over some bread. "Hooper, the pilot, he must have panicked, Snowy falling out like that, and he just ploughed right into this Albatros. Both of them gone then, it would have been quick, thank the Lord, smashed to smithereens. It was like a volcano, but in reverse. I could feel the heat blast."

They found out the other two men, who had only arrived at the base that day with less than ten hours flying time between them, had been unable to control their aeroplanes and crash landed on the enemy side. The observer and pilot had died on impact, both with broken necks. Twelve young men had set out, but ten of them did not return.

"Dear God." There was nothing more to say. They ordered a second bottle of brandy with more bread and cheese to soak it up. The food and drink arrived and the waitress, a young spirited looking woman, saw from their emptied and furrowed faces that now was not the time to make eyes with les aviateurs anglais. They would leave a large tip, these fliers always did. Several hours later the three men emerged from the bar, as if anaesthetised.

A little part still remembered why they had drunk so much and it was in a mutual silence that they both shook hands with Leadbitter. He clung onto Fred's hand cupping it in his own, but no more talking. They went their separate ways wordlessly. It was way past midnight and several miles to the depot. With luck a military vehicle would pick them up. Fred and Rutherford began the long walk back in the blackness, stumbling over each other as they tried to skirt the lumps of mud as large as beer crates pitting the narrow roads. Giddy with brandy and exhaustion, they had to stop each other from falling over.

In the distance they could hear the relentless boom-boom of the bombardment and see the occasional red flare light up the skies, as the shells found their targets. That night it felt as if this war might never end. That they had started a race which neither side could win and which neither would concede. At this rate there would soon be no pilots left to do any flying.

Chapter 22
Early Summer 1917

June came. In ordinary life, a time for lightness, for the throwing away of winter drabness, and for new growth, but not in France. The only certainty about the war in the middle of 1917 was that even if you believed it could get no more terrible, then it most certainly would. Depths of despair and hopelessness that knew no human limits had been mined. You knew somehow that there was always some other seam, more base and ghastly which could shake the very experience of being human. Perhaps though, the war was slowing down and after Arras, there would be a respite, enough to bring out some new machines and train a few more of these youngsters in how to handle them.

But the lulls were less frequent now. It was as if both sides were desperate to end the fighting and so forced to be even more reckless and brutal than before. One offensive would lead to another and inch by inch the Generals dug in for a giant tug of war where a slip of the foot could mean the loss of thousands of young men. An even larger offensive was planned and the relentless move to the north and the coast and the retreat of the German line was predicted. The nervous talk in the mess was of the plan to mine underground and blow up strategic ridges on the way to help capture high ground and push the infantry forward. He was one of the few people in the Royal Flying Corps who knew what conditions could be like underground, with the air pulled out of your lungs and the constant fear of tunnel collapse taking up every thought in your being until you heart would beat so loudly that you could feel it pushing against the walls to escape.

His father and uncles had worked in the mines in Wylam and he knew that even there, with the new machinery and extensive safety checks, life underground was unpredictable. Here in France there would be no deputy going down ahead of the shift, like his father, to ensure there was a safe passage for the miners. It would be a whole new version of hell below the ground.

The massive detonation of the underground mines which was the starting gun for the next assault shook the earth for many miles around. Deafening, single repeating booms. This vast drum display sent brown clods of earth the size of cows up into the sky until everything took on the aspect of a sepia photograph, ill-defined and rusty. Summer seemed to be hiding now, afraid to come out and shine light on such an unnatural, lumpen landscape. It had lost its contours, all ridges and large areas of high ground had become swampland. It was a whipped up sea of brown mud.

No green dared show its face here. Persistent rain had flattened everything which had tried to grow in its path. Pity the men floundering in the mud. The wretched bloody infantry. Even the rats were leaving them to it. The rain was constant, thick and cloying and it made flying difficult, so only the more experienced of pilots were able to negotiate it. Those months chronicled more and more machines crashing as the inexperienced new pilots failed to negotiate their air space in the grey featureless sky.

In the midst of this assault, Fred had been given a temporary duty back home to take a damaged machine back to Wye airfield in Kent, where he had to stay for a week training some new recruits, before bringing a new machine back over the Channel. Images of that first summer in the garden of England at Sutton Place took over his thoughts; to see colours of blue and green, to breathe unadulterated air, to sleep in a proper bed.

Not to be always surrounded by the mud and filth which seemed to have seeped into every part of Northern France. It would be five months since he and Kitty had last met. He still struggled to believe she was his. It was as if the rain had fused his memories like a camera left out in the rain, the images inside now all blurred and indistinct. He felt like he was writing to her for the first time.

Coming back July 22. In Kent till 29. Sutton Place nearby. Long to see you again, Fred.

He arrived back in England, battered and buffeted by the rain, and the fact that he had still not heard from Kitty. It took over an hour to fill in all the documents, and Fred noticed ruefully that as the war progressed his paperwork for a single flight could fill one folder. Just one simple trip over the Channel and fifteen sheets to complete. He doubted very much whether anyone would ever read any of it. It would probably end up in a bonfire. This funny little aerodrome, he thought ruefully, and hoped he would know some of the other officers, feeling once more that this war had gone on now too long.

"Captain Dunn. Wait a minute." The man in the office he'd just been in with the papers ran after him. "A letter came for you. Special delivery. It was brought by car yesterday. Must be someone important."

He could tell before the clerk handed over the thick cream envelope that it was from Kitty. Who else would write to him here on such paper and have it brought by car? He swiftly turned towards his hut, careful to open it away from anyone who could witness his reaction.

Sutton Place

July 21, 1917

My dearest Fred

I was beginning to fear I would never hear from you again. No letters seem to be getting through and the news from the Front just goes on getting worse and worse. My eyes filled with tears to see it was not the other type of telegram, but one with the very news I'd been longing for. I left for London the next day and came straight here. I can stay until the 25th but will have to return to London then.

Yours with my affection,

Kitty

Fred tucked the letter into his tunic and made straight for the hangar. He told a mechanic he needed to take one of the motorbikes as he had some business nearby. Within half an hour he was on the road to Ashford, towards Kitty. He felt a thrill of excitement and had to concentrate hard to remember the way. The English roads looked so unlike the straight French roads and their lines of ram rod erect trees which made following them in the air so much simpler. At first he found it hard to make out which way he was heading.

After twisting and turning, first heading west then bearing north, he finally arrived at Hawley. It looked just as he remembered it from two summers previous. Overgrown, verdant and untouched by war. It had a timelessness which Fred now found hard to take in. He stopped at the Chequers Inn and took the opportunity to freshen up. The landlord was the same curious man he remembered and he bought a pint of beer to calm himself, trying not to make it so obvious that he was hurrying to Sutton Place. "Back from the Front?" the landlord asked.

"Yes, just for a week. An airfield not far from here." Fred moved outside. He didn't want to explain why he was in Hawley and any talk of what was actually happening out at the Front was not something for pub chatter. It was towards seven when he made his way up the drive of Sutton Place, past the same hedges, crunching over the same gravel.

The sun was still strong, even though it was the early evening, and the house was bathed in that perfect dusk light. The wisteria was out and its purple beads framed the mellow cream stonework just as he remembered. He brushed down his tunic and carefully wiped the dust off his leather boots before pulling the bell chain at the front porch. Hickman let him in and appeared pleased to see him. It was hard to tell, as his years of service had made him discreet and ultimately unfathomable.

"Mrs Perkins and Mrs Burrell said you may be coming. I'm very pleased to see you again, Captain Dunn. They are in the drawing room if you would like to go straight there."

Fred followed Hickman across the hall, pulling at his

Learning To Fly 133

sleeves and flicking imagined bits of dirt from the front of his tunic. His nervousness and embarrassment had brought colour to his cheeks and perspiration to his brow. Edith was sitting in her usual chair by the fireplace, Kitty stood by the window. He noticed her lace covered high collared white shirt over a cotton skirt the colour of ripe plums, as striking and shimmeringly beautiful as ever. He thought of her long pale legs hidden under the plum skirt and felt his face flushing a deeper crimson.

Mrs Perkins would know nothing about their relationship, and he doubted she would welcome it, though surely she would notice he was a different person now? It was to her he moved first, trying to compose himself. He took her hand warmly and kissed it. They had not met since that summer in 1915 and he could see that the war, the loss of a nephew, a son-in-law and many other young men she had known, had left its mark on her. Her grey hair had wide streaks of white in it.

"Fred, my goodness, there you are. You do look hot. Kitty said she thought you may be stationed nearby for a short while. You should have written to say you were coming. Are you going to be staying for a few days? I do hope so?"

"I have to be back at the base tomorrow morning. I'm doing some training there. At Wye not far from here. It's a new aeroplane, the Sopwith Camel, you may have heard of it, so called because it has this hump just like a camel. Anyway, we've got to get these youngsters trained in flying it. Bit of a tricky one you see." He stumbled over his words.

"Fred, you must tell us all about it. Kitty, come and join us. Hickman, get Captain Dunn a gin, and some more for us. There must be something we can celebrate. I keep reading a corner has been turned in this war and that we are on the edge of victory." Edith busied herself with her glass, and Fred felt he could now look at Kitty fully, at her smiling upturned face, his back carefully placed towards her mother. She wore the same exquisite expression he remembered. He blushed again, then took her hand and kissed it, leaving his lips there on her skin just that moment too long. If only she would talk first and so give him chance to rearrange his expression.

"Fred, what a piece of luck you were able to get up to

Sutton Place. I do hope you can stay for dinner. Mother was just saying that it is so quiet around here just now. She needs someone to cheer her up. As I do, too." The last four words were said under her breath, for his ears only. Again he felt he had been caught in a searchlight and dropped her hand, as if it was a stolen treasure he had been caught with.

He hadn't worked out how he was going to behave here at all. How could he have just taken off without thinking how awkward it might be, the three of them together in the same room, yet kept apart by convention and tradition. He downed three gins like they were water before they went into dinner, and although he knew he had often drunk far more in the mess without any ill effects, the tension at being back with Kitty and with her mother between them made his head feel light and his thoughts jumbled.

"Ladies, I'm sorry, but I think I need some fresh air. Today has been a long one and if you will excuse me, I'll just go into the garden for a few minutes before dinner."

Quickly, ignoring Kitty's questioning look, he walked out of the front door, his feet crunching across the gravel toward the orangery. Here he knew he could gather his thoughts and would be well away from the dining room windows in case Edith happened to look out. There was a sweet smell of the lemons and the calming sound of water from the stone fountain.

The goddess of love it was. He stared at its naked form. Slowly, he drew on his cigarette, gratefully inhaling its smoke, enjoying the stillness and sense of calm it brought back. He was just about to stub it out and return to the house, when Kitty appeared through the open door. She grabbed both his hands and held them firmly, looking into his eyes. Fred looked at the ground.

"This is unbearable, Kitty. I want to grab hold of you and take you in my arms."

"I know. I feel the same. I feel like another person is speaking for me. But we have no choice Fred. Tonight we must carry on as if we are friends, nothing more. Now is not the time to tell anyone about us. It is too soon. You must promise me you understand this."

Learning To Fly

Fred nodded and kissed her again, on her lips this time. He felt surprised and disappointed by what he had just agreed to. He had made a mistake in coming here. It could never work meeting like this, always in secret, always on the look out for an unintended revelation. They could only have been there a few minutes, so keen was Kitty to make her way back to the house and not arouse any suspicion. It was painful to have to acknowledge how desperate she was to hide their relationship and to maintain the lie.

For the first time he felt a pang at the thought that it could be her snobbery. That she might feel somewhere within her that he was not good enough for her, her mother, or the life she had become used to, with its imitation castle and servants. Despite his success as a pilot, he was used to snobbery. It was all around him in the Royal Flying Corps. Men judging each other on where they came from, not who they were. He expected more of Kitty, though. Surely she was not ashamed of him?

Retracing his steps across the gravel, he walked slowly back to the dining room, carefully playing back her words like a gramophone record, trying to read something into them which might offer him some hope. But something had changed. He had felt so comfortable here at Sutton Place, where he had recovered his sanity, back in 1915. Now, suddenly, her words had made him feel like an outsider. An intruder into this closed world of wealth and privilege.

The war had opened doors for people like him, and now here was Kitty, the woman he had fallen in love with, slamming one in his face.

Chapter 23
The End of the Affair, July 1917

"Keep above the enemy. Keep the sun behind you to make your machine invisible. Hit him from behind. Aim for the pilot's head or petrol tank rather than general splurging and wasting your ammunition. If you are hit from behind don't look back, dive out and away. There is no shame in living for another fight."

Fred's pupils hung on his every word. The would-be pilots back at Wye were a new bunch, but not quite as wet behind the ears as he had expected. Four of them had transferred from the infantry hoping that life in the air would be less gruesome than the one they had lived through in the Somme, and just before in the battle for Arras.

But at least they were older, a few of them much older than Fred, and not so naïve as the young men he had trained in Croydon. These men knew how really horrific things were in France and were grateful for a chance to have a reprieve with the flying force. Officers like them assumed they were going to die in this war, and clung onto the chance that before dying in the air, so long as they weren't flamers, life would be more comfortable. Fred's new mood matched their war-weary fatalism.

"All it takes is a split second. That will make the difference between getting back to the warm fire and a stiff drink or ending up nose first in a field, with the Padre working out who you are so he can say another farewell. You could be 50 feet from the ground, looking forward to that steak and kidney pie, when whoosh, something breaks... you hit the joystick too hard, the wind hits you, and before you can say Jack Robinson, you're over." He slapped his arm against his thigh to emphasise the point.

"Never relax, not till you are tucked up in your bed." He thought of Robert Lillywhite and what had happened to him at 50 feet. A side-slip and oblivion in Catterick, not even at the Front in combat. Robert had the experience of hundreds of hours more than these men would ever get and still he'd gone.

A split second. It could happen to anyone.

"It's pretty gruesome out there, best not to go for heroics. Now the Americans are in, it will end sometime soon. No good getting yourselves killed and missing the victory party." He hoped his talk would not sound defeatist and it somehow get back to his superiors that he was being dishonourable. He meant every word though. It was too hard to train pilots, not to mention build their machines, to have them throw away their lives through a stupid sense of nobility or heroism. But these battle-hardened men were sensible and had already seen what this war was really about. None of them found anything strange or disloyal in his advice, and at the end of their day's training, he felt there was a real sense of comradeship in their group.

The next day Fred felt they were all flying as if they had taken what he had said to heart. He passed them all without exception. They would leave for France with him on Sunday and with a bit of luck at least half of the group might survive. For a new group of fighter pilots that meant success.

Not a word from Kitty though. She'd said would be leaving Kent on the 25th for London, and he would be returning to France in a few days. Was what had happened in the orangery a separation? Two minutes cancelling out two years. He couldn't bear to think that he would never see her again, but he couldn't bear to think of always being the secret that she was too ashamed to bring out into the open. Leaving Sutton Place before 6am quietly without waking anyone, he had been back in Wye eating lumpy porridge just over an hour later.

He and Kitty had not managed to speak privately since those two minutes. She had been friendly enough at dinner, entertaining her mother with stories of the hospital and Fred had marvelled at her ability to dissemble. Among her other talents, she was an impressive actress. It had not been the reunion he had expected or wanted, and the thought gnawed away at him. What was it that prevented her admitting to her family about their relationship?

She was a widow and he was an officer in the Royal Flying Corps. He had always thought of her as modern and uncaring as to public impressions. She had led him to believe that that was the case, hadn't she always argued passionately for women's suffrage and an end to stuffy Edwardian sensibilities as she put it, but now she had made it very clear that whatever they had had together to this point, would not be continuing after the war. Fred was an entertaining dalliance for her, it appeared, nothing more. The only solution would be to see her one more time to be certain.

"I have an important call to make Sir, something I have to do before going back to France. Can I use the telephone?" The ringing sound filled the small office and he could imagine a servant in the house in St John's Wood. rushing to pick it up.

"Hello, Mrs Perkins' residence"

"Hello, this is Captain Dunn, is Mrs William Burrell there?

"I'll just get her for you." He knew whoever answered would be asking if anyone knew a Captain Dunn later?

"Fred. Hello. I didn't expect to get a call."

Kitty sounded hesitant and her words betrayed surprise and perhaps even hurt that he had left without trying to say farewell or explain his action. He cupped the phone with his hand and spoke in a whisper. The Adjutant was listening, but feigned a polite disinterest.

"Kitty, I wanted… I have to speak with you. It wasn't like I wanted it to be. My going the next morning like that. I need to talk to you again." He slowed his words in an effort to stop sounding as if he was pleading.

"I'm so sorry," she said. "I didn't know how to take it when you left without leaving a note or anything." Why was she apologising? She sounded affected by his early morning departure. Perhaps it was confusion he could hear in her voice.

"I can be at the Café Royal by seven on the Saturday night. I leave for France at six the next morning."

Kitty was already in the Grill bar when he arrived. Sipping from her glass of champagne, she looked over at the other guests, with an eye constantly lining up with the door. She saw him before he saw her. Why had she fallen for this man, so unlike her late husband in looks, in background, and in attitude?

Learning To Fly

In his uniform, he was handsome, of course, and sensitive, she felt that radiating from him, trying to seek her out in the busy bar. What was stopping her from thinking of him as a husband? She pushed the thought aside and presented a wide open smile to Fred as he approached her table.

They embraced warmly and she let him hold her just long enough for anyone who happened to be looking up to have no doubt about the extent of their relationship. Another young couple grabbing some happiness before it was taken from them. One officer in uniform, one dazzlingly beautiful. It was a scene in bars and restaurants all over London that night. Their ease together had not changed, and over the first minutes of small talk they didn't refer to the awkwardness of their evening at Sutton Place until much later. By then they were in a room upstairs and midnight had long gone. Fred had to be back in four hours.

"I would marry you now," he said. He hadn't planned the clumsy words, and when they escaped his lips, he seemed as surprised as she was to hear them.

Kitty looked away and didn't speak for several minutes. Perhaps he would think she had not heard him. Fred had not said anything since those words. Kitty knew she needed to find some kind of response. "You must know I love you, but the war, the war has made me reckless,"

Fred looked bewildered. "Kitty, we are all reckless now, with our lives, with who we fall in love with, it's what war does, you cannot prevent that."

Kitty pushed her index finger across his lips to stop any further words. "You were there when William died," she said, "and I grabbed the chance to get to know you. I know that. It's made me the happiest I've been for years, but I'm not going to marry again." Her words hung in the air like a judgement, before she continued. "I've seen what I can do with the hospital and the estate and will not be able to give up on that. If you can accept that, we can carry on meeting like this, grabbing the times together and enjoying them for what they are.

"But if you want more, if you want to marry, then you

will need to find someone else." Fred had not expected such honesty, and it drew from him a confidence to say what was at the front of his thoughts.

"Of course I would want more. I would want to see you every day. Every minute. How can you think I would not? You have become everything to me. You are one of the few good, true things to come out of this miserable war. I love you, Kitty."

It seemed futile to speak further at that minute. Perhaps deep down Kitty did not want to marry someone who had such working class origins and even though he had left the pit village far behind, he knew now for certain her protestations were covering up a more unappealing snobbery. She couldn't see him as the Master of Middleton Hall. Yes, that was it.

To be honest, he couldn't see himself there either. There was nothing more for him here. He gathered up his uniform and pulled his boots on and left. Dawn was just coming up over Piccadilly. A shimmering pink glow which streaked the sky like candyfloss. Red Sky in the morning, Shepherd's warning. He hadn't thought of that since he was a child. Please God let it not mean a difficult crossing.

He would have to pay for a motor taxi to Wye now.

Chapter 24
Another Lucky Escape, August 1917

In the end, they were forced to delay their Channel crossing by another day as the rain was lashing down and the storm which had dumped its load over northern France was now heading towards Kent. Deep puddles had formed on the rough runway and were merging into each other to form a small river. No one was anxious to go over in that. They were glad for another night away from the war.

The new offensive, which had started in June with the mine detonations, was still going on, a see-saw of death and destruction. Whole swathes of farmland were now pock-marked and filled with watery craters. From the air it all had a surreal, unearthly look. Weeks of heavy shelling had transformed the landscape beyond recognition, with tanks and machines turned turtle in the brown sludge. Now and again Fred could see the legs of dead horses sticking up like stalagmites in a slimy cave. It all resembled the aftermath of a Biblical plague where the earth had turned against itself; men, machines, beasts, now all petrified in the mud.

He was on reconnaissance patrols again.

Throughout that August the rain had not stopped. It should have been a routine flight. The take-off was straightforward, a simple tilt into a colourless sky. He had not let himself think of Kitty in any detail since he had last seen her in the bedroom at the Café Royal, but that morning, flying solo to Candas, he allowed himself to think back and recall their last evening. The colour of her satin evening bag, the smell of the sheets which had infused tiny molecules of her scent, the sky at dawn over Piccadilly. But he struggled to put the whole scene together. It was as if it were a story with pages missing, a disjointed tale which had too many gaps to hold together properly.

As he puzzled on their conversation, which he replayed in his mind, he heard a quick sharp bang come from the engine.

He knew what he had to do: change the throttle, try to switch the fuel tanks over. Maybe a piece of dirt had got caught in the mechanics? He checked the controls, and tried everything he could to bring the engine back to life, but it was useless. The sullen putt-putt of the dying engine at 6,000 feet. It was raining, and his goggles had steamed up so it was difficult to make out where he was. He must be south of St Pol.

All he could make out was a brown rutted moonscape with its gaping man-made craters. The funny thing was that he didn't feel any panic. If this was the end, it was not a bad one. Not one in flames. He could try and make the crash landing as soft as possible. The options were not great, a broken neck or back the most likely. He tried the engine again, but still nothing. Now it was a case of steady the machine and just pick the best place to glide down to. Turning, to the left and right, like a rhythmic dance routine, he tried to lessen the angle of the descent, but he knew a crash landing was now inevitable.

An intense feeling of exhaustion and acceptance came over him. The face of one of the men he had taught at Wye just three weeks ago came back to him. An uninvited apparition, but so real, it was as if Harrison was there in the cockpit too. He'd gone down in flames in the end, after a grenade had been thrown into his machine from the enemy pilot who got just near enough. No training could have got him out of that as he and his gunner were obliterated over the very trenches he had tried so hard to get out of.

Fred saw he was at about 1,000 feet now when out of the grey thin clouds a raised circular wooded area loomed. He was heading directly towards it, almost on a line with the tree tops. Nothing could now bring the machine back up and over it. It had a momentum of its own.

The next few minutes blurred. The spires of the trees came up to meet him with the sound of foliage crushing against the linen wings. The machine was brought to a halt, ingloriously, crumpled and suspended, hundreds of feet above the ground in the bottle green vegetation. The summer covering of leaves had saved the machine from ploughing straight through to the ground and almost certain destruction. His head was forced

Learning To Fly 143

forward by the impact and hit the cockpit, and then everything disappeared. He lost consciousness.

As he found out later, his descent into the wood had been seen by a military tender on the road to St Pol. They must have driven back to the nearest base and radioed to Candas to see if one of their pilots was missing. It had all taken about three hours and the first Fred knew of it was some shouting from below. It was an English voice and momentarily he thought he was back in Kent. "Hello there. Can you hear me? Anyone up there?" The team below did not know if they were dealing with wreckage and a corpse or a survivor. A body was slumped forward against the joystick and the smashed windscreen.

Whoever was inside didn't appear to be moving. Sluggishly Fred raised his head, noticing the moisture on his face. He touched his forehead and his glove came away smeared with blood.

"Don't move too quickly or this bus will fall on top of us. You've got it nicely wedged in there," the same English voice. Fred wondered if it was a voice he recognised, and tried to move his arm. It moved, so it wasn't broken but his elbow, which he'd fractured once already throbbed with pain. He tried to wriggle his toes, which although numb, were still able to move. That was something. A sharp pain behind his eyes made him clutch at his goggles, which were now were smeared with blood which must have dropped from his forehead cut. If you can feel pain, you are still here, he thought to himself, and felt determined not to die, not this time.

The problem was how to get out of the machine quickly as the cockpit had crumpled in on itself, making any manoeuvre potentially treacherous, not just to him but to whoever was there below. With a heave he managed to pull himself out. The wing was torn and large chunks of fabric were flapping in the branches. Slowly he was able to crawl along the metal. Then a crashing sound coupled with a lunge forward of about ten feet threw him backwards until he was lying flat.

"Whoa! Steady on there, don't do anything. Wait a minute and we'll get a rope up over that branch and you can try and get down that way."

Eventually, it felt like hours, having used the ropes the team had thrown up for him; his boots touched firm ground again. The jolt made his legs buckle at the knees and he collapsed as if in prayer, before a mechanic he did vaguely recognise threaded his arms under him and hauled him to a sitting up position.

They must have got him on a stretcher after that and driven him to the base, as he next came to in a narrow iron bed in the sick bay, his head aching as if it had been fitted with an instrument of medieval torture, slowly being tightened by its screws. There was a bandage across his forehead and his hands were covered in white crisscrossed crepe too. The bed next to him was occupied. Whoever was in it was wheezing badly. It must be the middle of the night.

Unconsciously his eyes closed again and he tried to go back to sleep. He hadn't died. Not this time. His luck was holding out. A Dr. Williams, a man he hadn't seen before, came to stand at the side of his bed, explaining that he had lost blood, suffered concussion, and had a pretty deep head wound.

He knew without being told he was bruised and battered, and had a few more lacerations from getting down the tree. Williams sounded cheerful. Compared to the man in the next bed Fred had nothing to complain about he said. This man had pneumonia on top of everything else and would probably die before he got back to England.

"You'll be out of here in no time. We need the bed anyway and you can get better somewhere else. You're a lucky bugger, Captain Dunn. That tree was in just the right place. I'll leave some painkillers for later, but chin up. You live to fight on." With that Williams left, reflecting on how good it was to have a survivor. Less paperwork with this one.

Fred recalled he had been trying to remember something about Kitty. What was it? He had vague memories of a conversation they had had. A feeling that something had been said on which everything important now hung troubled him like an itch. If only the pain in his head would go away he could think clearly. The corrugated iron roof and closed windows

Learning To Fly 145

made the hut stuffy and he closed his eyes and drifted off to unconsciousness.

After one more day in the sick bay Fred hobbled back to his hut. His belongings had been rescued from the wreckage of the Bristol aeroplane and were set out on his bed. Carefully lowering himself down, he placed his crutch to one side and swung his broken ankle over the covers. He felt strangely light-headed. The other bed in the room was empty and he had the hut to himself. What he needed was a good mess binge. That would make him feel more alive than any of William's painkillers. He began to look forward to the evening and hoped the new crowd at Candas had some of the high spirits of the boys at St Omer.

That same afternoon two men in the patrol had been killed. They had come down on the other side of the lines, a fierce enemy artillery barrage having picked them out at the back of the formation like the weakest in a herd of struggling gazelles.

The German firepower had managed to crack the propeller, pierce the engine, and send the machine and its two airmen spinning into oblivion. The dead men had only arrived at the base a week before, so the drinks mixed that night were that bit stronger and the talk that bit louder and coarser than usual. Fred, with his broken ankle, was allowed a place at the top of the table with his foot resting on the chair opposite.

He wondered what they would have done if he'd gone the same way up that tree? How many of them would have got this drunk in his memory, or even referred to him by name? Those who had survived this far were programmed to live in the present only now, in that momentary snapshot of time with no head turning, and no capacity for future gazing.

The next day the effects of the whisky, port and wine coupled with his head wound and throbbing foot made it difficult to open his eyes, when Williams, who had been passing his hut, popped his head around the door. He had just finished sorting out the paperwork for the young airman who had finally died of his pneumonia.

"I heard you had a good night, Dunn. Trying your own version of painkillers now, are you?" Williams had given up trying to persuade the airmen not to drink so much and certainly not to drink and then fly. They all said a tot of brandy in the cockpit was the only way to get over the feeling of nausea which altitude, engine oil and cold brought on. He didn't believe a word of it. They were all alcoholics no doubt, but who could blame them?

"Thank you, Sir. Yes, feeling a bit sore this morning. Glad I was not up at dawn on patrol."

"Well I hear you are due a bit of leave anyway. I've suggested you get a break and the CO says you can go if you get back here for December 14th. You can go as soon as you're ready".

Two whole weeks away from this war. He'd go home to his parents of course, it would be good to show them he was just hobbling a bit and had not suffered anything more serious, but should he call on Kitty, or Edith? Did they even know if he'd been injured, and if they had, would it have caused even a flicker of upset?

The thought of Kitty distancing herself from everything about him was an ache far greater than any simple bone break. Not a word since July. He knew he had to get himself home. That was the only way he'd find out. His ankle ached as he swung himself out of his bed. He'd be in London by tomorrow night.

Chapter 25
Convalescing, London, December 1917

London was looking its most dark and dreary. A monotone dullness seemed to have seeped into everything. It would be the fourth Christmas, and the shops appeared to be ignoring anything festive. Not a light or sparkling novelty gave any sense that a holiday might be approaching. He'd always loved going to see the shops before, lit up and tempting, often displaying riches beyond his means, their sparkling attractiveness a wonder to his teenage self. Now all was drab.

Little pieces of glass from blown out shop windows were still visible on the streets even though they must have been swept. It was inconvenient, this damage from those Zeppelins, but it was only a small taste of what the men in France were suffering, so the shoppers stepped over the glass determinedly and businesses carried on.

The news about Passendale had been good. The Allies had taken the small town. There had been a huge cost of course, nearly 200,000 lives, but the newspapers' headlines dwelt on the victory, not the dead. For most of the people in London on that cold December the month couldn't end soon enough.

"How long do you think this will go on for?" his mother asked, trying hard not to display the anxiety in her voice. She knew her son was lucky to have survived this far, none of those bright young men he had brought home to meet them had been so fortunate. "I do think of those friends of yours, like poor Robert Lillywhite. So terrible for his poor mother, with only a letter of condolence and some old photographs now. For all their sakes, surely, the war has to end soon Fred?"

"There's no knowing, Mother. Winning at Wipers has changed things a bit, not in terms of the amount of land won, but the Huns are on the run now. They haven't enough recruits to replace those that went and there is a lot of talk of desertions. It might not be next year or the year after that, but it will be won. You can be sure of that, mother."

He could have made an effort to sound even more convincing. The fact was that no one in the Flying Corps could see the war ending anytime soon. Wars could last for 30 years or more, hadn't there been one which had lasted a hundred? Please God, not this one.

Fred spent the rest of the days of his leave walking with his stick as support around South Kensington and Hyde Park. Whenever his foot ached, he sat on the benches with his khaki woollen coat pulled tightly around him. Passers-by nodded encouragingly, seeing from his cap badge that he was in the RFC.

Everything looked tired and flat, out of kilter, like a seaside promenade in February. He rubbed his legs to try to give some heat to the stiff joints. He'd been tossing over in his mind whether he should contact Kitty or not. Her rejection of his marriage proposal had stung him deeply, and the hurt he still felt prevented him making the first contact.

He'd been home for eleven days now and was due to go back in two. If he was going to write, he had to do so soon. As he walked back down Exhibition Road, he resolved to send a Christmas card with greetings. Nothing more. He stepped into the museum and bought one of the few cards they had for sale in the small shop.

To: Mrs Kitty Burrell,
Middleton Hall,
Hampshire

With warmest Christmas greetings to you dear Kitty. I shall be back in France from 14th, my fourth Christmas there. I wish it were elsewhere and with others.

Yours affectionately,

Fred

ps. You may have heard I was injured, a small crash, nothing serious. Lucky old me.

Learning To Fly 149

There. He would post it tomorrow and would be on his way to France before she had time to reply. Yes, it had been right not to contact her earlier. It would have been too confusing, like scratching open an old wound. Best to let time be a healer. Whatever they had once felt for each other had been knocked off course, and he knew he must put any thought of Kitty from his mind. With his new determination, he stuck his arm out for a motor taxi and headed to Piccadilly.

A good dinner at the Grill, a drink or two at the club, and a few things ordered at Burberry to keep him warm in the months ahead. Yes, he thought to himself, an airman cannot get too involved with a woman. Flying solo was the only way.

The cold in the rattling train steaming through Kent numbed his flesh. Fred looked out of the window remembering the countryside in warmer times when he was travelling out to Sutton Place to stay with Edith. That summer 1915.

It felt as if two decades had passed. He thought about how he had changed since then. He'd been diagnosed with neurasthenia, and had felt like there was a tether and he had reached the very tip of it. Two years on, he knew there were many more depths to that depression of spirits a person could endure and still survive.

You could reach the end of one tether and take on the next and the next. How many people had he known who had died? Twenty, fifty even. Lillywhite, Bowyer, Barry, all long dead now. Here in this carriage for officers, would you say they were the lucky ones? Most of them looked already dead, afraid of what they knew was ahead of them There was a smell of the trenches which had seeped out of each one waiting for the train, even though they all must have taken advantage of a bath and clean clothes in their time back home.

The greatcoats could not expel the stink of mud and smoke, though, and it pervaded everything about them. The airmen must smell differently he thought to himself, petrol and engine oil. Less noxious, less a graveyard smell. Those in the carriage who weren't asleep kept up a constant buzz, their clipped accents cutting through the clatter of the train.

Most were showing off what they had got up to on

their leave. The usual embellishment; a third truth, two thirds fantasy. Just enough to keep them warm on the cold nights ahead. Naturally it sounded as though it had involved lots of alcohol and women. Women who had been keen to throw themselves at a young officer returning from the Front. Fred was amazed at how lightly his fellow officers were able to discuss their sexual conquests, real or imagined, in such detail. God, how he wished they would shut up. He tried not to think of the last time he and Kitty had been together.

Once he started, though, he couldn't shift the image of her naked. They had gone to the room in the Café Royal, not shyly, but openly, daring anyone to challenge them. He remembered. No embarrassment. He had a vision of her lean body. He remembered too her scent, how the pillow she'd made with her arm had seemed so comfortable. Suddenly, in the bleak train carriage, he felt a wave of arousal and pulled his coat about him willing the journey to end.

"Been home on leave?"

The chap opposite, no more than 25, ruddy cheeked with piercing blue eyes, seemed to want to chat, and although Fred had tried to make it clear as he got on the train that he was not in the mood, this person had a gentle face and it felt churlish to be anti-social.

"Yes. Ten days in London. And you?"

There were nearly at Dover. The conversation wouldn't be long.

"Alnwick, in Northumberland. This is the second train I've been on. Took hours yesterday, much colder up there, if you can believe that."

Fred sat up and looked at him more closely. Here was an officer, a Major by the look of it, in the Northumberland Fusiliers. 12th Battalion.

"Yes, I know it. I was born in Wylam, but moved to London when I was a teenager."

"You know the Cooksons, then? Smashing girls, I remember, quite a beauty that Sybil."

Fred smiled. Yes, he did know the Cooksons and, yes, the daughters were good looking. He did not say his mother had worked as a maid just up the road at the next big house next to theirs. Funny how the rich assumed everyone knew everyone else who was rich. It was like an elite club. You just assumed everyone you met was a member.

Fred found out that they had been in action in Arras, the Somme and Loos. Three names which spoke volumes. And here the Major was, still alive. He didn't need to say much more. It was obvious they'd seen the worst of everything and had suffered heavy casualties.

His new companion, Major James Willoughby as it turned out, gave his information softly as if not wanting to dwell on what had been an affront to everything he had once held true. He had seen men mown down like cut hay and bullets take away whole faces. Men in the middle of a curse, suddenly silenced by losing their mouths. He would not forget what he'd seen, and here he was, going back.

Willoughby had led a company with Wylam men in it. Fred mentioned a few names.

"There was a private called Turnbull and a couple called Appleby. I think that's what they were called. Gone now, of course, damned shame."

Fred stared blankly, not daring to show any emotion. The Turnbull must be Robert's brother. Was he in a different battalion? God, he must be dead now, too. Fred looked out of the window again and both men stopped talking. The resurfaced memories had silenced them. They were both relieved when the train juddered into its final destination and they could switch their attention to the gathering of kit bags, checking they hadn't left anything. They parted on the platform and Fred shook Willoughby's hand, warmly.

"Good luck. I wish we had met in better times. A drink in the White Swan without a war going on," Willoughby said.

"Good luck to you too." Fred doubted if they would have had a drink together in the White Swan or anywhere back in Alnwick. The likes of Willoughby didn't have drinks with the children of their servants outside of a war. Some barriers had been broken since 1914, but they had paid a very high price for the changes. Too high.

Fred thought of poor Henry Turnbull and his parents who would have seen not one but two telegram boys delivering the very worst of news.

The journey back to France had taken over 24 hours. He could have flown it in less than four. At least he was returning to flying. There up in the air, he was in control and not buffeted by his emotions. When you were flying thousands of feet up you could only think of keeping the machine going and how it was performing.

There was no time for thoughts about death, or Kitty. He went straight to the mess and had a large whisky and soda. This war couldn't go on for ever.

Chapter 26
Back in England, Spring 1918

Another New Year came and it was as if neither side could heave themselves over the line in what had become a grim tug of war. 'Tails up' they were told. In the same way as telling someone soaking in their own misery, 'Chin up', 'Tails up' seemed so inadequate an instruction. For Fred, now the longest serving Captain in the Aircraft Supply Depots, it meant more wrecks, and more ferrying of aeroplanes between fighter squadrons from north to south.

On some days he made nearly 30 landings, and arrived at the end of the flights, so cold and stiff, with icicles stuck to his face that he had to be helped out of the cockpit by the riggers. Sometimes in these wrecks, he noticed the remnants of a previous occupant, the now dead pilot in whose seat he was sitting. A torn piece of flying suit, a blood stain on the floor or the bullet marks at the height where they'd scorched the metal and wood.

Some machines were so riddled with bullet holes that the repair work made them look like patchwork quilts and at 10,000 feet he felt the wind whistling through the tiny gaps. Machines which should have ended up on the scrap heap, were being been coaxed back into the service of war. He was mentally and physically worn out, and a little deaf in one ear. A pilot's lot. If you didn't die, you would soon find out that one of your vital senses had disappeared. There was still no word from Kitty, not even a reply to his card. Fred knew he should not dwell on it, and had resolved to concentrate solely on his flying, but deep down he felt a biting disappointment.

The depot was reminiscent of the old days before they had lost so many men. There was a new intake of pilots, a mixed boisterous crowd, and not all public school types. It didn't go down too well with some of the old guard, but these men had brought a new liveliness to the mess. They knew the latest music hall songs and many evenings were spent around the piano bashing out songs which would have been deemed coarse in Fred's first days with No 3 Squadron. Fred had to admit he preferred this crowd with their strong accents and easy going attitudes.

"Clear as a bell I saw him. He'd been shot up all over. You could smell the petrol from three hundred feet away. He unstrapped himself and just bloody jumped. Must have taken a nerve to do that... Minutes later a big mushroom opened up and he was floating down."

"It's a wonder he didn't burn his toes on the way down."

"Wonder if we'll ever get them, they'd save a few lives around here."

The observer who'd witnessed the scene, this new phenomenon, Howarth, had come to the Royal Flying Corps straight from Catterick training, and wasn't afraid to voice a cynical view of the military machine. A few years ago, he would have been disciplined for such talk. Someone would have overheard and reported him for dissent. But not now.

"It'll save them a few lives, no doubt about it, Howarth. No reason why they cannot give our chaps them, too, though. Plenty of room in a Camel." Fred although the most senior there, and usually so careful not to say anything which could be misconstrued, had to agree with what was being said. He could see no reason why the British airmen did not have the same safety exit as the Huns. No doubt they would be ordered and the war would end. He didn't voice the last thought, which would almost certainly have been going too far.

A few hours later, he was told the CO wanted to have a word with him. The Adjutant who gave him this information gave no facial clues to suggest what this meeting was to be about. Unexpected meetings with the senior officer always made him nervous and he worried that the talk about parachutes had been reported back.

"Ah Captain Dunn. Good to see you in one piece." Hardie, wearied by the steady stream of replacements of the replacements, was not intending to spend long on this conversation. He'd been under pressure to step up the supply of machines, and for him, the officer before him was now someone else's responsibility.

"I've been told you are to be transferred to Home Establishment. You've done more than enough out here. Well done Captain, you are free to leave." He returned to his papers hoping that would be a sign for Fred to say his farewell and leave. If it was him he'd be on the next boat out and a sleeper back to Scotland. Fred had expected a very different conversation and was disarmed.

"Thank you, Sir, but why am I being sent to Home Establishment? I thought you might have a use of my experience with the Hun gearing up again."

"Not my orders, Captain Dunn. Just someone in the Air Ministry shuffling papers back home I suspect. They're fed up that all their pilots are dying before they get out to fight the bloody Hun, so they want to beef up the training squadrons again. You're off to 25 Squadron. Pretty good I'd say. Nice spot in Norfolk. If I were you, I'd be buying a round of drinks and thanking your lucky stars."

"Yes sir, but it feels like I'm going home with the job unfinished. Who knows how long it's going to go on for. I'd rather be out here in France."

"Dunn. Get yourself home and say no more about it. If we're still here in a year, you'll be back. Orders can change, you should know that. But, for now, 25 Squadron is expecting you. It's not going to be a picnic there, either." Fred knew he would cross a line in arguing further, saluted and walked out. Hardie had grown fond of Dunn and was actually sorry to see one of the more experienced level-headed officers in the place leaving.

He'd be sorry to say goodbye to Dunn, but it was amazing how quickly you forget a face out here. In a week or two he wouldn't even remember what he looked like. In a month he'll say that chap looks like someone who used to be here, Dobbs or Donn, or something like that. The war was doing it to them all. People were becoming expendable. Moving on was all that mattered. Very soon there would be no young men left that anyone had known for longer than a month.

Hardie picked up the pile of post. It had been given the once over already, but had been left for him to check. It was the post sent to those who were unlikely to be reading anything ever again. Casually, he flicked through it and saw that Adler had been sent a fishing magazine from his wife. Perfect, fill in an hour of this bloody war and Adler won't mind. He'd not be going fishing again. Best not let a good magazine go to waste. Hardie had already written to Mrs Adler. He allowed himself to wonder what she was like and what she would do now, widowed and alone, with no one to buy fishing magazines for. Her photograph had been among Adler's possessions, a pretty, cheerful looking woman, he remembered.

He hated writing those letters and tried to make them as personal as possible, but too often they sounded empty. Hardie picked up the magazine and headed for the latrines. In a month he'd have forgotten what Adler looked like, too. Dunn should be sending the bosses a case of something, not complaining he wanted to stay out in this hell hole.

The transfer to Home Establishment was one many pilots had longed for. But when it came, Fred felt strangely short-changed. He was leaving before there was anything resembling a victory in sight, when the Germans were regrouping and seemed to be getting ready for a big push themselves. Going before the job was finished felt wrong, as if he was cheating. The chances of being killed in training on home duty were just as high in England as they were in France, but still, the thought of being away from the action rankled with him.

He was due in Thetford in a week and had plenty of time on the journey back to think how he would spend this unexpected time off. It was now nine months since he had seen Kitty. Nine months. He couldn't decide if it felt like weeks or years. Sometimes the war elongated events, so that time might stand glacially still, and the weeks felt more like a lifetime, but more often the sheer monotony of flying and clinging onto life while you saw your friends and colleagues die, made everything accelerate.

He would be 24 in October if he lived that long. Every part of him felt tired. He knew he looked much older than those years, which in the Flying Corps, made him a veteran. These men on the boat and then again on the train had barely left school and already they were coming back injured or for their first leave, mud smearing their coats, an ugly smell of chlorine about them, and a blank stare into the middle distance, afraid to acknowledge what they had just witnessed. How many were going to wives or girlfriends? Not that many he assumed. They wouldn't have had time to get a wife. Who did in this war? Everything normal about life had been taken away from his generation.

Did anyone have a courtship anymore? Did couples still meet, go out, take walks along country lanes, a village fair, a local dance, grab a kiss behind a hedge? There were no young men in the villages anymore, and he guessed there would be no dances or fairs. No places to find a sweetheart and plan your life or have children. If you hadn't found a wife before the war, there was precious little chance during it, unless it was a lightning fast courtship and marriage on a home leave.

All the pretty young women, who should by rights have bagged a handsome young man, would have to make do with those left behind with their weak hearts, grey hairs or those other shady men left behind making a profit while everyone else was away fighting.

The train finally pulled into Charing Cross, filling the platform with its belching smoke, heralding another train load of men back for a breath of fresh air, as if the air in France had been too thin to feed their vital organs. The usual crowd of anxious relatives and lovers were there, craning their necks to make out their one person in a sea of khaki. Fred was making his own way to South Kensington intending to surprise his parents. They would be delighted that he was not expected to go back to France. The walk there would do him good, clear his head and put him in the right frame of mind to meet Adele and Thomas again.

He strode off down the Mall, towards Hyde Park and then along Knightsbridge to South Kensington and Harrington Road. Several other men in uniform passed him, trying to take in London, which although on the surface appeared as it always had, felt so alien. The men, those not in uniform that is, and the women were wearing dark, dismal clothes. All colour had been drained from the city, as if its citizens were trying to melt into the background so as not to draw attention to themselves or do anything which might appear ostentatious.

A group of nurses, their dark wool cloaks flapping about them, took up the width of pavement and he had to skirt around them. He tried to smile and catch the eye of the prettiest. She smiled in return and his spirits lifted. Perhaps they were from Kensington Palace Green hospital. None of them then were as pretty as the smiling one with the bouncy auburn hair, but he'd not been in the best of spirits back then, so he may not have noticed.

Even Kitty coming to his rescue, his personal angel of mercy, only became real to him when they had got out to Kent and away from the hospital. These women who had become nurses, with no experience of work which might prepare them for what they were now witnessing were angels too. He was outside the door in Harrington Road now. Twice he knocked, all thoughts of hospitals pushed from his mind. Here he was no longer a Captain, an officer in the British Expeditionary Force. He was a boy, who loved engines and his mother's cooking.

It was good to be home.

Chapter 27
Unexpected Meeting, London, Spring 1918

Fred woke, still wearing his tunic and breeches, and for a moment was unable to work out where he was. An old tartan travelling rug had been thrown over him. He could make out a glass of water and a few biscuits on a vaguely familiar bedside table. Slowly it all came back to him. He'd said he was just going for a nap after having arrived back in South Kensington and given as much of the details of his return as he felt he could. That must have been around 6pm last night.

It was now light outside and he could hear someone moving about in another room. He looked at the clock on the wall, the same one he remembered from his parent's room at their home in Hagg Bank, its gold leaves entwining a small glass face. Funny that it was now on this bedroom wall. He'd found it hard to read the figures of that clock when he was a child of ten, and now here it was before him. He had to squint to make out where the hands were pointing. They were pointing to twelve.

It couldn't be midnight. It was light outside. It had to be midday. He must have slept for seventeen hours. Fred jumped out of bed and noticed with affection how his mother had removed his boots and placed them neatly beside his bag at the foot of the bed. His overcoat had been put on the hook at the back of the door. She must have done that, too, as he couldn't remember tidying up like that. The sleep had nourished him and he felt a younger version of himself. Not his pre-war self, but a less wearied self, certainly. The smell of bacon frying came through the gaps in the door and he glanced in the mirror before going out into the narrow galley kitchen.

His mother was at the big house, so it was his father in his shirt-sleeves, who was frying bacon. Thick slabs of white bread with a good lathering of butter were on two plates by the side. It was a sight and smell he had often thought of in his hut in France. Now he was there witnessing it, breathing it in, he felt a kind of tranquility and composure he hadn't experienced for months. He could feel the muscles in his face relaxing, the rictus grin and tightness brought on by extreme cold and altitude which had become a permanent facial feature were being melted away. He was getting a new face.

"Morning, son. You look as if you needed that long sleep. Here, have something to eat. I'll bet you haven't been eating enough out there. Your mam was sorry she would miss you, but she will be back in a few hours. She wanted me to make sure you had something warm to eat."

Fred felt as if he were a baby bird back in a nest; secure and warm and protected from the world. It was a feeling he bathed in. Fred's parents had spent every day since he went back to France anxiously watching out for the telegram boy bearing bad news. They feared every squeak of bicycle wheels on the pavements outside Harrington Road. To have him here, alive, unharmed, untouched by war, was nothing short of a miracle.

Thomas said he had to drive to Victoria station and pick up some house guests who were staying in Queensbury Place, so after eating his bacon sandwich Fred found he had the afternoon ahead of him, alone in the house. He was not used to such absolute stillness. The tick of the clock, the slow and steady drips of a kitchen tap. The sound of feet on the cobbles outside. He'd never noticed such noises before. After an hour, he decided he needed some fresh air. It was mid-March and it was already feeling like spring.

He washed his face and changed his shirt, giving his leather boots a quick polish, before setting off towards South Kensington station. He turned left along Cromwell Place, crossing up past the museums and up Exhibition Road towards Hyde Park. This was his usual route. He remembered following it as a teenager to get across town. He looked up at the grand façades, admiring the grandeur of undamaged buildings bordering the wide streets. He'd been walking briskly and at the end of Exhibition Road, he stopped to get his breath back.

As he was about to cross over into the park, he noticed a tall, well-dressed figure in a knee-length brown coat and light coloured felt hat, its willowy arm extended out to hail a taxi. The face was slightly tipped towards the oncoming traffic, away from him, and he noticed a frown hovering above the eyes. The figure was beseeching the street to deliver an empty cab to get her to her destination. Fred would have recognised that look anywhere; purposeful with a slight irritation at this obstacle in her plans, but still so attractive at the same time. Fred let a second or two pass. He could easily at that moment have carried on walking across the road. Kitty was looking back up the road towards Knightsbridge so wouldn't have noticed a man in uniform crossing the road. He would have been in the park before she could have realised anyone had even been there. But in that split second, he decided to call out.

"Kitty, Kitty…" She turned. Momentarily, he noticed, she showed a nervousness and hesitation. Then she smiled the big, wide happy smile he remembered.

"Fred! Oh my goodness. What a surprise!" The awkwardness of their unexpected encounter had made them both shy and tongue-tied. How strange that two people who had known each other so intimately could feel that way.

"I got your Christmas card. Thank you," she said.

"I hoped you would. I was hoping to get something back…" He stopped the sentence, feeling angry at himself for sounding so petty. The last time he had seen her, she was naked in the Café Royal, and here he was complaining she hadn't sent him a Christmas card. It was as if they were dragging themselves through quicksand. A motor taxi was approaching. Fred saw it before Kitty and feared she would want to stop it to escape this new awkwardness.

"I've got an appointment in Holland Park and was going to walk, but I'm so late now, I was hoping to get a motor car." Who was she meeting in Holland Park? He hoped it was not a rich general, back from the Front, or an ageing diplomat or lawyer trying to bag themselves a rich, beautiful widow. He forced himself to push the thought away.

"Can we meet later? This is too hurried," he said. The last words tumbled out of his mouth and he had to stop before he said anything more. It sounded desperate enough as it was.

"Yes of course. Another time."

"A drink later then? The Ritz? At six?"

He managed to spit out the suggestion as the motor taxi drew up. She would have to refuse him now or make an excuse. He could see yet another brief hesitation cloud her eyes like a darting swallow. Gone quickly, but it had been there, he was sure of that.

"Lovely. Yes, at six." And with that she got in the vehicle.

He heard her say 'Holland Park Avenue' and watched as the car drove off towards the High Street Kensington. She didn't look back as it left. Feeling like he had taken a punch in the stomach, Fred crossed the road and made for the first bench. He had to process what had just happened, and work out if he had done the right thing. He had been rocked by seeing her again and had been reckless to call out like that. And Kitty, how did he feel about her now he had actually seen her? She was as elegant and beautiful as ever, even more so. There was an extra confidence about her, perhaps? Had she accepted his offer just to be kind, as you would with the relative of a trusted family retainer, or was it worse than that - she had accepted, but would not turn up. That she was too polite and too well brought-up to refuse, and accepting was the least cruel and embarrassing way to end the unexpected meeting.

Fred was in the Rivoli Bar at ten to six. There was a group of officers already there and from the looks of it, they had been there most of the afternoon working their way through the cellar. He picked a table in the furthest corner, but with a view of the entrance, and ordered a whisky and soda. The waiter appeared to be about sixteen or seventeen, not old enough to drink himself. Any older and he would have been in France.

Fred finished the drink quickly, too quickly, and hurriedly ordered a second. At twenty past six, just as he was suspecting his negative premonition was correct, he saw her approach. She looked around, the same quizzical beseeching look she had shown when trying to get a cab. He went over to where she was standing, and took hold of her hand. Deliberately he held on a couple of seconds longer than would have been usual if they were just meeting as friends. He could hear her breath quicken just a little.

At the table, Kitty unbuttoned her coat, revealing a grey open necked silk shirt and wool skirt the colour of heather blossom. A big black belt pulled in her tiny waist. They had not exchanged a word as the business of getting settled took over. He ordered champagne. Kitty looked majestic, nodding in agreement at the order. Fred felt short and untidy in her company. He had always preferred being in uniform, as it was his armour into her world of privilege and wealth, but sitting here with Kitty, he felt his tunic bringing back the smells of the Front and the oil and grease of flying. It did not match the opulent atmosphere and this sophisticated woman. Kitty spoke first.

"Fred, I'm so sorry it turned out as it did. It was never meant to. I don't know why I didn't write after you left in July. Your proposal took me by surprise. Months just passed, and after a while there was just too much left unsaid, and I felt we both must move on."

"I didn't write to you until that card in December. I now know, it was too late. I thought it was you who had moved on, found someone else." Fred said the last words carefully searching her face for a response, a clue if she had indeed found an admirer or a new lover. Moving on could mean so many things.

Kitty didn't reply straight away, but looked out beyond him as if trying to find the right words. "It was not a question of moving on or giving up. I think we had just got caught up in the war. The fact that so many people were dying, life was so perilous. It made what we had seem like a precious fragile, glass egg. If we dropped it, terrible things would happen. I was too scared all the time to hear you had died to think straight. You asking me to marry you, it somehow made everything too complicated. It was easier to draw a line."

Fred noticed her eyes were welling up and he could see that the last statement had been a difficult thing for Kitty to say. He understood the feeling. In this war, relationships had to remain superficial. Anything deeper and he knew where that might lead. To grief and unbearable sadness as one dear friend and another went. After a while, you had to teach yourself not to mind, not to feel it so much. Kitty had lost her husband in 1914, before he had even got to the Front. She had had to steel herself against mourning and being with someone who hourly faced so many opportunities to be killed. It had weakened her and had made her vulnerable again.

"I'm back from France now," he said. "On home leave. Out of danger." The last bit was not true. There was as much danger in training as being over the trenches, but a little white lie would not be too harmful. He took her gloved hands and kissed them, rubbing the back of her wedding ring with his fingers through the kid leather. "Let's get out of here," he said. "Let's go for a walk. I need some air."

For the next hour they walked in St James's Park, up and down the avenues, as darkness fell and the skies were lit by an occasional search light. The awkwardness had dissolved somewhat. They were not back to the ease they had felt before in Kent or Brighton all those months ago, but there had been a shift. A thawing.

By the time Kitty said she had to go to get back to St John's Wood for a dinner and hailed a motor taxi to get her there, Fred knew they would see each other again. She had not rejected him. If this could all end, he thought, we could have a real life, a proper life together. He could in time ask her again. He headed off towards Hyde Park corner, smiling to himself. For the second time that day he felt what he had thought was an extinct feeling.

He was now genuinely hopeful that something positive might come out of this ghastly war.

Chapter 28
Training at Thetford, April 1918

Fred and Captain William Hewett drove to Thetford rather than take the train. As they left London, the green fields and the open spaces, pancake flat, brought back memories of another age back in Northumberland. He'd grown used to being in a big sprawling city the past week, and before that the ruined lunar landscape in France. He had almost forgotten what country pastures could do to a mind starved of such sights.

"It's so quiet here. It's as if everything is waiting... Waiting to get back to normal. You forget when you're out there." His driving companion and car owner Captain Hewett didn't need anyone to tell him what it was like out there. The place where greens had become brown like a paint palette left out in the rain and fields had become lakes, where nothing ever grew, only died.

"You're right, but look at the crops and the hedges. They're not being kept like they would if there wasn't a war on. Who's left to work on this land, anyway? The grandsons the farmers will never have. I don't see how it will ever get back to how it was, Fred."

Hewett was a softly-spoken, sensitive fellow who in another life might have expected to be a gentleman farmer like his father and grandfather before him in South Devon. Like Fred, he was the only son, and the future of the farm rested on his shoulders. His parents had been against him joining up, and would have preferred him to go to Cirencester and learn about agriculture, not aviation at the Central Flying School. Now four years on, he wished he had taken their advice.

As they drove east, Hewett tutted loudly at the hedges bowing under the weight of blackberry bushes and cow parsley which was smothering the verges. They talked a little of what was going on in France and the latest German offensive. Both men had been there in the worst of times and knew what an offensive from either side meant. This latest German assault in the last days of March around St Quentin and Amiens, had pushed the Allies as near to defeat as they had ever been. The war still appeared to be one which would never conclude and it seemed that the Germans were putting new life into their efforts on the Western Front in this last gasp merry-go-round land-grab.

"You would have thought with the Americans in now, it would have quickened things up a bit, but if anything it looks like the Germans are gearing up again."

"It will end. I'm sure of that William. Just not yet. Maybe not even this year. We're lucky to be out here and not over there."

Both men knew as the fighting on the ground in France got more desperate, that the airmen above were being pushed harder and harder. Pilots were being instructed to fly low and pick out marching troops as if they were in a fairground shooting gallery. Mass slaughter was not what these boys had become pilots for. The war had made them all barbarians. Now it wasn't just taking out an enemy pilot in a matched fight in the air based on the skill of flying and presence of mind. This ground strafing and dropping bombs on moving troops, so close you could see their facial features, took them into another much darker, league of fighting. Norfolk was a sanctuary from all that.

The two instructors arrived at Thetford when the light in the wide skies was just beginning to fade and sought out their new Commander. Bowden barely looked up as they presented themselves to him. He'd lost six men the week before in training accidents. As the new arrivals walked in, his thoughts were remote and he did not have the will to drag them back to the present. The cruel truth was he had loved secretly, but passionately, one of those who'd died the week previously. Barely 20, he'd leapt from his machine in the air after the wing had snapped like an umbrella caught in a sudden gust, and his machine had hurtled towards the ground.

That day, Bowden had lost what little enthusiasm he still had for this interminable and dreadful war. He missed the cherubic Archie, whose crumpled broken body had landed in a field yards away from the wreckage, his face untouched by the horrible end, still beautiful. He could never explain to anyone else just why this death of this one airman, an old Harrovian like himself, could cause him so much grief.

When Fred and Hewett presented themselves to him, he hadn't left his hut for two days and had the haunted look of a man who had not washed or slept properly. His men had enjoyed a brief respite from the daily grind while he wallowed in his unmentionable sorrow with only his gramophone and Chopin for company. Bowden felt like putting an end to it all, he was so very sick and tired of this war.

When they had managed to get their instructions, the two new arrivals made for their accommodation. Fred as a Flight Commander had a separate comfortable enough hut, but was shocked to see that the conditions in the rest of the aerodrome were pretty basic. The mess was an old hangar shed with sacking to close off the gaps in the corrugated iron. No amount of decoration could improve the desultory air it had.

Even in France they had made their surroundings more homely than this, with their bartered sofas, gramophone and old furniture from their French neighbours. At least it looked like the bar at Thetford was well stocked and the food would be good, given they were surrounded by the best of Norfolk's farmland and near the sea. Fred made his excuses as Hewett went to get a drink and meet the other officers, and went back to his hut. He had a letter to write.

Thetford,
Norfolk

April 11 1918

My darling Kitty

You have been in my thoughts ever since we met again in London. For someone who does not believe in divine intervention, I truly believe we were meant to meet each other again on that day. It was the most welcome of reunions, and I am so perfectly happy that we have an understanding again.

I will keep myself safe and not be the cause of any worry to you. You have my word about that. I shall be here for weeks, maybe months, who knows.

It is a bit of a dreary place, but the other training officer Hewett, is a decent chap and a farmer. We shall get along just fine. He knows a lot about agriculture and I have been learning from him. I don't know if it will ever be useful for an aviator, although they do say that some of the most basic accidents for a new flyer is not to know a grass field from a field of wheat when trying to land. You would not believe how little some of these boys know! I am rambling, and it is late. Do write to me. I long to see you again.

Yours lovingly,

Fred

He underlined 'long' twice, sealed the letter and addressed it to Middleton Hall. Would she would receive it in the same spirit of expectation and excitement in which it was sent, now he had reason to hope she would.

It was at breakfast when Fred went to the canteen and found Hewett and another officer reading the newspaper. " 'Backs to the wall', he says. 'Bloody carnage,' I say. That is what it will be. Does he have any idea what it is like out there? We will be lucky to get out of this one alive."

Hewett wanted to get on with his life. Putting it on hold in uniform had been something honourable and glorious at first. Now it seemed never-ending and the ache of missing his home had become almost unbearable.

"Sometimes I think I will never see the farm again. They would have to sell it if anything happened to me, and I couldn't bear to think that."

"Come on Hewett, you will get back to your farm. Here take your tea and go outside for a bit. We're not going up for half an hour."

Fred knew the signs that his new friend was not in the mood for light-hearted banter, and to take his mind off the 'backs to the wall' image, he wondered when Kitty would have received his letter. He didn't have any leave until the end of May, which was the earliest he could hope to see her again.

They had parted with so much unfinished business, and although it had felt disarmingly like old times, something had been missing. Some intimacy had been lost. It would have been too much to hope that they would have spent the night together, but he had still hoped for more than a brief kiss, a touch of skin really. He felt again the burning desire for a woman, a feminine touch or even just a feminine presence. Aerodromes with their testosterone and the unmistakable smell of men who hadn't washed properly in days were beginning to get on his nerves. Perhaps he could ask her to send him one of her scarves to try to take away the terrible smell which seemed to be everywhere.

If the bloody war would only end they could start making machines that could do more than just shoot at people. Machines had already evolved so much since that first crossing of the Channel. Who knows what they could achieve next. That was something to hope for. Bugger that Haig, he thought to himself. Let's win the war so we can get on to doing some proper flying.

He popped his head round the door of the administration hut as he was passing. A lanky, spotty Scottish second lieutenant called John Donald was sorting through some mail, dividing it all up into piles. He had his hand on a pale cream envelope. Fred could see the writing he knew so well. Instinct told him to cover up whatever he was feeling as he saw Donald toss it casually to one side among the pile of other hand written letters on non-military paper.

"Donald, I think that one is for me. Let me have a look."

"Ah, Captain Dunn, yes. Looks like a right fancy one. Got a mistress in high places, have we?"

Fred reddened and didn't reply. Sensing he had an easy target now, Donald sniffed at the thick cream stationery. He made a face, a smirk crossing his lips and pretended to kiss the paper in a lascivious way, which made Fred want to thump him. Donald longed for some excitement in this war. He had been to France, but after an altercation in a bar, something to do with a bill and a fight, the local bar owner had had his skull fractured. He couldn't remember all the details, and nothing could be pinned on him, for the chair leg which had smashed over the Frenchman's head, could have been used by anyone in the group that evening. But he'd been court martialed and sent back to home establishment. Never darken my doors or this squadron ever again, were the last words said to him.

So here he was, sorting out letters and ordering sodding supplies in a hut in the middle of this flat, dull part of England. He had half a mind to rip the letter up and see what that did. The urge to do something vindictive, which usually came over him like a wave, suddenly receded as quickly as it had arrived, and he tossed the envelope at Fred.

"Rich and beautiful is she? Lucky bugger," he said, as Fred grabbed the letter.

"None of your bloody business, Donald. Best you don't think of women. Fat chance of you finding any round here."

He left before Donald could think of anything else lewd to say, and went straight to his hut.

Middleton Hall,

May 1st 1918

My dear Fred

Your letter arrived only yesterday, which is extraordinary. They came quicker than that from the Front. It brought back memories of when I got your wonderful communications and news from France. It seems so strange to be writing to you again, after all this time, when I assumed we were lost to each other. You are so right. It was as if the gods were willing us to meet again by the Albert Hall that day. We have been given a second chance, I really do feel that. Knowing you are at least safer here in England than in France, gives me great comfort. This war does seem to be dragging on. I hear the news is a bit better now, but still, you do wonder when or if it will end? Mother sends her best wishes. I did say we had bumped into each other

Learning To Fly 171

again in London and she was keen to know what you were doing now. She is keeping to herself in Hawley and rarely ventures to London.

Everyone is terrified of these night raids, so I haven't been back since we met there. Those Zeppelins are making us frightened of our own shadows The hospital here is full to bursting. We have 50 beds now, all taken. Some nights they have to put up camp beds in the hall to fit them all in. It is being run with ruthless efficiency by Matron, and I hardly dare walk along the corridors of my own home now. You know I think she even resents the fact I am there at all. But I forgive her a little as it is grim work. I have to steel myself when walking along the wards, which I do from time to time to hand out things and have a chat with some of the men, especially those who do not have visitors.

Oh Fred, they are the lucky ones to be here alive, but you can tell that they don't think that. I'm sure many of them would rather have died in the mud with their friends than come back, with a limb or two missing. One poor young chap has lost both his arms, and if I'm there I try to offer to feed him. He gets so embarrassed. Sometimes I think I only make him feel worse. Goodness knows how he will manage when he gets out of here. I shall be travelling to London at the end of the month and staying at St John's Wood for a few weeks. I shall wait to hear from you and you can rest assured I will be in a state of anxiety to see if a letter from you has arrived each day. Do not let me wait too long.

Yours with affection,

Kitty

Fred read the words for a second time to prove that the emotion he had dared to wish for was there, in black and white. The most important thing was that Kitty would be in London in a week, when he had some leave. They could be together again. The anticipation made him shudder and he wanted to reply at once, but a knock on the hut window reminded him it was time to go up again.

He felt as if he were flying without leaving the ground.

Swinging his leather cap, and humming a tune, a broad smile taking the years off his face, he passed Hewett.

"Something making you happy today Fred?"

"You could say that. Just getting my leave plans sorted."

Chapter 29
Reunion with Kitty, May 1918

The train which took Fred through Cambridge and to London was unbearably slow. He felt every mile, as the engine teasingly pulled him south. Two other passengers got into his carriage in Cambridge; a couple of aging academics in their thick tweed, smelling of pipe smoke and old books.

"Good morning. You don't mind if we join you do you? Are you headed for London?"

They had looked admiringly at an officer in uniform.

"Yes, of course. King's Cross, yes, though it seems to be very slow."

Apart from this initial conversation, which they hoped said they too would have fought for their country if only they were not so old, both men had kept their faces buried in their books, occasionally nodding off as the train and perhaps the words they were reading sent them to slumber. Fred envied them their knowledge and the security it had given them in their long lives. There were some other young men in uniform on the train, maybe passing through London before heading back to the Front. Their smiles and easy manner proved they were having at least a day or two in the capital before they had to face the journey to France.

Fred had arranged to meet Kitty at King's Cross. It was the same station he had arrived at from Northumberland all those years ago. The end of the line for anyone travelling down the eastern coast from Scotland. For him it had been the beginning of a new life and he welcomed this arrival as a talisman. As the train approached the grand edifice of the station, Fred tried to peer through the smoke mushrooming up into the domed roof, the air sour with the coal fired expulsions. That day he did not notice the towering glass and metal structure, another triumph of railway engineering. He was trying to make out Kitty's face in the crowd, gathered at the barrier.

It was hard to identify anyone, obscured as the crowd

were by the swelling smoke. There were at least twenty people gathered to meet his train or board the next one standing on the parallel platform. He gave each face of the women gathered a quick scan for signs of recognition. Kitty would have stood out among this grey, dowdy crowd, with her height, poise and love of hats, usually feathered or jewelled.

Today he could see no such hat, most of the women looking drained and colourless, their heads in scarves or simple cloth hats jammed down to just above their searching eyes. The train to the side whistled, and a number of those gathered moved off to board the train which would take them north, but still Fred couldn't make out Kitty. Familiar worries surfaced. She had not turned up. She had thought better of it and he would soon get a note to say she had made a mistake.

He was now walking along the platform, still nervously scanning those left at the low metal gate. The academics were met by an equally aged and tweedy looking man who shook their hands warmly. They turned back.

"Cheerio, good luck to you."

"Goodbye, thank you."

He felt an irrational anger and an envy that they had someone waiting for them.

Their lives were carrying on as if the war were a side show. Fred wondered how many of their students were left behind to receive the benefit of their wisdom, and reflected how so many would never be coming back to the ancient colleges to pick up where they had left off.

All that knowledge lost, like everything else, buried in France. At the barrier, he now had to accept that Kitty was not among the crowd, which had reduced to one or two stragglers looking beyond Fred, hoping to see a familiar longed for face. He stood still, deflated, all that built up expectation and desire leaving him like the returning tide dragging with it the lovingly made sandcastle.

Suddenly from the far corner, Kitty appeared. He saw her long arm waving, before he saw the whole person. She was wearing a large straw hat with a sapphire coloured velvet band. How could she not stand out in this place among these people?

Learning To Fly 175

He allowed himself the sweet thrill of pride that it was his face she searched for.

"There you are Fred. I'm so sorry. The roads are blocked on Euston Road with some bomb damage, and we took the wrong turning which was jammed with motors."

Kitty stopped her explanation. She realised she was babbling and speaking too quickly in her haste to explain her lateness. It was pointless now, she was here. Fred grabbed her and pulled her towards him. Enough talk. He kissed her neck and smelled that familiar lily of the valley.

"Kitty, let me look at you properly. I cannot believe it is you."

Fred pulled away, still holding her narrow gloved hands. He could feel her wedding band beneath the leather and experienced that moment of bittersweet recognition. They had not planned what they were to do once they had met, and without knowing why they made their way across the small neat garden to the Great Northern Hotel.

Lewis Cubitt's magnificent curved structure stood proudly as if waiting to impress any train passengers just arriving in the capital. That day it offered them a refuge to take stock and work out their next move. Fred, who had always felt a boyish wonder at anything to do with the railways, looked up at the sleek exterior and the way the building hugged the terminal like a Roman temple built to honour engineering genius.

They went inside and were ushered into a crowded bar, the clients mainly servicemen in uniforms with their girlfriends. Kitty spotted the most private corner, and led the way to a small booth. Fred ordered champagne and a plate of oysters. He hadn't eaten oysters since the bar in Amiens, and the sight of the hardy shells brought him back momentarily to the war and a memory of friends, long gone now, trying oysters for the first time. Dead in the first year of the war. Kitty saw the slight shadow cross his face, and raised her glass to divert him.

"To us, Captain Dunn."

Conversation had never been difficult between them, and Fred was soon making her laugh with stories of Donald and her letter and the other awkward irritations of life at Thetford.

Kitty threw her head back, her face opening up like a sunflower. Fred could not stop admiring her, she still looked like the head-turning beauty he had first met before the start of the war. She too had stories, of the hospital and the patients, seeing hope in what sounded like the most desperate of cases, and it was obvious that she had found a new depth to her compassion and personality, which without a dreadful war and injured servicemen to help, she would never have discovered.

The war had tested them all and for many, especially the women left behind, had given them a new occupation and purpose which women, of Kitty's class and privilege could not have experienced in a country at peace. Fred was drawn by her confidence and sophistication. By late afternoon they were both giddy with the champagne. The crowd in the bar came and went with the railways' timetable; new people arrived looking for a private space to grab a few moments with a sweetheart or someone who for an afternoon would make them smile and forget there was a war on.

The station was still busy when hours later they went outside again, and they had to wait to hail a motor cab. Secure in the back on its black leather seats they were finally able to hold hands and kiss, observed only by the driver. To him, it was heart-warming, a man in uniform and his sweetheart. He had a son at the front and another who had died in the Somme so he forgave a man in uniform almost anything, so long as he wasn't one of those stuck up Generals who had messed up royally and sent men like his poor Jack over the top to their deaths, while making sure they were back in their chateaux in safety.

When he dropped them off at the corner of Hyde Park, he smiled at how they climbed out, giggling and unsteady, like teenage lovers. Fred noticed the black edged photograph in the front of the cab as he fumbled with some coins in his pocket, and handed over a collection of them. It was a large tip, enough to make the driver open his eyes wide. Today Fred was feeling flush with happiness and wanted to share it with everyone.

They walked slowly, her arm through his towards the Serpentine, a silver streak in the green parkland. They passed nannies pushing prams, and young mothers holding onto the

Learning To Fly

hands of toddlers passed them as they followed the twisting paths towards the water.

Benches were filled with old men. Young girls sat in groups on the grass holding their pale faces up to the last of the day's sunshine. Because Fred and Kitty were feeling unburdened by care and wanted to make their time together stretch out like the glittering water before them, they made their way to the few boats and paid the youth there to let them take one out. He was glad to take their coins, business was not so good with all the young men away and even though he could tell they were a bit tipsy, he was a man in uniform, a pilot it looked like. They would be no bother.

Fred rowed well, almost effortlessly, his arms strong from flying and holding onto the controls of an aeroplane. He took them out into the middle of the water and then raised the oars and let them drift with its motion. They were on their own, watched of course by the youth who'd taken their money, but to anyone who did happen to look over they could have been another upper class couple capturing the last moments of a perfect Spring day.

Kitty trailed her hand in the water. If he'd one of the cameras they had used to capture the ugly scenes of marching troops and trenches in France, he would have captured her there at that moment for all eternity. At that instant he knew without having to ask that they were both uncomplicatedly happy.

Chapter 30
Armistice, London, November 1918

Everyone could feel a change coming, as if the barometer so long stuck on low pressure had started to drift to high and it was now irrevocable. Stuck there on high waiting for the consequences. Fred and Hewett were now with a new squadron at Chattis Hill to work on training pilots in using the new wireless telegraphy systems.

Flying was now reaching levels of sophistication which the pilots of 1913 could not have dreamed of. Then the rudimentary ways of communicating with the ground with hand signals and wiggling of the wings meant messages and instructions were misunderstood, sometimes fatally so. War which had ruined so much, had improved some things too. Since they had arrived in Hampshire the rumours of the impending German defeat were intoxicating.

They were called into the mess.

"We have had information today, gentlemen, that some men from 15 Squadron have flown over German lines and returned with the news that no enemy aircraft or artillery fire has been seen. The German air force and army have stopped fighting.

"Germany has surrendered, and we are now at peace. I want to thank each and every one of you here. Some of you have been involved from the very beginning. Some have just arrived. But you have all done your bit. You can be very proud."

The CO's voice was crackling with emotion. Then, almost as an after thought, he added, "There will be no instruction today. All officers can take the next two days as leave. You deserve to celebrate."

Fred and Hewett stood together. They had come through, not unscathed, but alive. It was an unbelievable feeling. They shook hands, almost formally, not daring to say anything which could jinx this moment. Within an hour they were heading to a car to join the crowds in London. Kitty had been staying there since October and he was determined to make a telephone call to her the moment he arrived in South Kensington.

For now, they had to get on the road. As they approached the outer reaches of London, the place was waking up to the news of peace, and appeared to be going wild with delight. They came through Twickenham, Richmond, and Chiswick. Flags were being hung from the houses and small crowds had gathered outside garden gates, waving and cheering, ignoring the cold, and clasping the hands of anyone they met.

Church bells were ringing. It was as if the country had come out of a deep sleep and was enjoying the feeling of daylight for the first time in four years. They left the car in Cromwell Place, calling on Adele and Thomas to share the moment with them. Adele held onto her only son, tears streaming down her face. He had come through the war which had taken so many, and her prayers had been answered. Even the residents of Queensbury Place were emerging from their grand homes, smiling and greeting everyone there.

A sea of revellers. Servants and masters mixing together, all shaking hands, all differences in class and position, for that one day at least, shelved. The noise levels rose as the hours passed. The cars on the roads hooted their horns and loud cheers went up. A group of young women outside South Kensington underground station were dancing a reel and pulling in any available man to their set. The sound of their heels clattering on pavements as they swung round each other in exuberance.

It was hard not to be caught up in all the madness. Fred was able to break away from the group and make his telephone call at Mrs Freemantle's. Her son had also survived and would be coming home from France soon, and she clung onto Fred as if he was an understudy for her beloved Arthur.

Kitty was at St John's Wood and would soon be driven to South Kensington with her mother and younger sister to join the celebrations. They would be there in under an hour. Back in the street, more people had emerged from their homes and shops and all business had been suspended for the day. The engineering works where Fred had started off as an apprentice was idle and the old men who had stayed were out in their shirt sleeves in the street, bottles of beer in their hands.

Fred approached them and the delight of recognition was sweet. This young boy who had left in his battered old grease-stained jacket, a hand me down from his father, was now a Captain in the smart blue uniform of the Royal Air Force. They slapped him on the back and more beer was brought out. Small boys and girls ran in and out of the group trailing streamers and trying to grab the beer and drain the dregs before the adults, lost in their happiness, noticed. In the melee Fred saw the sleek grey Daimler which he knew belonged to Edith Perkins, draw up, a driver and three women in the back. He watched as Edith then Violet get out, and saw them walk up to the Freemantle's grand entrance. He felt his pulse quicken. Kitty was holding back to see if he was there in the crowds. She was looking up and down the street, towards the museums and then back again.

He waited just that one minute extra to see the others were inside the house, then he appeared by her side. He did not wait to consider what the chauffeur might make of it, he grabbed her by the waist and in the street, they embraced, almost mad with the euphoric atmosphere around them. At that moment Fred felt the war had truly come to an end and all the hardships and grief it had caused could be shelved forever.

Kitty spoke first.

"Baynes, I'm going to be joining the celebrations with Captain Dunn, you can tell Mother and Violet not to wait for me." The chauffeur who had known Kitty since she was 12, tried to hide his amusement.

"Right you are Mrs Burrell. I will tell them. I hope you have a good time. Peace was a long time coming, but now it is here, you are right to celebrate the fact."

Kitty smiled and then she and Fred walked up the street, oblivious to the neighbours who called out as they passed. Everyone was too wrapped up in their own jubilation to notice a young unmarried and unchaperoned couple that day.

They walked towards the museums and turned right towards Knightsbridge. The crowds were ten deep in the streets now and any progress was difficult. Everyone wanted to stop and talk and share the good news. Buses were inching along, their passengers packed like sardines in a can, all laughing, waving, carefree as to how long it took them to reach their destinations.

Fred and Kitty boarded one heading east. They mounted the stairs to the top, pushing their way among the already drunk men in uniform, from the navy, the army, even the blue of the air force. Fred acknowledged them, a moment shared. They would understand.

"It takes a war ending to get you on a bus for the first time Kitty."

"I like it, you can see more up here. I shall go on them more often now."

At the corner of St James's Park, they got off, the area was now thronged with people wrapped in flags, strangers linking arms with each other, men in uniform trying to grab a kiss from the best looking girl they could see. They could hear Big Ben chiming, striking out above the din, declaring for all the crowds to hear, we have peace, we are victorious. It was as though the dumb had suddenly found speech and the clamour after each chime was louder than anyone could remember.

They were intoxicated with the noise; signing and cheering as if they were required to make a massive din to make sense of it all. The throng who had been outside Buckingham Palace wanting to share the news with their King and Queen were now moving up Constitution Hill and Fred had to hang onto Kitty to stop her being pulled away in the crush.

They took the path back towards Piccadilly, and began to make their way up the wide avenue towards the street and the Ritz. There the crowds were thinner, but the noise from the parks had permeated even the opulent inner sanctuary of the hotel. Officers and ladies, old gentlemen in top hats and their wives in fine silk, were in the lobby, smiling and chatting. The bar was a lively throng, and a group of officers, drunk and delirious with the thought that the war was over, were standing on the velvet banquettes and belting out music hall songs at the tops of their voices.

Fred and Kitty squeezed into the booth they had been in on their visit earlier in the year. If ever there was a day for champagne, today was it. They ordered two bottles and several glasses. Fred offered them to the crowd around and within minutes the room, which had been in separate groups was as one, singing and raising their glasses. More champagne was ordered.

"I never thought this day would come, Kitty," Fred said. "It was like the war was a death sentence for me, and survival was not allowed."

"I didn't expect you to survive, if I'm really honest," Kitty said. "As it dragged on it just seemed more and more likely that you wouldn't. This makes just being here that much more important."

Kitty took Fred's arm. She knew it was up to her now to set the course for whatever would happen to them from this moment on. "I've had enough of decorum, or whatever my mother might call it. We have a right to be together and it would be wrong, ungrateful even, if we did not take that chance. The gods have smiled on us Fred, we must smile back at them."

"We will. I promise you that, Kitty." Fred pulled her towards him. A wide, deep satisfied smile lit up her face. She looked the most beautiful he had ever seen her, as if a tautness had been released. A lightness and warmth infused her features.

She nodded gently, acknowledging that they were here, now, together.

Alive.

Chapter 31
After the War, Winter 1918

Fred woke, his mouth parched and eyes resistant to the daylight which was trying to force its way in the gap in the curtains, his mind couldn't adjust to his new strange surroundings. It took him several minutes to accept he was in a room at the Ritz. He had vague recollections of dancing with Kitty and drinking with some fellow officers from no 3 Squadron. The rest was a jigsaw whose pieces he had lost.

He looked to the side of the bed and saw he was there alone, its satin covers unruffled by another person. How he had got there or who had helped him was a troubling thought. It was a feeling he had felt many mornings in France and had managed to drive away the nausea and vague recollections of a night, where the excessive partying had lasted until dawn. Then he had been forced to push down a few boiled eggs for breakfast and hot sugared tea, before taking off into the unfriendly skies in France. Now he remembered the war was over and that he had been celebrating this wonderful fact.

Filling the basin with cold water, he immersed his face for several seconds, wincing at the rush of energy it released. Pulling his hand through his short springy hair he looked at the blue tunic, belt and breeches which were neatly folded on the armchair, the boots set in front as if a person were sitting, ready to step out of the chair and march purposefully to the door. Timidly he pulled on his clothes, breathing in the stale smell of alcohol and cigarettes, and catching a whiff of lily of valley perfume.

He sniffed his sleeve, drawing in the perfume again, rubbing his nose into it as if Kitty herself was there in the fabric. A quick check in the mirror and despite the redness around the eyes, yes, he looked like an officer. No one could mistake him for anything less, especially here in this bastion of hierarchy. The badge and the sleeve stripes said more for his new class than anything else could ever do. He headed downstairs, and having observed well his fellow public schooled officers for some time, he assumed the air of someone who often stayed over at the Ritz after a fulsome night.

At the reception desk not a flicker of either joy or unease passed the face of the uniformed man, who looked up when Fred gave his name. When attempting to settle the bill, he was told, with perhaps just the underlying hint of disapproval, that his bill had been paid by Mrs Burrell who had left a note for him.

My darling Fred

In case you are wondering, the celebrations were befitting you wonderful pilots. We danced till dawn. Captain Roden was there and helped me bring you to the room. You looked so peaceful sleeping that it was a pity to wake you to say goodbye.

Yours lovingly,

Kitty

Vague memories of the evening surfaced and added to the hazy picture which was forming in his head. He was glad to find they were good memories, none tinged with foreboding. How often in France had he woken in the same unsteady state, but coming to the surface of a new day, had to face the fact that the party had been to mark the death of someone, or several people, and that they had been quite literally drowning their sorrows.

This morning he felt thick headed but even the deepest throbbing hangover could not alter the fact that the war was finally over. He had seen things he would try to forget, but today, there was something jewelled and gilded about everything around him. Even the disdainful receptionist could not take that away as he headed out into Piccadilly and made towards Knightsbridge.

Outside, empty bottles and trodden flags littered the path. London had for too long been deprived of a party, and suffering from the excesses of the night before was waking sleepily to gauge the damage done. In the doorway of a side entrance to the hotel, the khaki deeply stained uniform of a sleeping soldier huddled, a hand still clutching his brandy bottle.

No room at the Ritz for him. The brandy had left a large patch on his trousers, and mingled with the stench of dried mud and sweat, it brought back previous unwelcome odors. In the park he could see couples still chatting and laughing, the women no doubt wearing their clothes from the day before, not caring that their coats were open, exposing white fleshy knees to the November cold.

The time for modesty had long gone. They could celebrate the fact the country would no longer be populated by old men and boys; the men, the real men, would be coming home. That is what they were thinking, these young women, the day after the Armistice. Fred hoped it would be true. It might take months, maybe even years to come to terms with the fate of the disabled, the dead and the missing. When would the last of those be accepted as really dead? When did a family give up hope?

He thought of John Milne, missing over Belgium for the past three months. He'd taught him at Hendon. Milne, ex-Radley College and in the Oxford and Bucks light infantry was a world apart from the 19-year-old Fred, but they had been friends, along with Lillywhite. Both now gone. Milne's attractive young wife Joan had written to him when he was at Chattis Hill to see if he could find out anything more about where Milne's Bristol Fighter had been brought down and if there was a chance, he could have been taken prisoner and maybe still be alive. When would Joan, have to admit that he wasn't ever coming home? He would write to her tomorrow. From her flat in Portland Court, she would have heard and seen the victory party all last night. How difficult to watch a country celebrate when she had nothing to cheer her. It must have been agony.

In South Kensington and the cramped but cosy front room of his parents' house in Harrington Road, no mention was made of his night out. They had been up for hours, but knew better than to say anything to Fred. A letter from the Air Ministry was on the table, propped up against the old cracked milk jug. He felt his mother's eyes watching as he carefully opened the brown envelope.

"It's the Air Force Cross, mother."

Wordlessly, not wanting to acknowledge the thrill it gave him, he handed the letter to his father. Although he knew these things were more for having come out alive than anything else, it was still an honour and recognition; for his parents, for Kitty, for whoever cared to cheer his success, more than for himself.

He had to be back at Chattis Hill in the evening, and for the first time, he wondered where Hewett had got to in the celebrations. He'd last seen him outside a bar just down the road talking to some shop assistants, who had been given the day off. The car was still there as he passed Cromwell Place, and unless Hewett turned up soon, he would have to drive back alone. He hoped for Hewett's sake that he had found someone to share the night with.

It had been dark for several hours when the bedraggled officer turned up at Harrington Road bringing with him the smells of the various public houses he had been in since they had last seen each other. His had been a very different night to Fred's. They smelt different. Hewett had a cut above an eye and his knee high leather boots looked as if he had been in the fields of his farm back in Hampshire. After strong tea, hot fruit scones, and a boot polish for both, Adele and Thomas waved the two men on their way. War or no war, they were still employed by the RAF and had a job to do.

But at least now it would be in peace time.

Chapter 32
Farnborough, January 1919

Fred's eyes darted across the bar trying to pick out a man who fitted the description of a Captain Percy Rawlings. Most of the customers in the Tumbeldown Dick Hotel bar looked as if they had something to do with aviation, and with the airfield just up the road, quite a few men could match the description of an officer who had flown in the war and won medals for it.

That had to be him on his own at the side of the oak bar; tall, stick-thin, and rather distinguished looking, in an ordinary suit with a large tweed cap still on his head. Fred waved, a confident salute almost, and went over to him. Rawlings was drinking sherry, which Fred thought was rather strange given he'd come from the Royal Flying Corps too, not many of them had drunk sherry in France. He asked for a whisky and the two men forced their way over to a small table by the window.

"I'm glad you could come along, Captain Dunn, I've been wanting to meet you for a while now." He raised his glass.

"Cheers! I'm very glad to meet you too, and call me Fred. If we are going to be working together on this aeroplane you are building, we can use our first names. It's is quite a thing I hear. Tell me more about it."

Percy Rawlings was working for a company run by a Mr Walter Tarrant to build a massive triplane which would be the largest aircraft ever built. It had started off as a fighting machine to drop bombs on Berlin, but now it would be used for pleasure not war.

"It's the height of a four storey house, you would not believe the size of it Fred. You could fit a full size cricket pitch in the fuselage."

"I read that. 131 feet long. Makes our little Bleriots look like dragonflies compared to an eagle!"

"We've come along way in aviation since 1914. Speed, height, weapons, and now size. This is going to change people's lives, you can mark my words about that. We could get to

Bombay with just one stop, to New York. Maybe, in time, to Australia."

"If we can do that Percy… Well, you hope don't you, that the war and everything that happened, will be worth it. We will have learned something."

Fred gazed out of the window, thinking how Lillywhite would have reacted to this giant machine, the Tarrant Tabor. He would have snapped at the chance to be involved. Proper flying, taking passengers, not just those ladies and the adventurers back in Hendon, but proper fee-paying passengers travelling the world. It would be just the job for him.

"It's a daring project, a triplane to trump all others, and if it flies, well, it will indeed change everything about aviation."

"It will do that indeed, Fred. You need to meet Mr Tarrant. He's quite a force, and very rich of course. You know he made his money from supplying those wooden huts out in France? His factory is now making all the girders for this giant. He's putting thousands of pounds into the Tarrant Tabor and he wants the very best men on the team. He's heard all about you and I know he wants you to work with us. Mr Tarrant is a man who gets what he wants."

It was arranged. The next day Fred was to meet Mr Walter Tarrant in his London offices at Clock House, Arundel Street. A brass plaque outside said *W G Tarrant, Aircraft Manufacturer*. He made his way up the wooden staircase to the first floor office ten minutes before their agreed time of 2pm. A smell of glue filled the air, which was strange given all the manufacturing must be done out in Surrey. Maybe all the visitors who came from there brought the aroma with them as they climbed the stairs. It took him back to Hendon and the workshops where the groups of women in their white overalls varnished the linen wings, their fingers turning yellow with the thick gloopy dope.

Walter Tarrant was a short, stocky man, with a thick grey beard, which made him look like an Admiral in the navy, not an aviator. He had a gold chain across his waistcoat which was pulled tight as he came out from behind his desk to greet Fred.

"Captain Dunn, hello. I've heard quite a lot about you. Rawlings was very complimentary and I know you had a distinguished war. The Air Force Cross... Very impressive."

"Thank you sir. I enjoyed meeting Captain Rawlings. This is a very exciting project."

"It will be an aviation first Dunn. The largest aircraft ever built, flying the furthest distance. To think it was only ten years since that Frenchman crossed the Channel. We've come a long way since then."

The conversation continued easily, as it always was between men with a shared love of flying. An hour soon passed.

"Captain Dunn, do excuse me, I forget my manners, I haven't even offered you tea." He called through the glass partition. "Daisy, bring our guest tea and some of those biscuits."

The placement of the china tea cups and biscuits took up a few minutes and gave Fred the chance to think about what he was being offered. Lead test pilot in an amazing adventure to fly across oceans in the biggest aircraft ever built. The prospect was indeed incredible.

"Thank you, Daisy." The slim blonde woman who had brought their tea smiled at Fred. She would be very glad to have this new visitor come to the office often and hoped he would get involved with this project of Mr Tarrant's.

"I know you're still with the Air Ministry, but they are interested in what we are doing with the Tarrant Tabor, and of course we can pay you rather more than they can."

Fred tried not to look over-interested in the financial recompense.

"We can pay you £1,000 a year. You'll have to live at Farnborough, but Rawlings says the hotel there is decent enough for a single man. So, what do you say Dunn?"

£1,000 a year. A small fortune.

Enough to set up his own home, and marry Kitty. Maybe even enough to buy a small machine for himself. A toy, a plaything, just like those men in 1914 who came to Hendon to learn to fly their latest acquisitions. If not an aeroplane, then a motor car. A gleaming sports car. He had a vision of himself, picking up Kitty, the door of this new car open to let her in.

Him in his driving cap and gloves, a picnic basket strapped on the back.

"Captain Dunn, what do you say then?"

"Sorry, I was just thinking about your offer, Sir. I shall think it over tonight and you shall have my answer first thing in the morning." He surprised himself at such coolness.

"Well, I do hope you will accept. We will make aviation history, Dunn, it will change the world."

"Yes sir, I think it could do just that."

Fred almost ran up Arundel Street to the Strand, narrowly missing a horse and dray as he crossed the road at Aldwych. Kitty would be waiting in the Waldorf. He had been talking to Tarrant for over two hours. He was going to be over half an hour late. She was sitting in the sunken pink columned room surrounded by dowagers and their unmarried daughters, up from the country for shopping and a show.

He stopped nervously at the top of the stairs, feeling slightly out of place in this grandly feminine domain. Kitty waved him over, lifting her face to him. There was no sign of any irritation at his lateness. The war years had not aged her, but she had changed.

She had been a woman of the last century, now she was a modern, fashionable woman of the new one. The war had not only opened her mind to things she could do, independent of the men in her life, but had changed her attitude to how she looked and dressed.

Kitty was never one to be afraid of convention, but now she delighted in the frisson a navy blue knee length wool dress with a tight thin belt emphasising her waist and the effect her now short styled hair could create among the old dinosaur dowagers in the Waldorf.

Fred kissed her hand, and ordered a drink. He'd had enough tea for the day. It was an occasion for celebration and it was hard to celebrate with black tea. £1,000 a year, and the world's largest aeroplane.

"It is something which is going to change everything, Kitty. For flying. For me. For us." He stopped, noticing her cheeks colour at his reference to their future. Too soon, he

Learning To Fly

191

told himself. His excitement was making him rash. "It's being built in Farnborough, so I'd have to live down there of course. Rawlings will be there too and he's a good sort. Most of the people working on it during the war were women. All the men were away fighting so they did all the varnishing and working on the fuselage. Even Mr Tarrant's daughter was involved."

Kitty laughed out loud at that, glad to have moved the conversation onto safer ground than their future. She threw her head back, and took Fred's hands in hers, causing the dowagers to look over and tut.

"Well, Fred, then of course you must take the job. It will be a great adventure. I will come as your passenger. I've always wanted to go to America."

That decided him. If Kitty was this enthusiastic, it was the stamp of approval he needed.

He would write to Tarrant tomorrow.

Chapter 33
What a Hope, May 1919

In his new maroon touring car, its roof the colour of soft caramel, Fred drew up outside the Tumble Down Dick hotel pleased with the impression he made. He hoped the hotel, whose name marked the failure of Oliver Cromwell's son Richard, would not prove a bad omen for him. Omens had seemed so bizarrely important to the fliers in the war.

He was still compelled to see portents in everything he did and shrugged at the absurdity of it. He had taken a room above the public bar where he and Percy Rawlings had first discussed Tarrant's project. From there it was a short walk up the hill to the Farnborough aerodrome and to the sheds in which the giant machine was being put together.

Rawlings was sitting at the bar leaning on over sized white sheets of paper, creasing them with his arm. He was holding his head in his right hand and a worried expression gave his face a grey sickly palour.

"Fred, just in time. We have got to change the engines. All a bit last minute I know, but those four 600 horse power Siddeley Tiger ones aren't going to be ready and Mr Tarrant wants to push on." Fred sat down on the stool opposite Rawlings and glanced at the sheets. A cross section diagram of the Tarrant Tabor showed the positions of the four engines they had expected to use.

"That is a disappointment, we will need all that power to get the Tabor up"

"We're going to have to use six less powerful ones and put two between the middle and top wings." Rawlings pointed at the diagram.

"I see, but will it be as stable that way - they will have to be set further apart…"

"We have no choice Fred. Tarrant wants us to go with six."

Learning To Fly
193

Rawlings stood up and rolled the plans into a thin tube. He tapped the end.

"Let's get up there and see what the rest of them say."

The two men were silent as they walked up the road to the aerodrome. Each calculating what this change in the engines could mean for their test flight. It was a bit late in the day to be changing thought Fred. That, coupled with the disagreements about the balancing of the machine was troubling. He could feel the air in the small office at the airfield, heavy with apprehension. A young woman he had not seen before was sitting at a desk in the corner, a pencil behind her ear and another clutched in her hand as she scribbled tiny figures in a thick black book. Her long brown hair was drawn back severely and held tightly in a bun. She was chewing her lip as she wrote.

"Miss Letitia Chitty, can I introduce you to Captain Frederick Dunn, who is our lead pilot. Miss Chitty is a brilliant mathematician just down from Cambridge."
Rawlings made the introduction and then left as someone else called him over.

"Miss Chitty, pleased to meet you. You seem to be deep in concentration here."

"Captain Dunn, yes I am." Miss Chitty looked annoyed at having to stop her work. She was not pretty, not compared to Kitty of course, but she had an interesting face, if a bit stern. It would be good to have a woman around the place.

"Well, I will leave you to it then." Letitia didn't look up, but added another figure to her long list.

The centre of gravity test was set for May 8th. The Sunday before was a day off, so Fred decided to take his new car to London, anxious to show off to his parents and meet Kitty again. The test the next week was a tiny itch which wouldn't go away, and he kept wanting to return to it, to give it a scratch, but he also didn't want to worry his mother or Kitty with the technicalities of the building of the vast aircraft. He'd learned how to hide his true feelings when he was out in France, he could do it again.

"It has to be built in the balloon sheds it's so big, even getting the engines up to the wings requires a lifting platform.

You will be amazed when you see it Kitty. A man can stand on the middle wing and still be dwarfed by it."

"It sounds incredible, an aeroplane the size of several houses. I do worry about you Fred though, something this huge has never been flown before. You do think it will fly don't you?"

"Of course Kitty, I will be flying you to New York by the end of this year, didn't I say so?"

He could not tell Kitty that he was worried about the gravity test. Men who had been so confident just two months ago, now looked nervous and agitated at the mention of it. Their fear was infectious. He could not say how he often went back to his tiny room at the Tumble Down Dick hotel, his head throbbing with the complexity of the task they were setting for themselves. Kitty was right, never before had an aeroplane of this size been flown. They were at the forefront of something he knew could herald a new age for flying. What if they did manage to get the great beast to fly? Could it really take passengers across 2,000 miles of open water?

The day after the test, Fred intercepted Captain Wilson as he was going into the Air Ministry Office at the western end of the Aerodrome. He'd not served in France, instead staying behind his grand oak desk in the Ministry, where his spidery writing covered the memos which had decided the fate of hundreds of young men. Perhaps because of this, Wilson's office was kept well away from the main offices of the engineers and Tarrant's consultants, most of them had served in the war and mistrusted anyone who hadn't. A friction between the two sides had clearly grown over the past few weeks.

Wilson, cantankerous at the best of times, had been hoping to avoid speaking to anyone in Tarrant's employment in person. He'd wanted to put the new findings directly into a letter to his superiors at the Air Ministry. Seeing Fred looking so positive was temporarily unnerving, as well as irritating.

"Dunn, I've not got the time to talk to you now. I'm just off to draw up my report for the Ministry. You will have it soon enough".

The war had taught Fred to accept orders and not question his superiors. They'd won the war in the end, so

Learning To Fly

somebody must have known what they were doing then, he would have to accept that cleverer minds than his were working on the Tarrant Tabor. He was just the pilot. If only he didn't feel as if they weren't telling him everything.

Mr Tarrant of course, was full of confidence and as affable as ever. The conflict between the two sides of the project was irritating to a man who had found it so easy to deliver wooden huts to the soldiers in the war that he saw no need to delay an ambitious project such as this over some minor technicality. Obstacles were to be leapt over or knocked down.

"This model they built for the gravity test, well how can it be accurate, the Tarrant Tabor is too vast for a mere model to represent it. If the machine is too heavy, we will just put lead ballast in the nose to balance it out. We've told the Press we would be ready by the end of May and they will want to know why, if we delay them further. It won't do."

Fred saw Letitia Chitty standing with her back pressed against the corrugated iron wall of the balloon shed. She must be getting a breath of fresh air, all those figures making her dizzy.

"Miss Chitty, how are you? It looks like we are all set for the end of May. Mr Tarrant is keen to press ahead and he's inviting the Press."

Letitia looked up, blinked twice, and tried to smile at Fred. She liked him, but now was not the time.

"Good morning, Captain Dunn. Yes, I heard about the Test flight."

Fred wondered why every time he tried to make conversation with this severe looking woman, she wanted to end it as quickly as she could.

The trouble was Letitia knew something she couldn't share with Fred. She had been asked to work out the stress on the wood used in the giant Tarrant Tabor. When she was a student at Newham College, her figures had been just that figures on a paper, they hadn't really signified anything beyond what they were, beautiful numbers. Now her figures did mean something, something awful, and she didn't know what to do about it.

What she knew was that changing the supply of wood from spruce to tulip at the last minute because top grade spruce was in such short supply because of the war, had changed everything. She had given her report on the variations between the two wood types, her carefully worked out calculations, to her manager. But she was just 22, he'd said dismissively, and he'd asked her more senior colleague to do the figures again.

The trouble was Letitia knew she was right, her figures did add up. She had already concluded for herself that the Tarrant Tabor was just too big, and too heavy. It hadn't a chance of safe flight. She couldn't tell Captain Dunn that.

Chapter 34
The Test Flight, May 1919

The flight was set for Monday May 26th, and a select band of journalists and photographers were sent invitations. Fred decided not to tell his parents or Kitty about it. He would wait a short while before he let them know how it went. He hoped to be able to visit Kitty the following weekend. Far better not to worry her unduly. The Saturday night before, he received a call at the hotel at nine in the evening from Mr Tarrant. The test was on.

They had decided to set aside the conclusions from the model test, after its dubious result, and he should be at the balloon shed just after dawn the following Monday morning. There was no going back now. It was the same feeling he had experienced many times in France when a patrol was set for the next morning. An excitement certainly, but matched in its intensity by a dull dread that maybe this one patrol was to be his time, his last. His overriding feeling now was to get the trial over and done with, as only by putting it behind him could he relax.

The following day Fred went for a walk on his own. The air was light and fresh. Everything in Empress Woods had sprung into new life. At times like these, he preferred his own company. He felt he needed to be away from prying questions and inconsequential chatter. Nagging away at the back of his mind like a worm devouring small pieces of a leaf, tiny bit by tiny bit, was the knowledge that the press had been invited. He knew a journalist from *Flight* magazine would be there, and didn't want to disappoint anyone connected with the magazine where he had first learned of the wonders of aviation. Clearly Tarrant was expecting him to put on a show for them. He felt his life was coming full circle. The nineteen-year-old showman at Hendon was now being expected to impress a far more serious and judgmental audience.

Uncharacteristically, Fred went to bed at around eight, avoiding the crowd in the bar where he would have enjoyed a drink and a smoke. He felt the need to prepare himself and that could only be done alone. Again he reflected on the memory of France and the cocoon of silence which every airman needed before those patrols from which they knew a few would never return. He hung his old greatcoat over the window to keep out some of the light the thin curtains were not able to block, and he covered his ears with his pillow to stop the noise from the public bar downstairs. He wished he had had a drink after all. Both the pillow and the greatcoat blocking the light failed to help him get off to sleep and it was just after midnight when he finally drifted off.

Four hours later he woke with a start. Carefully, as if following a newly nurtured superstition, he dressed in his old flying tunic, breeches, and leather boots, and in the now lifting darkness, he walked slowly up the hill towards the airfield. The air felt linen fresh and he took large lungsful of it as he walked. People still slept, unaware of the event that was about to occur in their own town. It was fine and calm, as Rawlings had predicted, although still cold, as the sun had not had been up long enough to give any warmth. He hadn't wanted to eat anything before he left the hotel, and worried that had been a mistake. He should at least have had some tea, sugary tea. He felt cross with himself for worrying about such trivialities and looked ahead up at the grey metal fencing around the aerodrome, which he was fast approaching. One more minute and he'd be there. He felt a sudden shiver run through him. In France they would have said these were the ideal conditions for flying, a perfect Spring day.

In the airfield, the massive machine had already been winched out of C shed on a special railway track, laid down to move the huge construction, like a submarine, slowly being hauled out of the deep water. Its size away from the confines of the balloon shed was overwhelming.

The press would have something to write about now, conjuring up some imaginative comparisons to describe this giant. Mechanics used a motor on the plinth to start each of the four engines, one by one.

As Fred arrived outside the shed, the noise was

Learning To Fly

deafening, even with the engines operating well below their full capabilities. He pulled on his leather helmet. No use trying to talk in this racket. He went over to see Rawlings, who had just arrived, and he had a word with Edey and Grosert, the engineering foreman and his assistant. Edey was going to be behind the bulkhead, which separated the pilots' cockpit from the fuselage, with Wilson and another observer, Adams. Rawlings, Fred and Grosert were to climb into the open cockpit from a ladder propped at the side. He wobbled a bit as he climbed and hoped nobody had noticed. Fred took the pilot's seat and examined the controls. Rawlings squeezed his long body in beside him and Grosert sat behind the two pilots. From Fred's seat he could see the small group of reporters and photographers across the field. Several pictures of him getting into the triplane had already been taken, but he waved again, hoping they could pick him out, a tiny head just visible in front of the huge body of the machine. He checked his watch. 6.10 am. Fred increased the power to the four lower engines and the press group moved back, surprised by the wave of noise rolling towards them. Slowly he inched the beast forward for about 90 yards, with the bottom throttles half open, and the top engines just ticking over.

The plan was to take the machine out and turn left, but when he tried to manoeuvre the giant machine leftwards, he could not turn the beast. He throttled down the starboard engine and throttled up the left hand ones. The machine went into a 270-degree circular turn, crossing the path it had taken when it first came out of the shed.

He was now on a straight course to the right of the balloon shed and already building up speed. It felt exhilarating now it was moving to be in control of such a powerful beast, taming it by his actions, and willing it to perform. Rawlings, who had left the controls to Fred, had not said anything since they had taken their seats and glancing over at his co-pilot, Fred realised it was too noisy to say anything meaningful so he gave him the thumbs up and smiled. Rawlings looked pale and didn't return the gesture.

The speed was now 45 mph with the four lower engines at full power. At this point the tail was rising, almost effortlessly. This was unexpected, as he had been led to believe the tail would be hard to get up. Fred turned the giant triplane to the right, towards the middle of the airfield, and kept taxiing. Just at that moment, he would have said he felt calm, and in control. They must have already travelled for about a mile. The ground was rough and bumpy, and the machine bounced grumpily. It was like a giant woken from a long sleep and angry at the disturbance, rolling from side to side in protest.

Fred knew he had to counter the tail, which had now risen to flight height. If this machine was ever to fly, he would need to lift the nose and its heavy lead ballast. The wheels were now just inches above the grass, flicking at it with their rubber tread. He put the top two engines on. Another wave of sound filled their cavity. The control lever was already as far back as he could pull it, and the effort to drag the monster up was enormous and almost overpowering. Small beads of sweat had gathered on his forehead and he brushed them away. He had never sweated like this on a flight before take off. His arms and body ached at the pressure and force the machine was exerting over him. He looked again at Rawlings. Again he said nothing, but now looked ghostly white.

Fred realised, with a numbing, sickly feeling, that the machine was too heavy for one man to handle. Its momentum was now relentlessly forward and he alone could not counter the lifting tail no matter how much he pulled back on the control wheel. He checked the speed. 45 mph. He had a brief vision of Kitty, smiling as usual, willing him to raise the machine. Suddenly, he felt the giant nose go over, inexorably, determinedly, down towards the earth. At that split second he knew that the Tarrant Tabor would not fly. It was too heavy. It was a whale which could not survive in the air. No chance. Something, some memory of the flamers, made him turn the engines off. The giant nose was now crumpling up like paper, its Tulip wood splintering into the ground, eighty feet of tail flipping into the air, creating a massive, unnatural, lop-sided tower. The two rudders still flapped helplessly, as if uncertain what to do now.

Their job was over. Fred had not even a single moment to acknowledge that this time, after every stumble at death's chasm, this was it. The falling in.

This was how it would end.

Afterword
The Funeral, May 1919

The air was still sharp with the smell of cordite and grey wisps of smoke hung in the air. A hundred rifles had fired their volleys over the open grave. Just two Mondays ago, Fred was alive. Unconscious, and with his skull fractured, but alive and breathing. The fortnight since had passed slowly; tear-stained, and desperate. Thomas and Adele Dunn had moved into the Tumble Down Dick hotel to be near the hospital at Aldershot, drawing what comfort they could from the fact that Fred had spent his last uninjured night here, in this room, in this bed, his blue uniform folded on the same chair. Adele felt his presence there still, even in the thin curtains as she drew them each night.

It had taken him a full three days to die, three days when it had been thought that he might rally, only to watch him float back and fall away again. The day of the funeral was incongruously, relentlessly sunny. The thick dark overcoats and the black heavy drapes of the mourners looked out of place in the heat. The sun's glint off the black caused shafts of light to twinkle. Before, the coffin had been draped with a Union Jack flag and placed in the chancel of St Mark's Church, the local church to the airfield at Farnborough. His parents were the chief mourners, the starring role that no one wants. To be burying your only son, to be alive when they were dead. It was as unnatural as their mourning clothes in the bright sunshine. They could take some comfort perhaps from the fact that the church was full. Old friends from South Kensington, pilots, airmen, mechanics, and those who had come through the war, were all there.

The crash of the largest aeroplane in the world had been the talk of the town and many of those now crowded into the small stone church were there out of curiosity even though they had not known Fred personally. All shared a fellow feeling with the parents of its dashing young pilot. They all sang gustily; a hymn which had had many outings in these past few years.

Onward Christian Soldiers. Too many soldiers had followed its calling. Onward Christian Soldiers, Marching as to War. With the cross of Jesus going on before. They had sung it often enough in France. It was one of the few hymns they could all remember which seemed to fit the occasion, given it mentioned war and Jesus in the same verse. Fred's funeral was a far grander, more solemn affair than those rushed out in the flat fields of northern France, when the Padré might struggle to remember the names of the soldiers or airmen he was burying and from which no one could return quickly enough to the mess for a drink.

Later, the newspapers would call Fred's passing a 'tragic end to our brave and brilliant airman'. They would describe how he was given a funeral with full military honours. How the King's Royal Rifles and the Queen's Regiment were represented. How six officers had carried his body in its coffin to the gun carriage to make its way to the cemetery, led by the bands of the regiments playing the 'Dead March'. They had stood in the sunshine as the shots were fired to signal the final farewell and flowers, perfumed and bright, were strewn over the flagged coffin, alongside, the wreaths. It would be commented on for weeks to come just how many people there were there, from the very top of the British establishment to the very lowest, from decorated airmen and military commanders to the shopkeepers and railway men from back in Northumberland.

Fred had amassed so many friends and associates, more than seemed possible for his 24 years. Adele and Thomas stood at the graveside weeping, heads bowed, diminished by the occasion. Thomas's brothers David and Edward stood behind them. Mr Walter Tarrant and his wife were there too, but to the side, their figures covered by the tree which hung over the open grave. It had been an awkward acknowledgement when he had passed Adele and Thomas. His ambition for this flying machine was the reason for the funeral, and although he had told his wife they had to go for appearance's sake, it was not a comfortable feeling to be the one many of those present held responsible. It was not his fault, but all the same he had held onto his stick throughout to steady himself, his hands clasping its decorated silver shaft tightly, so that afterwards he saw the red marks left on his palms.

It wasn't just Fred who had been lost. Poor Rawlings had been killed outright and £60,000 of the wrecked giant triplane had been left in the corner of the airfield as a reminder of the terrible crushing accident. Walter Tarrrant felt a wave of relief when the notes of the Last Post finally sounded, and he was able to slip away. As he left, stumbling slightly on the soft mud dug out for the coffin, he knocked the parasol of a tall, elegant woman who had been standing behind him. He bowed slightly, apologised and caught sight of the side of her face under the black lace shade. A beautiful woman, even her obvious grief could not alter that. Tarrant wondered who she was. He would ordinarily have noticed someone like her around the airfield. Her clothes spoke class and money, though her eyes were red, and crying had left her face looking raw and scrubbed.

Kitty hadn't spoken to anyone in the church. She had slipped into the back, intending to leave the graveside before her presence was discovered. Her grief was too unspoken and personal to stomach the funeral party at the hotel, with its tea and sandwiches. People would mutter about how she was overreacting and how she was just a casual acquaintance of the family. In fact, wasn't her mother the young pilot's benefactor after all? Kitty held the parasol in front of her like a shield, warding off imagined questions and conversation. It had been wrong of her to come. She turned, crossed over the grass and left the cemetery by a side gate.

She stood at the wall, leaning into its coolness. She was glad of its age-smoothed and rounded stones, holding her up and hiding her. She had overcome grief before for her first, her only husband, but perhaps this time, her immunity against misery had been lost. Fred had been her cure. He had said, 'I would marry you now,' and she had ignored the words, which must have hurt him. Now, here at his funeral, she was not a wife, not even a sweetheart. To everyone gathered there, she was no one.

Their relationship had been doomed from the start of course, shrouded in secrecy and cursed by the war. Her shaking shape cowered behind a wall, mourning the passing of the man no one would ever know she had once loved.

Author's Note

Most of the events in this book did happen and I have tried throughout to keep it as historically accurate as possible. Nevertheless, I have taken the liberty of creating several characters and events to give the story additional latitude.

Frederick George Dunn was indeed born in Wylam, Northumberland in 1894. A miner's son, he and his parents moved to South Kensington, London where Thomas and Adele worked as domestic servants for a family in Queensbury Place. Fred's flying career is followed as accurately as I could, drawing from his records at the National Archives in Kew, his own meticulous log book and photographs and various newspaper reports. His Air Force Cross is still treasured by our family.

Fred's early flying career at the London Aerodrome in Hendon is recorded in many of the programmes and newspaper reports of the time. He knew a Robert Lillywhite there and the bomb dropping prize on the August Bank Holiday Monday 1914 was tied between Fred and Lillywhite. The motor crash in Coventry was discovered during my research at the British Library newspaper archive. Fred was charged with dangerous driving after young Private Hibbert was killed, impaled on railings having been flung from a tender driven by Fred. The Coventry Telegraph reported the crash and subsequent court cases. Also unearthed was the fact that Fred suffered a nervous breakdown in June 1915, or neurasthenia as it was then known, and was sent to the Palace Green hospital in Kensington to recover.

The Perkins existed as a wealthy landowning family in the North-East, but the romance between their daughter and Fred is fictitious. As he never married and no love letters were found among his possessions, we will never know if there was a love affair. We know from other accounts that the men in the Royal Flying Corps lived life to the fullest.

I have tried to reflect other events from the Great War as accurately as possible. The terrible deaths of young pilots, including the explosion at a squadron base in March 1915 around the time of the Neuve Chapelle battle all happened. I feel sure Fred would have been affected by such a terrible loss of life. The training regime put in place in 1917 after the losses in Bloody April also fit in with Fred's work. I have tried to reflect how the machines were tested and trained on as well as I could.

There is much documentation and several photographs concerning the crash of the Tarrant Tabor in 1919. Some accounts suggest it was pilot error (by Fred) putting on the top engines too soon. I think that is unlikely. My strong impression is that the aeroplane was just too heavy. The build process had certainly been plagued by problems. On the occasion of its first test flight in May 1919, the aeroplane was unable to get off the ground and the lead ballast in the nose played a part in it crashing into the ground, throwing both Captain Rawlings and Fred out of the cockpit. It is too often the case that when a plane crash happens, it is the dead pilot who is blamed.

After Fred's death at just 24, a letter was sent to his parents by Major Gen Brooke Popham, then Director of Aircraft Research at the Air Ministry, later to become the Air Chief Marshall. Fred had been his chief test pilot in France in the first years of the war. He wrote: 'He was undoubtedly the best all round pilot I have ever seen, and was equally at home in every type of machine, whether large or small, British or foreign. His death is a distinct loss to British aviation and I lose a personal friend.'

Bibliography

Appleyard, Rollo (1933), *Charles Parsons, His Life and Work*, Constable and Co

Barker, Ralph (1995), *The RFC in France - from Bloody April to Final Victory*, and *A Brief History of the RFC in World War One* **(2002)**, Robinson Publishing,

Cooksley, Peter G (2000), *The Royal Flying Corps Handbook 1914-18*, Sutton History Handbooks

De Groot, Gerald (2014), *Back in Blighty, The British at Home in World War One*, Vintage Books

Eisele, Ron (1918), *Blue Skies Aloft*, Ron Eisele

Gunston, Bill (1991), *Giants of the Sky*, Patrick Stephen

Gilbert, J (1975), *World's Worst Aircraft*, Michael Joseph

Hadingham, Evan (1968), *The Fighting Triplanes*, Hamish Hamilton

Hart, Peter (2007), *Aces Falling*, Phoenix

Laffin, John (1964), *Swifter than Eagles, Biography of John Maitland Salmond*, Blackwood and Sons

Lee, Arthur Gould (1970), *No Parachute, A Classic Account of War in the Air in World War One*, Pocket Books

Levine, Joshua (2009), *Fighter Heroes of World War 1*, Collins

Lewis, Cecil (2009), *Sagittarius Rising*, Frontline books

Mackersey, Ian (2012), *No Empty Chairs, The short and heroic lives of the young aviators who fought and died in WW1*, Phoenix

Martyn, Thomas J C (2015), *Aviation Adventures, The True Story of WW1*, Anne Martyn Alexander

McCudden, James (2000), *Flying Fury, Five years in the Royal Flying Corps*, Greenhill Books

Mountjoy, Desmond (1923), *The Melody of God*, Constable and Co.

Norris, Richard (2008), *The Life and Work of Walter George Tarrant*, Ian Allen Printing

Patterson, James Hamilton (2015), *Marked for Death, The First War in the Air*, Head of Zeus

Paxman, Jeremy (2013), *Great Britain's Great War*, Penguin

Robinson, Derek (1971), *Goshawk Squadron*, Pan

Robinson, Derek (1987), *War Story*, Macmillan
Robinson, Derek (1999), *Hornet's Sting*, Harvill Press
Sloan, Carolyn (1998), *The Story of of Alcock and Brown (Incredible Journey)*, Silver Burdett Press
Smith, Alisdair (2013), *Images of War - Royal Flying Corps*, Pen and Sword
Tilley, Brian (2015), *Tynedale in the Great War*, Pen and Sword
Winchester, Jim (2005), *The World's Worst Aircraft*, Grange Books
Wallace, Graham (1955), *The Flight of Alcock and Brown*, Putnam
Winter, Denis (1982), *The First of the Few*, Penguin
Yeates, V M (1962), *Winged Victor*, Jonathan Cape

Gallery

1) Railway bridge for the mine over the River Tyne,
Wylam, Northumberland.
Hagg Bank (where the Dunns lived) is in the background

2) Brothers Tom (Fred's father), David and Edward Dunn

3) Fred, Hendon, August 1914, given to his cousins Emily and Eva Dunn

4) Fred (centre) and other instructors, London aerodrome, Hendon, 1914

Learning To Fly 211

5) Fred in the uniform of the Royal Flying Corps
(probably late 1914)

6) 'My first loop on an Avro…'
The Avro was used mainly as a training aircraft

7) Fred in uniform, cane and cigarette in hand

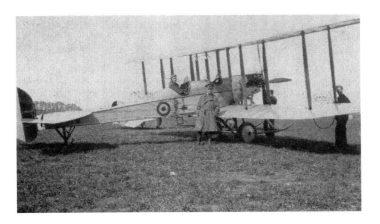

8) Croydon 1916, in a BE2B two seater biplane, designed by Geoffrey de Havilland

9) 'I wonder what is wrong…' (Probably 1915)

10) Fred and Pentland, known as 'Snowball'

11) Fred in flying helmet and goggles,
seen through arm of General Longcroft, 1916

12. Above the clouds, France (Probably 1916)

13. Early cameras for aerial photography, France, 1915

14. The Tarrant Tabor tri plane, Farnborough, May 1919
Fred standing on cockpit, leaning on lower wings

15. Crash site of the Tarrant Tabor, May 1919

Learning To Fly 217

16. Gravestone of Frederick George Dunn,
AFC, Farnborough, May 1919

Proof

Made in the USA
Columbia, SC
02 October 2017